DATE DUE

4/2011			

Also by William Colt MacDonald in Large Print:

The Phantom Pass
Restless Guns
King of Crazy River
Powdersmoke Range
Rebel Ranger
Action at Arcanum
Alias Dix Ryder
Blind Cartridges
The Comanche Scalp
Ridin' Through
Sunrise Guns
Two-Gun Deputy

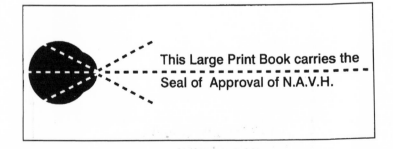

This Large Print Book carries the
Seal of Approval of N.A.V.H.

The Riddle of Ramrod Ridge

William Colt MacDonald

Willimantic Library
Service Center
1216 Main Street
Willimantic, CT 06226

Published in 2005 by arrangement with
Golden West Literary Agency.

Wheeler Large Print Softcover.

The text of this Large Print edition is unabridged.
Other aspects of the book may vary from the original edition.

Set in 16 pt. Plantin by Carleen Stearns.

Printed in the United States on permanent paper.

Library of Congress Cataloging-in-Publication Data

MacDonald, William Colt, 1891–1968.
    The riddle of Ramrod Ridge / William Colt MacDonald.
      p. cm.
    ISBN 1-58724-949-9 (lg. print : sc : alk. paper)
    1. Outlaws — Fiction. 2. Ghost towns — Fiction.
    3. Large type books. I. Title.
PS3525.A2122R53 2005
  813′.52—dc22   2004052026

The Riddle of
Ramrod Ridge

As the Founder/CEO of NAVH, the only national health agency solely devoted to those who, although not totally blind, have an eye disease which could lead to serious visual impairment, I am pleased to recognize Thorndike Press* as one of the leading publishers in the large print field.

Founded in 1954 in San Francisco to prepare large print textbooks for partially seeing children, NAVH became the pioneer and standard setting agency in the preparation of large type.

Today, those publishers who meet our standards carry the prestigious "Seal of Approval" indicating high quality large print. We are delighted that Thorndike Press is one of the publishers whose titles meet these standards. We are also pleased to recognize the significant contribution Thorndike Press is making in this important and growing field.

Lorraine H. Marchi, L.H.D.
Founder/CEO
NAVH

* Thorndike Press encompasses the following imprints: Thorndike, Wheeler, Walker and Large Print Press

CONTENTS

I

Missing Gold

After the second day the Deacon commenced to grow impatient. For two days he and his companions had remained in Paraiso, terrorizing the small population that had settled a few miles from the banks of the Gila River. Paraiso couldn't be termed a town; rather it was just a collection of adobe huts. There was a sort of general store and a cantina. The settlement was made up of Mexicans and a few Yuma Indians; there were some half-breeds. Very little work was done in Paraiso: there were a few tiny corn fields; here and there chickens scratched in the dusty roadway; there were a number of sheep and goats to be seen. All in all, it was peaceful there; a man could doze in the shadows when the sun grew unbearable; true the nights were chilly at certain seasons of the year, but "the poor man's stove" always rose bright and clear to pour down its benevolent heat.

But Deacon Trumbull had had enough

of Paraiso and of a certain stubborn Mexican. The Deacon said as much to his two companions as their booted feet scuffed up dust along the sun-drenched roadway as they headed toward Paraiso's single cantina. Dark, furtive faces peered nervously from partly opened doors as the three proceeded along, intent on the subject of their conversation.

Deacon Trumbull said sourly, "I'm sick and tired of waiting longer. Either that greaser comes across for us today, or I'm aiming to know why."

The Deacon was a tall, gangling man with long, sour features. He wore an ancient "stovepipe" hat from beneath which wispy gray hair hung raggedly to the back of his collar. His nose was long and inquiring and tended toward a reddish hue at the point. His knee-length frock coat was unbuttoned and thrown back to reveal the cartridge belt and holstered forty-five that encircled his middle. His shirt may have been white once — that part of it that could be seen between the grease-spattered fancy vest and knotted bandanna about his skinny throat. He affected a pious manner in which very few took any stock. The Deacon was, in short, an unmitigated scoundrel.

His two companions also carried six-shooters. They were costumed like cow-men: battered sombreros, faded overalls, riding boots, woolen shirts. One, the Deacon's bosom pal, was known as Limpy Bristol. He was stockily built, with an evil, unshaven face and a slight impediment in his right leg, the result of having, one time, been nearly captured when indulging in a bit of cattle stealing. The bullet in his leg was there for life, but it in no way impeded the nefarious course that life pursued.

The third man, Hedge Furlow, was more or less a recent acquaintance of Trumbull's and Bristol's who had placed himself in their good graces through the simple me-dium of shooting in the back a deputy sheriff who was engaged in taking the pair to Tucson, having picked them up in Yuma on a hold-up charge at least two years old. Furlow was a coward at heart and looked it. Only the fact that he hated law officers had prompted him to fire the murderous shot. The three had proceeded on to Paraiso from there, leaving the stiffening body of the deputy to grow cold on the sandy and cacti-studded wastes of the Ari-zona desert country.

"But how," Bristol was saying, "do you figure you can make that Mex talk, Deacon?"

"There are many ways to bring the errant sheep into the fold," Trumbull replied smugly.

"A hot slug o' lead might loosen his tongue," Furlow growled, kicking savagely at a stone in the road.

"And thus," the Deacon reminded, "still forever the tongue that can tell of untold treasures. Nay, there are better means."

They walked along under the hot sun, perspiration trickling through the whiskers on their unshaven faces. A near-naked child, almost the color of the roadway in which it played, rose suddenly from beneath their feet and scurried frightenedly toward a near-by adobe shack. Bristol jumped at the sudden movement as though he'd been shot, and commenced to curse. "Damn' brats!" he snarled. "Always gettin' underfoot where you can't see 'em."

"Suffer little children . . ." the Deacon murmured piously.

"Damned if I wouldn't make all these dirty oilers suffer if I had my way," Furlow growled. "By Gawd, they ain't no good on earth. We've done our best to make 'em miserable — threatened 'em, forced 'em to cook our meals, and even" — he leered evilly, "— and even —"

"Mention it not, Hedge," the Deacon interposed dourly. "The sins of the flesh are an abomination in the eyes of your Maker —"

"But what I'm getting at," Furlow insisted, "is that if these greasers had any guts they'd have run us out long ago."

"I don't reckon they got any guns, pro'bly," Bristol commented. "Some greasers make damn' good fighters. I've seen 'em."

"They are a stiff-necked people," the Deacon muttered, half to himself, "but now we shall see if the spirit of one is not to be broken. Come on."

They turned in through the open doorway of the cantina, a blocky adobe place with the only porch in Paraiso. Within the building the air was cool and shadowed. The walls were bare. Two small square openings allowed light to enter. At one side was a single wooden table flanked by four rickety chairs. At the opposite side of the beaten-earth floor was a heavy board plank resting on two whisky barrels. A small fly-specked mirror and a shelf containing a row of bottles and glasses were on the wall back of the plank bar.

Behind the bar stood a young Mexican in overalls and a faded shirt. His feet were bare; his face was round and swarthy. His heavy, blue-black hair was neatly parted at one side. His dark eyes watched the three men narrowly as they entered the cantina. Then, without a word, he turned to his back bar and reached for two bottles, one of tequila and one of whisky. Glasses were set out, together with a saucer bearing a small bit of salt and a slice of withered lemon.

No word was spoken. Furlow and Bristol poured full glasses of whisky. The Deacon placed a pinch of salt on his tongue, tilted the tequila bottle to his lips, and drank deeply. Replacing the bottle on the bar, he drew the slice of lemon through his teeth, then flung it on the floor. There was considerable smacking of lips on the part of the three drinkers.

Still no one spoke. The Deacon belched heavily and stared intently at the Mexican. Finally he drew out his six-shooter and with trigger finger through the guard, spun it easily, the butt dropping into his palm with each revolution, the barrel coming momentarily to short pauses to bear on the Mexican. The Mexican stiffened slightly, but his dark eyes were steady on those of the Deacon. Finally the Deacon replaced his gun in its holster.

"How's about me taking a hand?" Furlow asked eagerly, one hand starting toward his six-shooter.

"Leave be, Furlow," Deacon Trumbull said coldly. "This is my show." He bent his chill gaze on the Mexican. His voice didn't raise above normal. "All right, Jiménez, it's time you started talking."

The Mexican raised one hand in quick protest. "But, señor, I'm already tell you — I know nozzeeng."

"Liars are an abomination unto me," the Deacon said sourly. "I've come to the end of my patience. Today, Jiménez, you tell what you know. We've already wasted two days. I'm not intendin' to see the sun set in this sink of iniquity another day. You'll talk or else!"

"Look you, Señor Deacon, I'm already tell all what I'm know —"

"Jiménez," the Deacon scowled, "you know where that money went to. Fred Vincent rode into Quithatz Canyon with thirty thousand in gold dollars. I want to know two things: where did Vincent disappear to and what became of the gold."

"I'm tell you I do not know, señor —"

"And I'm stating you do!" The Deacon sounded ugly. "A man doesn't just ride out of Ramrod Ridge with thirty thousand dollars and disappear into thin air."

"I'm repeat," the Mexican stated earnestly, though his voice shook a little, "that I'm not see the Señor Fred Vincent since the night he leave —"

Limpy Bristol ripped out a curse and drew his gun. Furlow swore and kicked the plank from the two whisky barrels, sending the bottles and glasses crashing to the floor.

The Deacon looked pained at the violence displayed. It seemed to recall him to his earlier mildness. "That is enough of that," he stated quietly. "You can't thread a needle with a rope, nor yet utter subtle words in a bellow —" He stopped short. His eyes glistened. "A rope," he murmured half to himself, "a rope." A sour smile twisted his lips. "Truly I have an answer for my guidance." He turned to Bristol and Furlow. "Furlow, you go bring up our horses — and be sure to fetch our ropes."

"You going to string up this greaser?" Furlow queried eagerly.

The Deacon nodded. "In a way, yes."

"Choke the life outten him," Bristol growled. "You got the right idea, Deacon."

The Deacon shook his head. "It may be we won't have to employ such extreme measures. A slight pressure about the throat will often cause words to issue from the lips. Perhaps Jiménez will feel more inclined to talk. . . . Furlow, the horses."

Furlow hastened out. Jiménez didn't say anything. Bristol turned back to the Deacon. "There's a roof beam sticks out from the porch outside," Bristol stated eagerly. "We could toss a rope over that and —"

The Deacon shook his head. "I think it will be best to go out from town a short way. After all, we can't push things too far. Somebody may rebel; somebody may have a gun. It is quite probable Jiménez has friends here, even though they haven't yet seen fit to come to his rescue. But it seems to me one of those sahuaro cactus might make an admirable gallows —"

"You mean those giant cactuses with the big arms sticking out? Hell's bells, yes! You've hit it!"

The Deacon turned back to the Mexican. "Well, Jiménez" — he spoke in a manner that was almost cordial — "it's up to you. You've listened to the plan. Ready to talk?"

Stolidly the Mexican shook his head. "I'm tell you I'm know nozzeeng."

"Ah, well," the Deacon sighed, "a hempen loop about your gullet may change your mind for you. I feel our feet

17

are set upon the right path, Limpy."

"Me, too, Deacon."

Within a short time Furlow was back with the three saddled horses. The men forced Jiménez outside. He made little resistance; there wasn't any use in that now. The Deacon and his companions mounted. Certain orders were given. Bristol shook out a loop in his rope and tossed it over Jiménez' head, pulling it just tight enough to force the Mexican to follow when the horses started. The Deacon led the way from town, Jiménez stumbling at the end of the rope.

As the little procession left Paraiso, heads were stuck furtively from doors, but no one protested, no one made an attempt to follow.

A quarter mile out of town the desert and its growths closed in on the riders and their victim as they entered a veritable forest of giant cacti, some of which stretched nearly forty feet into the air. Paraiso couldn't be seen from here. Nothing to be seen in any direction except a few paloverde and ironwood trees, desert shrubbery, some prickly pear clumps and the huge sahuaros rising from the sandy wasteland toward the sapphire sky above.

The Deacon drew his pony to a halt; the

other two followed suit. The Deacon sat eying a tall sahuaro with giant arms lifted in a great curve on either side. "I figure," the Deacon said contemplatively, "that one there will prove a right good specimen to work on, Limpy. That right-hand arm isn't too high, so's we'd have to knot our ropes . . . Uncoil and throw the other end of that string over that nigh arm. Then dally to your horn and give this stiff-necked greaser a mite of elevation. He'll talk or I miss my guess."

Bristol obeyed orders. Knotting one end of the rope about his saddle horn, he touched the pony lightly with his spurs. The beast moved into a walk. The rope went taut over the arm of the big cactus. The loop tightened about Jiménez' throat. Imperceptibly, his feet commenced to lift from the earth. Involuntarily, his hands went to the rope about his neck.

"You, Furlow" — the Deacon spoke swiftly — "take your piggin' string and tie that bustard's arms behind him."

Furlow got down from his pony. It took but a moment to execute the order. The Deacon spoke to Bristol. Again Bristol started his pony. The Mexican's feet left the earth. His body twitched and his legs commenced to kick. Strangling sounds

19

issued from his lips.

"Let him down!" The Deacon spoke sharply. "You want to kill him right off, Limpy? We've got plenty of time for that — afterward."

The Mexican's feet again touched earth. At a word from the Deacon, Furlow loosened slightly the rope about the man's neck and supported his limp form. After a time breath returned to the Mexican. He opened his eyes.

The Deacon said, "Feel more like talking now, Jiménez? You might as well. We can keep this up as long as you can. Ready to tell where that gold went to?"

Jiménez eyed the Deacon steadily, refusing to speak. His lips were tight; a slight pallor had crept into his skin. There was no fear in his manner. Overhead the breeze lifted and made soft whistling sounds through the spines of the giant cacti; the huge plants swayed slowly, stiffly in the breeze. Still Jiménez kept silent.

The Deacon's eyes narrowed. "And he shall be lifted unto me . . ." the Deacon murmured softly. Then his voice took on a harsher tone, "Limpy! Give that Mex son another taste of dancing on air!"

Limpy's horse moved forward. Jiménez' feet once more rose slowly from the earth.

II

"Jerk Your Irons!"

Two riders moved leisurely through the giant sahuaro forest, their bodies moving easily to the motions of their ponies. They followed a faint trail winding through the big cacti. Occasionally great outcroppings of rock were passed, but for the most part the way led through a thick growth of cacti, paloverde trees, and lower forms of desert shrubbery. The horses' hoofs made soft clumping sounds in the sandy earth. Now and then a shoe struck a spark from a loose bit of stone.

One of the riders, Nogales Scott by name, was a tall rangy man with red hair, a slightly aquiline nose, a firm chin, and an infectious smile that lighted up his candid gray eyes like a clear spring morning. His companion, Caliper Maxwell, was shorter, barrel-chested, with sleepy blue eyes and tousled blond hair that always looked as though he'd just climbed down from the hurricane deck of a pitching bronc. His features were deceptively good-natured and didn't at all agree with his given name, which happened to be Cadwallader. Ignorant of the fact that Cadwallader signified "Battle Arranger" — and how appropriately the name fitted — Maxwell felt there was something sissy about the name, and always signed his pay checks plain C. Maxwell. People who wanted to know what the C stood for were always greeted with a growled retort that furnished no information. One man meeting with such reproof took one look at Maxwell's saddle-warped legs and announced loudly that the name must be Calipers. Somehow the name Caliper stuck to the cowboy.

Both men wore Stetson hats, woolen shirts, unbuttoned vests, denims cuffed at the ankles of their high-heeled riding boots, and bandannas about their necks. Each had slung about his hips a well-filled cartridge belt attached to which was a worn holster carrying a walnut-butted Colt's six-shooter.

These two were pards of long standing; in a crisis they worked beautifully together — as many law busters had already discovered to their sorrow. Their friends called them fondly, "The Twin Saddle Tramps," though their physical aspects flatly denied the primary part of the name and they were far from being hoboes; quite the contrary, in fact. Nogales and Caliper were inseparable, though they disguised their deeper feelings toward each other through the employment of rather insulting terms in their daily conversation. For instance, Caliper at the present moment:

"Sometimes, Nogales, I think that if your brains was nitroglycerine you wouldn't have enough to blow your hat off."

"You think?" Nogales retorted scornfully. "Now what in the name of the seven bald steers would you use to *think* with? That takes gray matter — brains! Ever hear of 'em?"

"Not from anything you ever said," Caliper drawled. "You talk a heap, but it don't make sense."

"Not to you it wouldn't. But what's eating you now?"

"That is."

"What?"

"Eating. I'm hungry."

"I never saw the time when you wasn't. Howsomeever, we should be coming to that place called Paraiso that feller told us about right soon."

"If I had any sense I'd never be 'way over here in this country."

"Oh, so you finally admit you ain't got any sense?"

Caliper nodded. "I admit *that* every time I go any place with *you*. Cripes! When we going to get that outfit of our own and settle down?"

"Now, look, Caliper, if we had our own outfit what would you be doing right now?"

Caliper smiled blissfully. "Riding around easy, watching our cows put on weight."

"You see," Nogales declared triumphantly, "there's very little difference. We're riding around, and the way you've been stowing away grub, I'm watching you put on weight. Cripes! It's only about four hours since you had breakfast."

Caliper looked dubious. "Seems like four days."

"I reckon you'll survive," Nogales grunted. "But if we're going to have a ranch of our own, we've got to look over a heap of spots first."

"For a right long time now," Caliper growled, "I've seen plenty spots —"

"In front of your eyes," Nogales said quickly. "You're probably bilious. I notice you have dizzy attacks right frequent. You should consult a doctor — a horse doctor. One that's specialized on mules. I hope what you got isn't contagious."

"If it is, I caught it from you —" Caliper abruptly paused, then added a sudden exclamation, and jerked his pony to a stop.

Nogales went on a few paces, then glanced back. "What did you see, pard?" he asked swiftly. He reined in his horse.

Caliper raised one arm to point through a narrow-aisled vista of desert growth. He spoke, low-voiced, "See? Yonderly a couple of hundred yards. Looks like a necktie party."

Nogales' gaze followed the pointing finger and glimpsed a twitching form being hauled aloft at the end of a rope, while a burst of sardonic laughter reached his ears. After a moment the hanging man was lowered again. "Looks like somebody's dancing funeral," he said quietly. "Maybe it's none of our business, but I got a hankering to see what it's all about."

They spoke to their horses, moved forward at a quicker pace. After a time they pulled to a halt, dismounted, and crept noiselessly forward on foot, the sahuaros looming high above their heads and quickly closing in about them as they advanced across the dry, sandy soil. . . .

The minutes passed. Deacon Trumbull, seated on his pony, eyed the dangling figure at the end of the rope. "Better let him down again, Limpy," the Deacon growled. "Mebbe he'll talk this time."

"Gesis! I sure would," Hedge Furlow commented, his eyes wide. "That greaser is tough. Four times now we've h'isted him and he still refuses to talk."

"Coming down," Limpy Bristol grinned, exposing a line of tobacco-stained, broken teeth. He backed his pony and the rope slid quickly across the arm of the giant cactus. Jiménez' feet touched the ground, then his legs buckled and let him down. A choked moan left his throat as Furlow stooped over him and loosened the hempen loop.

After a minute Jiménez gasped out a request for water. Furlow's grin widened as he glanced over his shoulder toward the Deacon. "We got him begging for a drink, anyhow," he said. "That rope has softened him some all right. He'll be talking right soon, I'll betcha."

The Deacon's thin lips twitched at the corners. "And straightaway the string of his tongue was loosed and he spake plain," he quoted softly.

After a few minutes Furlow helped the Mexican to his feet. The man swayed helplessly for a moment, then squared his shoulders and gazed defiantly at the Deacon. The Deacon's mouth tightened.

"You, Jiménez," the Deacon said cruelly, "you'd better make *habla* right quick. I'm sick of waiting. This is your last chance. What became of that gold?"

"Even if I'm know, Señor Trumbull," Jiménez choked out, "I'm see you and your buzzards in hell before the word pass' from my lips." His words sounded half strangled.

Limpy Bristol ripped out a curse that was paralleled by one from Furlow. Furlow whipped the back of his hand savagely across Jiménez' pale face. Hot pin points of hate burned in the Mexican's eyes, but he didn't wince from the blow, only glanced contemptuously at Furlow.

The Deacon sighed. "Better lift him again, Limpy — and maybe we won't let him down for a long time."

Limpy prodded the pony with his spurs. The horse moved forward, taking up the slack in the rope. The noose tightened slowly about Jiménez' neck. His form stiffened, lifting him to tiptoes.

And then a new voice intruded on the scene: "Go easy on that rope, feller!"

Nogales Scott and Caliper stepped out of the brush through which they'd been approaching. At the edge of the clearing they halted, leisurely surveying the scene, their thumbs hooked in gun belts.

"In fact," Caliper added his words to Nogales' command, "I'm suggesting you loosen that rope right pronto until we learn what this is all about."

Limpy Bristol had halted his pony in surprise; the rope slackened, letting Jiménez to the earth but holding him erect. One of Bristol's hands strayed toward his holster.

Nogales snapped, "Don't you, feller!"

Something in the tone forced Limpy to restrain his draw. He looked to the Deacon for orders. The Deacon twisted about in his saddle, coldly eying the intruders. Hedge Furlow gave a sudden gasp, swore, and then started to back away.

"You, Furlow," Caliper jerked out, "stay right where you are!"

Nogales laughed softly. "It is our old friend Furlow, isn't it? Didn't recognize him at first —"

Here the Deacon interrupted, speaking for the first time, his tones pious, "Ah, my friends, you have arrived in time to witness the punishment of a sinner. If you'll just stand to one side and —"

"What's his crime?" Nogales demanded shortly.

"Er — uh —" The Deacon cleared his throat. "It's a matter having to do with a horse. One that didn't belong to this son of iniquity —"

"That's it, that's it!" Limpy burst in. "This greaser stole the Deacon's horse and —"

"I don't believe it," Nogales said flatly. "There's some skulduggery here some place."

The Deacon looked pained. "Now, my friends, you wouldn't doubt our word, I hope."

"We sure would," Caliper snapped, "just as we'd doubt the word of any man we found in the company of Hedge Furlow. Coyotes always run in packs!"

The Deacon assumed a look of righteousness. "You know not whereof you speak, I'm sure. We want no trouble with you. Pass on, and —"

"Pass on be damned!" Nogales growled. "You, Furlow, take the rope off that feller's neck —"

"Furlow," the Deacon said sharply, "don't touch that rope."

Furlow stood undecided, his eyes darting nervously toward Nogales and Caliper.

"Move smart, Furlow!" Caliper ordered grimly.

Furlow gulped and removed the noose from Jiménez' throat.

The Deacon's eyes narrowed. "I don't like to become involved in a misunderstanding," he said mildly, twisting around still farther in his saddle, one hand stealing beneath his long coat. "At the same time, if you insist on an explanation —"

A burst of gunfire from the vicinity of Nogales' side cut short the words. The Deacon felt a lead slug cut through the flaring lapel of his coat. His skinny frame stiffened; one hand was removed hastily from within the coat. His eyes widened a trifle as he gazed at Nogales. There wasn't any gun in Nogales' hand now, but a wisp of smoke still spiraled from his holster.

"Rather impetuous, aren't you, my friend?" the Deacon inquired. His eyes were hard on Nogales.

"I'm not your friend, you mealy-mouthed old hypocrite," Nogales said, his words wintry. "I saw you reaching for that gun. Next time my slug will come closer — if you want a next time. It's up to you. I'm suggesting that you three sidewinders vamose pronto. But it's your move!"

The Deacon didn't speak at once. Hedge and Limpy looked to him for leadership. Jiménez stood rubbing his throat on which was a raw red welt made by the hempen noose.

"It's your move!" Caliper was grinning widely now.

"You're apparently looking for trouble," the Deacon said in injured tones, while his mind moved swiftly, seeking a way out of the fix.

"Yeah, we are." Caliper's grin widened.

"May I remind you," the Deacon pointed out, "that we are three to your two? We have the advantage."

"That's just lovely." Nogales chuckled. "All right, go ahead and jerk your irons!"

Hedge Furlow was making violent signs to the Deacon, but the Deacon failed to see them. Furlow finally made himself heard. "Look, Deacon, mebbe we'd better drop this matter for the present." Furlow's tones sounded shaky.

The Deacon shifted his glance to Furlow. Furlow was violently shaking his head.

"Judging from Furlow's actions," Caliper laughed, "maybe you don't hold the advantage, Deacon. I can see he don't want any more of our game. But make up your mind fast. What's it to be?"

Furlow's actions had somewhat unsettled the Deacon; plainly, the thought coursed the Deacon's mind, Furlow knew these intruders and was advising against a fight. Perhaps Furlow knew whereof he spoke. After a moment the frown was smoothed from the Deacon's face. "I don't want any trouble," he said unctuously. "I go through the world avoiding such whenever possible. Perhaps it would be better to withdraw. However," fixing Nogales and Caliper with a stern glance, "you two shall live to repent this day. I'm not speaking idle words. I'm a peace-loving man, but there's a judgment for evildoers. Mark what I say."

"We'll mark it with lead, if you like." Caliper sounded disappointed.

"On your way, then," Nogales said disgustedly. "The sooner you clear the atmosphere, the better we'll like it."

Bristol was coiling his rope. Furlow was already leading his horse off to one side and preparing to mount. The Deacon spoke again. "Limpy, Hedge — bring that Mexican with us."

"You leave that Mex here," Nogales thundered. "If you don't leave pronto you'll find yourself leaving on the end of a forty-five slug. Now git! Scat!"

Led by Hedge Furlow, the three men "scatted." In an instant the desert shrubbery had closed about them as their ponies' hoofs drummed softly across the sandy wastes.

A long sigh of relief lifted from Jiménez' lips. Color flooded back into his face as he stumbled toward Nogales and Caliper, his hands still bound behind his back.

"Señores," he cried, "you have save' my life. Everytheeng I'm owe to you. What can I do to repay?"

"Tell me where I can get some grub," Caliper grunted. "I'm hungry."

"And a drink." Nogales smiled, untying the Mexican's bonds.

III

The Land Without Law

Two hours had passed since the Deacon and his companions left the scene of their attempted hanging. For twenty minutes they had pushed their ponies hard, heading west. After a time they had slackened pace. From then on Hedge Furlow had done most of the talking, the ponies dropping to a walk as the Deacon and Limpy became more and more interested in the conversation.

The Deacon finally said slowly, "Perhaps it is best that we sidestepped the encounter, if Scott and Maxwell are all that you claim."

"I'm telling you I was there," Furlow insisted earnestly. "Them two is hell on wheels when they get started. Me, I was plenty lucky to escape with a whole skin."

"It's right hard to believe," Limpy commented unbelievingly. "Those two might be good, but after all — Well, you say there was the four of you waiting at this Tip-Top Corral and those two cleaned you out."

"I'm telling you," Furlow said huffily. "You don't have to take my word for it. Ask anybody in Orejano about them two. I was plumb lucky to be just wounded slight; I might have been rubbed out complete. When they told me to get, I grabbed a hawss and got. And that ain't all they done. Feller named Krouch had a right nice cattle scheme worked out in the Orejano country, but Scott and Maxwell cleaned him and the gang up plenty."

The Deacon said sarcastically, "You sound like an admirer of their efforts."

Furlow swore savagely. "Like hell I'm an admirer! But, like I said, next time I cross guns with that pair I want to be sure they're plenty outnumbered. Why! The first day those two hit Orejano they cleaned out the Apache Saloon and it was full of tough hombres too."

"Those two alone?" Limpy demanded.

Furlow shook his head. "There was a cowman we were set to rub out. We was doing all right, too, until those two happened to ride into town and took a hand. Damned if I know why they did it, but they immediate set to and give this cowman backing. That's the trouble with Maxwell and Scott. You can't figure 'em. They'll jump into anybody's battle, without even knowing what it's about — just like they did with us today."

"And where were you when this fight at the Apache Saloon was going on?" the Deacon demanded. "Don't tell me you faced the guns of such paragons on two occasions and each time escaped with a whole skin."

Furlow flushed. "I stood it as long as I could, then I hightailed it. I ain't a fool."

Limpy let out a guffaw. "Just brave when you can plug 'em in the back, eh? Like you did with that deputy over near Yuma."

"Dammit!" Furlow said hotly. "You two would have been in the clink by this time if I hadn't rubbed out that deputy. I got as much nerve as the next man, but you can go plumb to hell, Bristol, if you think —"

"Peace, brethern, peace," the Deacon interposed firmly. "We'll settle with Scott and Maxwell in our own good time, I reckon."

"When'll that be?" Limpy wanted to know.

"I've been doing a mite of thinking," the Deacon said. "We'll cross the Colorado tonight — though I don't reckon we'd better cross at Yuma — and get back to Ramrod Ridge. If we're not badly mistaken, there's thirty thousand in gold thereabouts. I figure that Jiménez will tell Scott and Maxwell about that gold. From what Hedge tells us, Scott and Maxwell will be keen to get in on it. They seem to be the sort that's always looking for adventure and cutting into other folks' arguments. I've a feeling they'll follow us to Ramrod Ridge. Once there, we'll have things our own way."

Furlow said dubiously, "You're right about the adventure and cutting in on other folks' arguments, but that thirty thousand gold will never tempt 'em. I already told you they're well heeled."

The Deacon said sarcastically, "Well heeled, or no, I've yet to see the man thirty thousand wouldn't tempt."

"You don't understand," Hedge said earnestly. "That missing gold would be just a drop in the bucket for Scott. Must be you never read in the papers about where he fell heir to old Angus MacLaren, the Chicago meat packer, when he died. Funny part was, Scott hardly knew him, but there wa'n't any other relations. Scott got a lot of various interests. Cripes, this cowman I was telling you about in Orejano, they backed him in an outfit —"

"Great Jehovah!" the Deacon ejaculated.

Limpy finally found his voice. "And with

all that money, those two go riding about the country —"

"I'm telling you," Hedge insisted. "They give it out that they're looking for the ideal place for a ranch. If you ask me, they just got itching feet and like to see new places. Shucks! All that stuff came out after they'd cleaned up Orejano. It was in the papers."

The Deacon's eyes narrowed in thought. "This," he said at last, "is better than I hoped for. We'll get back to Ramrod Ridge, Limpy. There's never any law officers bother that neck of the range. I feel right certain Scott, Maxwell, and the Mexican will show up there before long. Simon Crawford will be waiting there for us to show up too. This is something that needs another head beside my own. But I think Simon will see it my way. We'll get the thirty thousand and more, too, or I miss my guess. Not to mention squaring accounts with that pair —"

"Look" — Furlow had a sudden idea — "if Scott and Maxwell follow us to Ramrod Ridge they'll be almost sure to cross the Colorado at Yuma. After we cross, we could swing back and wait until they came along the trail, then get them from a hide-out spot."

"Don't talk like a fool," the Deacon protested. "That would be biting the hand that feeds us — I plan they will feed us — and more. No, we'll get to Ramrod Ridge as soon as possible and wait for them to walk into our little trap. That's the way I see it, and I reckon Simon Crawford will agree with me. Come on, let's show a little more speed."

IV

California Bound

Caliper sat at the rough board table in the cantina in Paraiso. Before him was a bowl of chili, a foot-long piece of sausage, some tortillas, and a half-filled bottle of warm beer. By this time Jiménez had set the bar to rights and was engaged in sweeping out the broken glass which littered the floor. A Mexican woman entered the door bearing a platter on which were some fried eggs and more tortillas. She was barefooted and clad in a voluminous skirt and shawl.

Caliper grinned. "Right good chow, señora. If this second course is as good as the first, this little snack will hold me until suppertime — maybe."

The Mexican woman's eyes bulged at the inroads he'd already made on her first serving. "*¡Madre de Dios!*" she exclaimed to Jiménez. "This one, he eats like the caballo!"

"Except," Caliper pointed out gravely, "the horse eats hay."

"*Sí, sí.*" The woman laughed. "And the oat, also, no?"

"If he don't," Caliper chuckled, "he oat to."

The woman stared blankly, frowned, and left the cantina. Jiménez gazed reproachfully at Caliper then sadly resumed his sweeping.

Caliper said between mouthfuls of sausage, eggs, and tortillas, "All right, Jiménez, get on with your story — Say, what's your first name?"

"Esteban, señor."

"Huh, Steve, eh? Steve Jiménez. Danged if I know whether to call you Steve or Jimmy. All right, Jimmy-Steve, get on with your story."

"Is all, Señor. No more to tell." The Mexican's face was blank now. To change the subject, he asked, "Where is your pardner go?"

"He's out around the town some place," Caliper said carelessly. "Probably giving away ten-dollar bills. The minute we hit this town he mentioned something about it being poor-looking."

"I do not understand, Señor Maxwell."

"Nobody else understands Nogales either — 'cepting maybe me. And I'm not always sure. But he likes to help folks."

41

At that moment Nogales strode into the cantina, his spur rowels clinking musically across the beaten earth floor. He dropped into a chair across from Caliper, seized a tortilla and, drawing his knife, cut off a chunk of sausage. Jiménez brought a bottle and glass and placed them on the table before him.

Caliper said, "Been out whitting down your capital again, I'll bet."

"Hell!" Nogales said disgustedly, "I can't even seem to catch up to the income. . . . You learn anything much?"

Caliper lowered his voice. "I'm wondering if this Mex has been smoking marijuana. Damned if he don't spill some queer *habla*. He's from a place called Ramrod Ridge over in California. Out on the desert it is."

"What's so funny about that?"

"This desert he tells about. It's surrounded by mountains and you don't go far before you see waterfalls —"

"Sounds goofy."

"— and palm trees."

"Palm trees? Cripes! They just grow in Egypt and places like that."

"Not according to Jimmy-Steve they don't. Furthermore, I'm inclined to believe him."

"Now I know you've blowed your top. Do you feel all right, pard?" Nogales queried anxiously.

"I know it all sounds crazy, but I'm telling you what he told me."

Nogales shook his head skeptically. "Palm trees and waterfalls! Of all the —"

"And gold," Caliper said solemnly.

"I suppose that grows on the palm trees."

"Nope. There was a shipment of thirty thousand headed from San Diego to a place called San Bernadino. The shipment was raided by stick-up men before it got there. Now, get this, one man got away from the raiders, leading a pack mule that was carrying the gold. It's known he entered a box canyon but he never came out. So far as anybody knows. Neither did the gold. Both just plumb disappeared."

Nogales laughed skeptically. "The pack mule, I suppose, was found sliding down the waterfall. Look, Caliper, don't be so gullible. I reckon so much food must have gone to your head instead of your stomach."

"Don't believe me," Caliper said heatedly. "Ask the Mex."

"I intend doing just that." Nogales called Esteban to his side. The Mexican put down his broom and approached the table.

43

He listened respectfully while Nogales talked. Nogales concluded. "Now, I want to know, is that a straight tale you're slinging?"

"*Sí*, Señor Scott. But more I cannot reveal to you. Eet ees not my story, but the secret of the Señor Vincent of Ramrod Ridge. I'm not tell even you, excep' you have prove to be my frien' and save my body from thees *cabrón* who is call' Deacon. He and hees pals they try to learn from me what goes with thees gold. Even if I'm know I not tell heem, though. But I am not know."

"This Vincent you mentioned — does he know?"

Jiménez shook his head. "Eet was hees son what make the disappear weeth the gold. He like ver' much to know too."

"As I get it," Caliper broke in, "the Deacon and his pards trailed Jimmy-Steve here and tried to force out of him information he didn't have after he left Ramrod Ridge."

Nogales asked directly, "Why'd you come here, Jimmy-Steve?"

"I'm come to visit my brothair what own thees cantina. Eet was hees wife what cook the food for you. But my brothair have gone to Mexico, so I'm stay here to operate thees place ontil he return'. I am — how you call heem? — bread-winnair for the family of my brothair, no? When he return', then I'm return to Ramrod Ridge where I'm work for the Señor Ethan Vincent."

Nogales felt the Mexican was holding back something, but he didn't press the matter. Instead he said, "I'd sure like to see those palm trees, if you're telling the truth."

"I'm swear I'm tell truth, señor," Jiménez said eagerly. "You come weeth me. You see for yourself."

"Hey," Caliper interposed suddenly, "don't dates come from palm trees? Or is it cocoanuts?"

Nogales sighed. "Always thinking of your stomach. I can see we're headed for California. Hey, Jimmy-Steve, when do we leave?"

"When my brothair return'. I mus' stay and make the money for hees wife and little ones."

Caliper said, "No telling when this brother will return. If Jimmy-Steve knows what he went to Mexico for, he won't say. I questioned him about it, but he got plumb reluctant to talk."

Nogales considered. "I'd like to get rid-

45

ing if we're going," he said slowly. "Suppose we buy out this cantina? The money should keep her going for some time."

"It's an idea." Caliper nodded. "But you'd have to have someone run it for you —"

"Cripes," Nogales grunted, "I'd give it back to her. I don't want to be burdened with just one cantina. When I go into the liquor business I'll buy me a distillery."

Jiménez' sister-in-law was called in, the matter was discussed. It appeared her husband already had valued the cantina for a prospective customer — valued it at one hundred dollars, with the stock and good will thrown in. The matter was speedily settled and the money paid over, much to the Mexican woman's bewilderment. She still didn't understand quite how it came about and stood at the bar, clutching the bills in her hand. Jiménez ran to catch up and saddle his pony. Nogales and Caliper moved out to the street and stood near their mounts, waiting, and rolling Durham cigarettes.

By this time there were numerous Mexicans on the street. Many of them bowed and smiled at Nogales. Caliper said, "It's plain to be seen you passed out some of your money in this town. One of these days you'll wake up and find yourself broke."

"Sometimes I wish I would," Nogales said. "Cripes! I don't even get any fun out of playing poker any more; I know it won't make any difference if I lose or win. As for this town, hell, there's a lot of folks here don't know what it means to eat regular. If I've got plenty, why shouldn't they have some?" He smiled. "Ever hear that saying, 'It's more blessed to give than receive'?"

"Darned if you don't sound like that Deacon feller — except that you're sincere."

Nogales chuckled. "I had an old granddad once that was always spouting gospel-talk like the Deacon. Only he was sincere too. Me, I used to know some of those sayings by heart. One of these days I'll be cracking back at the Deacon with some of his own talk."

"You figure to cross his trail again?"

"If we don't meet him in Ramrod Ridge I'll be plenty surprised, Cripes! Yes, he'll be heading back there all right. He's after that gold. You know that."

"You figure there'll be some lead-slinging?" Caliper asked eagerly.

"I'll be plumb disappointed if there isn't."

"Me, too, pard."

A sudden surprised exclamation left

Nogales' lips. "Look what's coming," he said.

It was Jiménez, riding to meet them on a sleek bay gelding. The man had changed his overalls and wore riding boots. On his head was a steeple-crowned sombrero with considerable embroidery around the rim. A gaudy yellow neckerchief encircled his neck and a forty-five six-shooter hung at the cartridge belt that encircled his slim hips.

"Well, I'll be damned!" Caliper gasped. "Geez! He sits that saddle like he was born to riding. Me, I'd figured him for just another greasy-faced Mex without no ambition above running a bar. Gosh, Nogales, he looks like all man."

"He does that." Nogales nodded. "He won't hold us back any on the trip. And I'm betting he'll back us to the last ditch in a jam too."

The horse came nearer. Jiménez greeted them with a flash of even white teeth. "Ready, *amigos?*" he asked.

"Gosh, Jimmy-Steve, you look plumb elegant," Caliper said.

"*Gracias,* Señor Maxwell. I'm surprise you — no?"

"You surprised us — yes!" Nogales grinned. "Well, let's ride."

The horses responded to the touch of spurs and drummed rapidly out of town. That night the riders entered Yuma on the Colorado River. The following morning they crossed the river by ferry, then headed their ponies up into the great Colorado Desert. They talked but little now, but each of the three wondered what lay in store for them at Ramrod Ridge. That there would be danger in plenty, no man doubted.

V

Gunfire!

During the week that followed Nogales, Caliper, and Jimmy-Steve (as they'd fallen into the habit of calling Jiménez) made considerable progress toward their objective. The Mexican had fitted well into the companionship of the two cow-pokes and they liked him more every day. They hadn't pushed their ponies hard. As Nogales had said, "No telling, when we reach Ramrod Ridge, we might need some fresh horse flesh. No use killing off our mounts crossing this desert country."

And hot desert country it was. The spring sun hurled down waves of heat that only men conditioned to hot climates could withstand. Two days before they had passed a great salt sink, a dazzling expanse of gleaming white that stretched north and south for nearly fifty miles. Salton Sink, Jiménez had called it, at the same time pointing out along the rocky bluffs some distance away the visible lines etched in the rock, marking the point at which, ages ago, an ancient sea had washed the cliffs.

"You mean to say," Nogales had asked curiously, "that at one time this desert was an ocean?"

"*Sí, amigo,*" Jiménez had replied. "So it is that the Señor Ethan Vincent has told me."

"Hmmm," Nogales mused. "Must be Vincent has a heap of education."

"The Señor Vincent is one very wise man."

Caliper had put in, "Seems danged queer when we think how we crossed the Colorado a few days back, there was so much water. Now, here's this Salton Sink and there isn't any left. Too bad somebody can't dig a canal over to this sink, from the Colorado, and let California have an ocean again. Then we could go fishing."

"Mebbe so," Nogales had conceded, "but I'm danged if I ever heard of anybody digging worms out of desert sand. And you can't fish without bait."

There had been plenty to see on the trip. The three headed north and slightly west, passing along the great desert valley sunk between twin mountain ranges. Far to the north, two mighty peaks reared precipitous heads: San Jacinto Mountain and San Gorgonio Peak, forming a pass that marked the way to the still distant town of San Bernardino. Desert willow and mesquite, both screw bean and honeypod, dotted the great sandy expanse. Now and then the riders passed an ironwood tree or a joshua lifting its weird daggers toward the sky of flaming blue.

"I'm danged if I know how anything can grow in this heat," Nogales panted, mopping perspiration from his brow with an already soaking bandanna.

Caliper chuckled, "I'll betcha it gets hot here in summer."

"Cripes!" Nogales growled. "What do you call this?"

"Anything I'd call it would come under the head of profanity." Caliper smiled. "You're right, pard, it's plenty hot — hey!" He paused and pointed ahead. "What's that? Looks like somebody had set the brush afire."

The other two followed his pointing arm. Huge puffs of smoke appeared to be rising from the plain, near the edge of the mountains. Jiménez shook his head. "Eet is not fire you see," he explained. "Where you look, there is a smoke-tree forest. True eet does look like the smoke from this distance, but eef you come close then you make the admire of the so beautiful

52

flowers on theese trees."

"Damn' if we don't learn something new all the time," Nogales grunted. "Are we heading through that forest?"

Jiménez shook his head. "From here we bear more to the left. We head for the hills. Prett' soon you see theese palm tree', like I'm told you."

"Hills sound good to me," Caliper said. "It should be some cooler over thataway."

They guided the ponies in a more westerly direction. Gradually the mountains came nearer. The way lay over firmer footing. More rock was to be seen as they made the slow, gradual ascent. Creosote bush, flame-tipped ocotillo, and deerhorn cacti dotted their path. Ahead lay a great rocky ridge thickly covered with spiny growth of beavertail cacti and catclaw. An hour later the three riders had swung around the ridge and started a long descent into a gently winding canyon. It was cooler now; now and then a cottonwood tree was to be seen. The canyon grew narrower as they progressed. On either side high walls reared rocky ledges from many of which sprouted yucca plants, their delicate white bells lifting high above the daggerlike leaves.

Suddenly, as the three riders rounded a

turn in the canyon, Jiménez exclaimed, "There ees the first palm. Now, *amigos*, am I the liar?"

Nogales and Caliper gazed in wonder at the palm tree ahead, its leafy fronds spread sixty feet above them, its slender trunk clothed in a thick cloak, composed of the dead fronds of previous years, hanging from its sides.

"Well, I'm dam'd!" Nogales ejaculated. "I'm even commencing to believe about the waterfall now. Gosh, it's not more than an hour or so since we were broiling out in the desert. What a country!"

They drove their ponies slowly through the winding canyon. More and more palm trees appeared, still taller than the first one they'd seen. The way grew shady and cool. A thin stream welled from the earth, and increased in size as the three advanced until it was a broad, babbling brook, coursing its cool, singing way along the boulder-strewn watercourse. Overhead the breeze made dry, rasping sounds in the clashing palm leaves.

They stopped the horses in the middle of the rapidly running creek and got down themselves for a cool drink. Palm trees cast black shadows around them, intensified by the blazing sun above.

Caliper rose from the stream, wiping his mouth. He gazed in some awe at the palms towering overhead. "Gosh, it's nice here," he sighed. "At the same time, those dry leaves sound sort of spooky rustling in the wind thataway."

The others were in the saddle again. Nogales said, "Now that you mention spooky things, I've had a feeling that somebody was watching us ever since we entered this canyon. Mebbe I'm crazy, mebbe it's just hunch. But once or twice, as I glanced up at these sloping canyon walls, I thought I saw movement in the brush."

"Birds, yes?" Jiménez asked.

Nogales frowned. "Might be. Still, I don't think so."

"Nogales," Caliper said, "here comes somebody now."

They looked ahead through the forest of palm trunks and caught a glimpse of a figure on horseback. As it came nearer Jiménez said, "It's all right. It's only Johnny Two-Horses."

"Who's Johnny Two-Horses?" Nogales asked.

"Johnny ees one of the Cahuilla tribe — ees Injun."

"Oh, an Indian. Peaceful?" Caliper asked.

Jiménez nodded. "Nowadays the Cahuillas are for peace. Johnny Two-Horses ees good hombre."

They sat their horses, waiting, while the Indian approached. As he came nearer they saw he was clad in overalls, with a colored cloth bound around his forehead to hold back his raven-black hair. He wore no shirt; his muscular torso gleamed with perspiration. His feet were covered with tattered moccasins. The horse he rode looked like a definite advertisement for a boneyard or glue factory. It was gaunt, rib-thin, swaybacked, with a mangy tail and mane.

"He should be called Johnny Half-a-Horse," Nogales chuckled.

The Indian came up and greeted Jiménez. His face was flat and brown; he was of medium height; his black eyes looked intelligent. Jiménez talked to him in a mixture of Spanish and the Cahuilla dialect before introducing the native to Caliper and Nogales. The Indian gravely shook hands, then resumed the conversation with Jiménez. The two talked seriously for some minutes; finally the Indian nodded in friendly fashion to the two cowboys, kicked his pony in the ribs, and moved on.

Nogales looked curiously after the man a

moment, then swung back to Jiménez, saying, "I don't savvy that Injun talk, but I managed to pick up some of your Spanish. To me it sounded like Johnny Two-Horses mentioned something about a wild man."

Jimmy-Steve nodded. "Johnny tell me he is go for visit his grandfather who raises the few of sheep in a canyon not many mile' from here. About thees wild man — you are correc'. Johnny says for many weeks theese wild hombre have inhabit theese hills and thees canyon." The Mexican shrugged. "Maybee what you call — how you say heem? — the superstition, no?"

"Indian superstition, eh?" Caliper nodded. "That's probably right. Has this wild man hurt anybody yet?"

"Is harmless," Jimmy-Steve said. "But he has steal of the Injun food. The Injuns scare' of him, like he not human."

"Many Indians hereabouts?" Nogales asked.

"Is small tribe — fifty or sixty — of Cahuillas, live a few mile' thees side of Ramrod Ridge. Ver' peaceful."

They rode on for half an hour, Nogales and Caliper still marveling at the palm trees. Nogales suddenly drew rein where the palms were thickest. Caliper, noticing a

57

frown on his face, asked, "What's up, pard?"

"I still feel like somebody was spying on us from that hillside to the right," Nogales said uneasily. "I don't like it. You two ride ahead. I'll wait here a spell. Maybe if whoever is watching us thinks I'm alone, we'll get some action."

Caliper protested Nogales remaining, but Nogales had his way. "No, you two go on. I'm waiting," Nogales said firmly. "Only don't get too far ahead. If you should hear a fuss break out, come a-running. I'll yell if I have time, of course. Go on, now."

Somewhat reluctantly Caliper and Jimmy-Steve spurred their horses on. Nogales drew out Durham tobacco and rolled a cigarette. He sat his saddle, eyes darting along the hillside, eyes alert for the first sign of danger. There was nothing to be seen or heard except the sounds of the running stream and the dry clashing of palm fronds overhead. Nogales scratched a match for his cigarette and the sound rasped sharply against the sounds made by the breeze through the palm trees. Caliper and Jiménez were beyond view now, having passed beyond the next bend in the canyon.

Five minutes passed; ten. Nogales drew deeply on his cigarette and the gray smoke from his lips drifted swiftly off among the shadows. Finally he pinched off the glowing end of the butt and dropped it on the ground. "I must have been mistaken," he muttered, still unconvinced.

His eyes strayed through the trunks of the palms to a spot on the hillside to his right. Was there movement up there, or did he just imagine it? At the point under his scrutiny the brush grew high. There were tall clumps of beavertail cacti and creosote bush. Two huge barrel cacti reared heavy, ponderous forms against the landscape. Nogales started to glance away, his gaze seeking movement still higher. Then it happened.

The roar of a forty-five shattered the silence. Nogales felt the Stetson jerk on his head and knew the hat's crown had been pierced by a bullet. Close on the first shot came another burst of gunfire. This time the bullets didn't even come close.

Now, from up near the two barrel cacti, Nogales saw powder smoke curling from the brush. Whirling his pony, he plunged in spurs and headed for the hillside. Far up the canyon, ahead of him, he heard the shouts of Caliper and Jiménez. They'd heard the shots and would be coming on the run.

"Cripes!" Nogales gritted through set teeth. "I hope they get here soon enough. I may have my hands full!"

His horse splashed through the stream and raced up the hillside. Shooting again broke out as Nogales urged his pony up the slope. Suddenly he felt the straining animal lurch to one side. Nogales twisted about in the saddle as the pony crashed down, then leaped to the brushy earth, his six-shooter already in hand.

VI

The Wild Man

Somewhere, beyond those two barrel cacti, rose a huge granite boulder and beyond that was a small hollow; it was from behind this boulder the shots were coming. As Nogales mounted up the slope, he could hear the sounds of his pony thrashing in the brush below and behind him. From beyond the boulder there came a high-pitched half-yell, half-scream, then the sounds of cursing.

An ugly, bearded face peered around the corner of the boulder. The barrel of a six-shooter, trained on Nogales, slipped into view. Nogales threw himself to one side, thumbing one swift shot from his Colt gun as he moved. There came two explosions, close together. Nogales felt the breeze of a leaden slug whip past his face. The man behind the boulder gave a shrill cry of agony, then pitched into full view to sprawl face down in the brush.

The next instant Nogales had leaped around the corner of the boulder, past the body of the man he had just shot. Three men were in sight. One man was running swiftly toward some horses tethered back of a clump of mesquite trees. A second man lay prone on the earth, blood seeping from a wound in his head. The third man, six-shooter clutched in his right fist, was slowly backing away from Nogales' approach.

"Damn you!" he snarled. "Keep outten this. This ain't your business —"

Without stopping to complete the words, he pressed trigger. Nogales fired at the same instant, then threw a hasty shot toward the man running to the horses. His second shot missed, but the man who had fired on him was down on hands and knees now. Nogales threw a third shot at the fleeing man, but the fellow was out of sight by this time. There came the abrupt sounds of a rapidly leaving pony.

From the earth in front of Nogales came a sudden explosion. The man he'd downed was struggling up, getting back into the fight, when Nogales threw one swift shot, shooting by instinct rather than careful aiming.

That last shot did the work. The man groaned and once more sank down. From the opposite side of the hill came the noise made by a horse crashing through brush. Nogales started in that direction, then checked the movement: the man would be beyond shot before he could sight him.

Powder smoke thinned and drifted away on the breeze. Nogales plugged out his empty shells and reloaded the six-shooter. Two men were sprawled at his feet. Another man — the first one he'd shot — lay just beyond the edge of the boulder. There were more sounds now as Caliper and Jimmy-Steve came plunging up the hillside.

"You all right, pard?" Caliper yelled anxiously.

Nogales stepped into view from behind the big rock. "I'm all right," he called back. "I'm damn'd if I know what all this ruckus was about, though." He glanced down past Caliper and the Mexican. His horse was up again, peacefully cropping at certain tender leaves in the brush. Nogales gave a sigh of relief; anyway, his pony wasn't injured.

Caliper and Jimmy-Steve reached Nogales' side. They glanced at the still form sprawled in the brush, then at Nogales.

"What happened, pard?" Caliper panted.

"First I knew," Nogales said, "somebody slung a slug that ventilated my Stet hat. It come from up here. I started up to see what it was all about. My pony stepped in a hole, or something, and threw me. I came the rest of the way on foot. I was nearly to this rock when that hombre" — motioning toward the form at his feet — "started pouring lead at me. I made a lucky shot and downed him. There were three more hombres beyond the boulder. One high-tailed it away. I tried to get him, but missed. The other feller and I exchanged some slugs and he lost out. The third man was down when I arrived." He concluded by giving a few more details regarding the matter.

Jiménez stooped down, grasped the hair of the dead man at his feet, and pulled the man's face into view. Then he allowed the head to drop back. "Tim Church," he said shortly.

"Who's Tim Church?"

"Bad hombre. Hangs around Ramrod Ridge."

"He ain't bad any longer," Caliper said shortly. "What about the other fellers, Nogales?"

Nogales led the way around the corner of the rock where two men lay in the dust. Jiménez recognized one of them immediately. "Jack Schmidt," he said. "He's pardner with Tim Church. Just as bad." The other man he didn't know. "Looks — what you call heem? — familiar, I'm theenk."

The man was white-haired; his face lined and drawn. He was thin to the point of emaciation; his clothing was in tatters; the sole was missing from one of his boots. His white hair was long and tousled, partly covering his face; his beard, while not so long, was matted and dirty. His bony hands were like claws; one of them still gripped a Colt's six-shooter.

Nogales knelt at his side. After a moment he raised his head. "There's still some life in this old hombre," he announced.

"Schmidt isn't quite finished yet," replied Caliper, who with Jiménez had been making an examination of the other man. "I figure he ain't long to live though."

Jiménez said, "Maybee we can make one of these hombre' talk. I go for get the canteen on my saddle."

He disappeared around the corner of the rock.

Nogales moved over with Caliper, kneeling at Schmidt's side. It was plain to be seen Schmidt hadn't long to live. His breath came with difficulty; a frothy red foam had formed on his lips. Nogales braced the man's head in a more comfortable, higher, position. After a moment Schmidt opened his eyes. He gazed vacantly about, then a groan parted his lips. "Water," he gasped feebly.

"It's coming, feller," Nogales said, not unkindly.

"This is the . . . end . . . eh?" Schmidt asked.

"I reckon it is," Nogales replied. "If you've got anything to say, you'd better talk fast. What was the idea of throwing down on me?"

"It wasn't your scrap." Schmidt spoke with difficulty. "We were out . . . looking for the . . . wild man. Well . . . we found him . . . or he . . . found us . . ." Schmidt's voice faltered, and his eyes closed once more.

"Wild man?" Caliper exclaimed; he glanced toward the silent, white-haired form stretched on the earth a few yards away. "Hey, Nogales, that must be the wild man that Johnny Two-Horses mentioned."

"That's a right good guess, Caliper."

At that moment Jimmy-Steve came hurrying around the rock with the canteen in his hand. They forced some water between Schmidt's pallid lips, then at a word from Nogales Jiménez went to see what, if anything, could be done about the wild man.

Within a few moments Schmidt re-opened his eyes. They gave him another drink. After a time his breath came stronger.

"Like I'm tellin' you," Schmidt continued, "this wa'n't your fight, feller. We'd been lookin' for . . . the wild man. We'd sighted him . . . once or twice . . . in the past two weeks . . . but could never . . . get close enough . . . to catch him."

The halting details continued. Schmidt and his companions had sighted the wild man earlier in the day, making his way through the brush along the hillsides. After a time Nogales and his companions had been sighted and Schmidt had realized the wild man was watching Nogales, Caliper, and Jiménez.

"We seen you three," Schmidt continued, "ridin' through the canyon, under them palms. We'd get a glimpse of you . . . every so often. Somehow . . . we lost sight of the wild man. . . . Then we see your two pards . . . ridin' on . . . and figured you was with 'em. Didn't know you was below a-tall. Just about the time we was set to start lookin' . . . for the wild man again . . . I happens to look up the slope above us. There he was . . . with a gun in his hand.

The minute he sees me . . . he cuts loose with his fire. Missed me, but I reckon his shot must have come close to you . . . 'cause you came charging up the slope . . ."

"Plugged the crown of my Stet hat," Nogales said.

". . . and then," Schmidt continued, "he come bargin' down on top of us. We . . . had to shoot . . ." He paused, and asked for more water. His eyes were growing glassy now. Jiménez brought the canteen.

"All this don't explain," Nogales said grimly, "why you fellers started hurling lead in my direction."

"Don't talk like a damn' fool," Schmidt muttered. "I reckon Jiménez knows the wild man. That gold is as good to us as it is to you —"

"What gold you talking about?" Nogales asked. "Who is this wild man?"

Schmidt feebly shook his head. He tried to say something but words failed him. "How — how about a cigarette?" he finally gasped out.

Caliper started to roll a cigarette. Nogales asked, "Who was your pal that escaped, when I arrived here?"

"Think . . . I'll be . . . fool enough . . . to tell . . . ? Wish I . . . had a drink . . . of liquor. . . ."

"Look, Schmidt," Nogales spoke earnestly, "tell us what you know about this. You haven't much chance. You might as well go out clean —"

The scratching of a match intruded on Nogales' words. Caliper said quietly, "I reckon I'll smoke this cigarette myself now."

Jack Schmidt was dead.

By this time Jiménez was back working over the wild man. He had cut away the man's tattered shirt and was examining a wound in the right side, just under the ribs. Blood flowed from another wound in the man's left arm, though Jiménez, by this time, had nearly stanched the flow. A third bullet had creased his scalp.

"I'm theenk, thees man, he pull through," Jiménez said.

Nogales and Caliper moved over to Jiménez' side. "Maybe we can learn something from him when he comes to," Nogales said, making a brief examination of the wounds. "There's not much we can do for him here, though. How far is Ramrod Ridge, now, Jimmy-Steve?"

"Oh, 'bout 'leven-fifteen mile'."

Nogales nodded. "We should make it in a couple of hours. Schmidt's and Church's horses are back yonderly a spell. We can load them on one horse and put this wild man on the other. I reckon we better get moving as soon as possible."

Jiménez poured some water from the canteen into his bandanna and commenced bathing the wild man's face. Suddenly, as he mopped back the tangled white hair from the man's forehead, Jiménez leaped to his feet with a sharp cry. Then he knelt down once more and closely examined the wild man's features.

"What's up, Jimmy-Steve?" Caliper asked curiously.

For a moment Jiménez didn't reply. He appeared almost frightened as he gazed intently at the wild man's features. Then, abruptly, *"¡Madre de Dios!"* Jiménez exclaimed. "It is indeed he!"

"What you talking about?" Nogales asked sharply. "Who is it?"

"I'm tell you" — Jiménez pointed one shaking finger at the wild man's unconscious form — "thees hombre what look so old, weeth the white hair, he ees not old. I'm know heem!"

Caliper snapped, "What you talking about, Jimmy-Steve? Who is it?"

Jiménez gulped. "Thees one you call the wil' man — he is the one what disappear with the thirty thousand in gold —"

"But wasn't he a fairly young feller?" Nogales asked, puzzled. "It seems like you said he was around thirty."

"*Sí, sí.*" Jiménez nodded. "But thees one is the same. By all the saints I'm swear it. Thees ees the Señor Fred Vincent!"

"That being the case," Nogales nodded, "I reckon we'd better get him to his father's place at Ramrod Ridge as soon as possible. Maybe we can get medical aid there. Look smart, pards. We'll bring up those horses and get moving."

VII

Simon Crawford

There wasn't any excuse for Ramrod Ridge — at least for the existence of such a town there was very little good reason. In the beginning, when the T.N. & A.S. railroad had planned to construct a line through California, it had seemed a reasonable site for such a settlement. Men poured in, expecting big wages, and the building of houses got under way. Land salesmen talked glibly of the big profits to be made, when the rails came through. Speculators bought up acreage in the expectation that Ramrod Ridge would someday become a metropolis.

It drew its name from a near-by mile-long ridge of sand. Someone remarked that it looked like a ramrod. The name, Ramrod Ridge, was adopted. And then, abruptly, the T.N. & A.S. company abandoned its plans when the news broke that the Southern Pacific had already commenced construction of a line down through the eastern part of the state. In those days there wasn't enough business, or so the T.N. & A.S. officials considered, to warrant their going through with plans.

That was the end of the boom at Ramrod Ridge. Men left as quickly as they had poured in, leaving behind what practically amounted to a ghost town. Even the long, sandy ridge commenced to disappear under the devastating force of vagrant desert winds that shifted the dunes from one section to another from year to year. Remained only a collection of wooden shacks, the general store, and the single dusty main street. Oh, yes, and Simon Crawford, owner of the general store. Crawford always said he was too fat to make another move, but his intimates knew better. Where there was easy money to be picked up, there was found Simon Crawford.

In time, with Crawford's assistance, Ramrod Ridge became known as a mecca for lawbusters. There wasn't any law in the town. Lawbusters stopped there, feeling secure that they wouldn't be molested by peace officers, or that, at least, Crawford would give them ample warning and assist in their getaway. Meanwhile, so long as such crooks stayed, Crawford was more than willing to help them dispose of their money, or to assist in acting as a sort of "fence" through which stolen goods could be passed. Sometimes such goods consisted of pilfered jewels, marked bank notes, rustled cattle; in short, Crawford was interested in anything in which he might turn a dishonest penny.

His general store had a private back room for his intimates. The big outer room carried an ample stock of supplies at one side and operated a bar on the opposite. So far as the empty board shacks in the town were concerned, anybody was welcome to use them — so long as they gained Crawford's permission. Crawford had set himself up as a sort of a boss in Ramrod Ridge. Mostly the shacks provided stopping-off places for bandits, holdup men, stage robbers, and rustlers. Wanted men were sure of sanctuary there. Now and then honest prospectors stopped off for a day or so in one of the shacks and replenished their stores at the general store. These, too, were welcome, so long as they minded their own business.

Occasionally one of the small sheepherders from up in the hills came into town for supplies. Within a radius of twenty or thirty miles there were small cattle outfits whose punchers at rare inter-vals dropped in for a drink or some canned goods. But it wasn't considered good cow country thereabouts those days. Water was too scarce for one thing; fodder for another. And yet these small outfits managed to exist.

All of Crawford's stock was hauled in by freighters from San Rivedino, county seat of Rivedino County. That was expensive hauling and Crawford charged accordingly — as he even charged for water from the well back of his building. It was a good well; there was no danger of it ever running dry. But it was the only well in Ramrod Ridge.

The only other water in the vicinity was back about two or three miles from the shabby town and flowed in a cool stream from the waterfall in Quithatz Canyon across the acreage owned by old Ethan Vincent. Vincent had taken up the land many years before Ramrod Ridge came into existence; with Indian labor he had laid out and built his house as well as the canal that carried the water from Quithatz — water that, until Vincent's plans came to fruition, had flowed out into the desert to seep out of sight into the sandy waste.

Simon Crawford had many objectives in mind but one stood out foremost: someday, by hook or crook — probably by crook — he would own old Vincent's property. At present he was well on his way to achieving that objective.

There weren't any honest customers in his general store at the moment — just men who worked for or with him. One was Deacon Trumbull who lounged at the bar with a glass of whisky in one hand. Hedge Furlow stood next to the Deacon, and beside Furlow was Limpy Bristol. Farther down the long bar were half-a-dozen men in corduroys or denims wearing battered sombreros and six-shooters. They made an ugly-looking group and the bartender serving them looked to be the crook he was described as in certain reward dodgers circulating at present throughout Montana.

Crawford, himself, lounged in a big armchair not far from the bar. He weighed in the vicinity of three hundred pounds, though it may have been even more. His jowls bulged over his soiled white collar; his double chin hid from view part of the black string tie he affected. His tiny pig eyes were almost lost in creases of fat; the mouth was a thin, straight, cruel line. He wore a fancy vest, striped trousers, and flat-heeled boots. His coat was of the type known as a Prince Albert. On a hook against one wall rested his big black sombrero. He was nearly bald, though a few wisps of stringy brown hair were plastered across the top of his huge head. He looked flabby but he wasn't; he was strong as an ox and nearly as huge. At present the gun belt about his big waist had been loosened to allow ample expansion of his girth.

The Deacon stood facing Crawford, elbows resting back of him on the edge of the bar. ". . . and it seems to me," the Deacon was saying, "that you should make up your mind right soon, Simon." The words didn't carry to the far end of the bar where the other men stood. Only Furlow and Bristol were listening in on the conversation. The Deacon added, "I sort of look for them hombres to reach here nigh any day."

"Might be," Crawford conceded weightily. His heavy voice seemed to well up from the depths of his ponderous being. "At the same time I ain't no hankerin' to make up my mind about things until I've seen these fellers. Maybe this Maxwell and Scott has got money —"

"No doubt about that," Furlow put in.

"— but that's no sign we could get it as easy as you say —"

"The Deacon's scheme ought to work,"

Bristol put in eagerly. "We can make friends with 'em, like the Deacon said. After they've hung around with us a month or so it should be easy enough to bump 'em off. Then the Deacon forges Scott's name to a will and we collect —"

"I know, I know," Crawford rumbled impatiently. "You've said all that before. But I want to see these hombres first. Now quit picking at me."

"Sure, Simon, sure," the Deacon said hastily, recognizing the danger signs. "We won't say another word." He and his two companions gave their attention to drinks standing on the bar.

Crawford glowered at the backs of the three a moment, then gazed ominously toward the farther group of men at the bar. "You, Pilcher," he growled heavily. "You said you wanted to talk to me. What's up?"

A loose-jointed individual with an unshaven lantern jaw rocked up and stood before Crawford. His face was flushed with drink and he looked angry. "I'll tell you what's up," he commenced, when Crawford raised one ponderous hand like a ham to stop him.

"Wait," Crawford said, and the heavy tones carried a sneer. "I'll tell *you* what's happened."

By this time everyone in the room was watching.

Crawford went on, "Three months ago you came here with twenty cows you'd picked up from one of the coast outfits. Stolen cows! I told you I figured I could get five bucks a head for 'em, and I gave you a hundred dollars gold. Now I suppose when you passed through San Rivedino today you learned, someway, that I got ten bucks apiece for them cows. Now you want more money. Am I right?"

"You're damn right you're right! I ain't going to be cheated. I figure you should split that other hundred with me, and by Gawd! you're going to do it!"

Crawford's small eyes rested balefully on Pilcher before he spoke. "You, Pilcher," and Crawford's voice was dangerously calm, "you're new around here. Maybe you don't understand my ways —"

"By geez! You cheated me out of my rightful profits."

"Call it that if you like." Crawford shrugged his shoulders and the movement was something akin to a mountain shuddering under the force of an earthquake. "The fact remains that you get no more money from me. Now go back to your drink and shut up!"

Pilcher's face crimsoned. Throwing caution to the winds, he burst out, "Why, you great big toad, you can't do that to me —"

Then Crawford moved! The man's speed was unbelievable as he surged up from his armchair, took one quick, light-footed step. His right fist flailed through the air, catching Pilcher just below the left ear. The impact was like the kick of a mule. There came a sickening, cracking sound as Pilcher was lifted from his feet by the savage force and flung several yards before his limp body struck the floor. He lay without movement.

There wasn't a sound in the room now as Crawford, without a backward glance at his victim, turned toward his armchair again and wedged his bulk between its arms after gathering up the gun and cartridge belt he'd dropped when rising.

"So falleth the wrath of the mighty one," the Deacon murmured.

Crawford glared at him and the Deacon shut up.

Limpy Bristol and a couple of others went to examine Pilcher. After a moment Bristol glanced up. "I think you've broke his neck, Simon."

"I don't *think* so," Crawford growled. "The lousy bustard! A couple of you hombres get him out of here. If he should be able to travel by night, make it clear he ain't wanted in Ramrod Ridge. If he's all through traveling — well, you know what to do."

Two men stepped quickly forward and carried out the limp form.

"A hasty temper," the Deacon said sweetly, "is a bad thing to possess, but a good thing to keep."

"Never got me in any trouble," Crawford rumbled, "losing it."

"It might someday," Limpy Bristol pointed out. "Suppose Pilcher ain't hurt bad. He's going to be mad when he comes to. For revenge he might bring some law authorities here and —"

"In the first place," Crawford said scornfully, "he'd be afraid of cutting his own throat if he done that. In the second, supposin' he did, I'd just deny it. There ain't ary man here what's got the nerve to cross me up."

His small eyes glinted swiftly about the room. The men at the bar watching him suddenly turned back to their drinks. After a few minutes normal conversation was restored. Pilcher wasn't mentioned again. An hour slowly passed. The two men who had taken Pilcher out returned after a time.

They didn't say anything; Crawford's first glance had warned them to keep silent.

Suddenly Hedge Furlow lifted his head. "Sounds like somebody running the hoofs off'n a hawss," he offered. The room listened. The sounds of drumming hoofs came closer. A man stepped to the broad porch fronting the general store. In an instant he was back. "It's Ten-Spot Nance, boss!" he announced.

"What's bringing him back in a rush?" Crawford grunted. "He was with Tim Church and Jack Schmidt. Ain't they along?"

"Ten-Spot's alone and riding like all the devils in hell was ridin' his horse's tail," the man said.

The Deacon offered quietly, "I don't exactly like the sound of that. Maybe I can make a guess —"

"Hush up your caterwaulin', Deacon," Crawford said irritatedly.

The Deacon hushed. The sounds of running hoofs came nearer, then halted before the general store. Flying dust floated through the open doorway. There was the noise of booted feet on the porch and Ten-Spot Nance rushed in. He was a mustached individual of medium height with eyes set too closely together.

"Boss!" he cried, panting hard, "there's hell to pay! We nearly had young Vincent when Jiménez showed up —"

"I knew I could make a guess," the Deacon said wearily. "Coming events cast their shadows before. Scott and Maxwell butted in and —"

"Damn you, hush!" Crawford bellowed. "I want to hear what's happened."

VIII

"That's Fighting Talk!"

"It's just like I've been telling you," the Deacon said sometime later. "Scott and Maxwell are bad medicine, Simon. You won't be able to push them around like you do the rest of us fellers."

"Never pushed you around none," Crawford rumbled peevishly. And added quickly, "That ain't meanin' I wouldn't was I a mind to." The Deacon didn't say anything. Crawford continued, "I still don't understand, Ten-Spot, how this Nogales Scott hombre downed both Schmidt and Church. They were both right good with their shootin' irons."

"That's the way it was." Nance shrugged his shoulders.

"What were you doing?" Crawford demanded.

"I went to get a horse," Nance explained glibly. "I figured that maybe Vincent wa'n't dead, and if I could get him back here, you could question him like you've been wanting to."

"You're sure for certain it was Vincent?" Crawford growled.

"It's him. He ain't shaved for months and his hair's white —"

"And you ran to get a horse to bring him to me?"

"That's it, boss. I figured sure that Tim and Jack could handle this Scott hombre before his pals got —"

"You're a liar!" Crawford rapped out savagely. "You run for a horse so you could hightail it. Don't lie to me, Nance —"

"Aw, Simon," Nance said lamely, "you wouldn't figure I was yellow —"

"Figured that a long spell back," Crawford said heavily. He gave a deep sigh. "I still don't see what Vincent was pulling that wild-man stuff for. If it was really him, why didn't he go home to his father's place?"

"Probably not him," the Deacon interposed. "I wish I could have got a look at him once."

Crawford interrupted, "I wish you could. It's like I told you, some of the Indians around here spotted him at a distance once or twice, and claimed it was Vincent. Then I sent out Schmidt, Church, and Nance to comb the hills. They spied him a couple of times. This was when you went over to Arizona in search of Jiménez."

"If they spied him," the Deacon wanted to know, "why didn't they grab him?"

"Cripes!" Nance put in. "That wild man was wilder'n a locoed bronc. We couldn't get near enough. We could have plugged him, maybe, but Simon wanted him alive. Then today he bust down on us and started shooting. We had to shoot back, or the crazy fool would have wiped us out. Then Scott came charging up the hill and —"

"And you snuk off with your tail between your legs," Crawford growled. "All right, you told us that before. Go get a drink and shut up." Nance slunk off to the bar.

Crawford said to the Deacon, "If Jiménez recognized the wild man as Fred Vincent — if he is Vincent — I figure he'll bring him to his father's place as soon as possible — either him or his body. That being the case, Jiménez will be coming through here. And Scott and Maxwell with him. We'll wait."

An hour passed. By this time the sun had dropped low; long shadows streaked the dusty main street of Ramrod Ridge. Then the man Crawford had posted as lookout at the doorway of the general store saw three riders, leading two loaded ponies, making their way through the sea of creosote bush that surrounded the town. The lookout hastened inside to tell Crawford.

"They're comin'," he announced. "Looks like they got Schmidt and Church tied across one horse. On the other, it must be that wild man. I figure he's tied in his saddle 'cause he's all slumped down like he couldn't fork it proper."

Crawford raised one huge paw to signify he had heard, but didn't say anything. Gradually the men in the store gravitated toward the outside porch, until only the Deacon and Crawford remained inside. Pretty soon the creaking of saddle leather was heard, then the Deacon caught Nogales' voice: "Yes, you keep going, Jimmy-Steve. Get Vincent home to his dad as fast as you can."

"But, Señor Nogales, maybee eet is bes' I remain weeth you and the Señor Caliper."

"Get going," Caliper's voice chimed in. "There won't anything happen here that we can't handle. . . . Look, Nogales, it looks like a reception committee here."

By this time there was a buzz of voices on the store porch. Somebody protested at the leading away of the horse bearing Vincent's still unconscious body: "Hey, that Mex is taking Jack Schmidt's horse!"

Then Nogales' voice again, "The horse will be returned, hombre."

Further words were drowned in surprised and angry cries at sight of the other bodies.

"Deacon," Crawford rumbled, "you go out there and tell those two hombres I want to see 'em."

The Deacon looked troubled. "It won't do no good, Simon. I know they won't come."

"Do as I tell you!"

"I'd just be wasting my breath. You can't order them two around. They're not that kind."

Crawford swore, and lifted his mighty bulk from the armchair. There was something elephantine in the stolid, heavy tread that carried him to the doorway and out on the porch, where he pushed aside those who impeded his way.

At his arrival with the Deacon, looking anxious, close behind, the men on the porch fell silent. Nogales and Caliper still sat their saddles, their horses drawn up close to the porch which was elevated above the earth. To their rear was a third horse to which had been roped the bodies of Jack Schmidt and Tim Church. Already some distance along the main street of the town rode Jiménez, leading behind him Schmidt's horse with the unconscious Vincent lashed in the saddle. Once Jiménez looked back; Nogales urged him on with a wave of the hand. Then Nogales and Caliper turned to stare at Crawford who stood looking at them, a heavy frown on his face. The men were silent, waiting for Crawford to speak. Still Crawford didn't say anything.

Nogales spoke cheerfully to Caliper, "Cripes, Jimmy-Steve said he was big, but he didn't even mention the word mammoth."

"There's our old friend the Deacon too." Caliper grinned. "And Furlow and Limpy Bristol. Well, well, what a reception committee — not to mention that one feller who's a crowd all by himself. Imagine him coming out here to say hello."

Nogales chuckled. "Know something, pard?"

"What do you mean?"

"This is just the right time," Nogales continued, "for the Deacon to pull that old saying about the mountain coming to Mahomet."

A sour look settled on Crawford's fleshy features. "You two," he rumbled, "what do you want here?"

"Just passing through, mister," Caliper said meekly, "and figure to drop this dead meat off at your door. I understand these two worked for you. By the way, Nogales, do you see the feller that had the wings on his heels?"

Nogales pointed toward Ten-Spot Nance. "That looks like him, though he was leaving so fast I don't think he could stop this soon —"

"You listen to me, you two," Crawford thundered. "Those two never worked for me. I don't know anything about 'em. And don't get lippy. As for passing through — Well, I say who'll pass through Ramrod Ridge and who won't. Where you heading for?"

Nogales said coldly, "That's none of your damn business, though you probably know we're heading for the Vincent place."

"Now, young feller, don't get smart. You might get too smart and then you'd be sorry. I'm trying to be friendly. Now just calm down a mite. Did I hear somebody say something about Jiménez taking young Vincent home?"

"You might have," Nogales said noncommittally, and added, "if your ears are as big as your carcass."

Crawford let that pass, though his frown deepened. "Where'd you find him?" he asked.

"I reckon one of your own men has already told you," Nogales said quietly.

"Dam'd if I know what you're hinting at," Crawford said, assuming a cordial tone of voice. "What did Vincent have to say?"

"You really interested?" Caliper asked seriously.

"Certain I am," Crawford grunted. "I've known that boy for a long spell. We've all worried about him, wondered what had happened to him. Why, I even spent good money sending Deacon Trumbull clear to Arizona. You see, I had an idea that that Mex, Jiménez, knew something about him. But the Deacon couldn't get a word out of the Mex. Oh yes, that's right, you and the Deacon have met before. Now I recollect he told me about it. That was all a misunderstanding. But I'm interruptin'. What did young Vincent have to say?"

"Well," Caliper drawled, "he told us that when we got over this way we'd see two big mountains, one called San Jacinto and the other ran the general store."

Blood crimsoned Crawford's huge face.

He started to speak, stammered, then fell silent, choking down certain orders that had risen to his lips. Behind him Deacon Trumbull whispered, "How about it, Simon? Say the word and I'll set the boys on them. We can wipe them out —"

"No, you fool," Crawford gritted furiously. "They may know something. We've got to go slow." He again faced Caliper and Nogales who were openly laughing now.

Forcing a thin smile, Crawford said, "That may be funny to you boys, but my size is no comfort to me. Look, I'm trying to be friendly. I don't want to make enemies. But you've got to meet me halfway. Now I could stop you from entering this town —"

Caliper said, "You just think you could."

"Now, don't get huffy," Crawford protested. "I'm telling you what I could do. I'm the boss here. One word from me and you'll never see another sunrise. But —"

Nogales drawled languidly, "I'm not familiar with California."

Crawford frowned. "What do you mean by that?"

Nogales explained, "I mean I don't know what your code is here, *but* back where we come from, that's fighting talk! If you want trouble, you can have it. But we're going through Ramrod Ridge and we're not waiting for your permission. Get that straight. All right, Caliper!"

At his word both cowboys pulled their six-shooters and covered the men on the porch. Arms shot hastily into the air. There was a sudden thundered protest from Crawford, to which Nogales and Caliper paid not the slightest attention.

Nogales went on, "We're not taking chances of being shot in the back when we leave here. Sorry to do it this way, but we're outnumbered and we can't take chances. Now, you hombres, get back in that building and close the door. When that's done, you can unleash your lead or do as you see fit, but right now, move!"

The men on the porch were quick to get the idea. They lost no time getting inside the building. Only Simon Crawford remained on the porch, eying them defiantly and shaking one huge fist at them. "By God!" he bellowed, "I'll not forget this!"

"An elephant never forgets!" Caliper shrieked with laughter.

The two cowboys wheeled their ponies, touched spurs to the animals' ribs, and raced out of town in the direction Jiménez had taken. No shots followed them from the general store. The men had been waiting for Simon Crawford to give the order and Crawford still stood as before, his face crimson with anger and one raised, knotted fist shaking insanely after Caliper and Nogales.

IX

Polly Vincent's Story

Back on the desert floor the sun still blazed, but here, on higher ground, the towering mountain peaks shadowed that fierce heat. Ramrod Ridge was nearly three miles to the rear by this time. Caliper and Nogales had drawn their ponies to a walk that took them through a miniature forest composed of mesquite and paloverde trees, with occasional clumps of catclaw and creosote bush. They were following a well-defined but little-used trail. Ahead, bordering the way they came upon a double line of cottonwoods. On either side of the cottonwoods was a big fig tree orchard, though neither Caliper nor Nogales recognized the genus.

"What sort of trees are those?" Caliper frowned.

Nogales shook his head. "You got me. Those gray trunks and big leaves remind me somewhat of a sycamore, but they're not sycamores. Jiménez said something about Vincent growing figs here but I don't know whether to believe him or not. I always understood that figs grew in Asia and countries like that."

"Can't tell what might happen in this California country," Caliper put in. "After seeing those palm trees, I'm ready to believe anything. Imagine stepping off the desert and finding yourself by a cool stream with palms shading you overhead!"

"I know, pard. The whole dang country seems twisted around. I reckon that stream and those palms go to make up one of these oases like you read about in the Bible."

"O-aces, huh? Mebbyso. Me, I haven't read in the Bible for quite some spell now — and I'd like to know when you ever did."

"It's quite a few years back, but I got a good memory." Nogales frowned. "Lemme see — it's something about being brought into a good land of brooks of water that spring out of the hills — a land of wheat and barley and fig trees — or something like that. I forget the rest."

"Thought you had a good memory," Caliper said scornfully.

"Cripes! What more do you want?" Nogales demanded with assumed irritability. "You want I should go on and tell you the place is called Ramrod Ridge."

"It couldn't be," Caliper said definitely, "not with Simon Crawford in the neighborhood — if what you said comes out of the Bible."

"Oh, Crawford! Well, there's sayings in the Bible that fits him too."

"What, for instance?"

Nogales pondered. "We-ell, it goes something like this, 'He was a murderer from the beginning and — and there was no truth in him.' "

Caliper eyed his pardner in admiration. "Danged if you can't sling that parson talk. You and Deacon Trumbull should get along —"

"We should get a long ways from each other if he wants to keep a whole skin. I can't stand that mealy-mouthed hypocrite —"

"There's the house," Caliper announced suddenly.

Nogales' gaze followed the direction in which Caliper pointed, and above the tops of the fig trees he could see the Vincent place, situated on slightly higher ground. The slope of a huge mountain rose gradually at the rear of the building.

Ten minutes later they were riding through the gateway of the white fence that enclosed the house, having crossed a wooden bridge over an irrigation ditch a few moments before. The house was of adobe, with a long gallery running its full width. There was a sort of garden plot on either side of the gravel path that led to the entrance, planted with cacti of various kinds — prickly pear, cholla, visnaga, and the well-known fishhook cactus — ocotillo, and Spanish dagger; also several geraniums with bright red blossoms. An Indian worked steadily about the plants with a rake. He glanced up as Caliper and Nogales passed through the gateway and pointed toward a stable at one side, toward which they headed their ponies.

There were other buildings scattered about, also of adobe with tile roofs; a sort of barracks where the help lived, a tool-shed, and two or three other miscellaneous structures. At the stable entrance a second Indian, dressed like the first in overalls, denim shirt, and a bandanna about his head, greeted the two cowboys in Spanish and told them he would take care of their horses. Near by stood the two ponies Jiménez had brought to the house; the Indian had been engaged in rubbing them down when Caliper and Nogales arrived. Paloverde trees grew in profusion about the buildings, giving the place an air of peace and contentment.

"Darned nice layout Vincent's got," Caliper commented, as he and Nogales made their way back toward the front of the house.

"Sure is. I even hate to think of that Crawford hombre being in this same neighborhood. He sort of destroys the peaceful atmosphere."

At that moment Jiménez hailed them from the long front gallery of the house. Another man stood at Jiménez' side, a tall, spare, clean-shaven man with a wealth of bushy white hair and steel-blue eyes that looked as though they had never viewed anything except the vast open spaces; tiny wrinkles at the corners of the eyes indicated that; a perpetual squinting against strong light and the winds of wide ranges gave one that look. He, too, was in denim overalls and woolen shirt and cowboy boots.

Nogales and Caliper mounted the stone steps to the flag-paved gallery where Jiménez introduced them to Ethan Vincent. Vincent greeted them cordially; his grip was firm and friendly.

"I should have been in the gateway to greet you when you first arrived," he said courteously. "Usually my guests receive better treatment, but you'll understand, I hope, that we've all been occupied with Fred —"

"Don't let that bother you," Nogales replied. "How is your son?"

Vincent's face was sober. "Not too good, I fear. Oh, his wounds don't worry me. A good doctor could fix them up. But his memory is gone."

"He's conscious then?" Caliper asked.

Vincent nodded. "We got him right to bed when Esteban brought him home. I did what I could for him. Polly — my daughter — is with him now. Yes, he regained consciousness, but he doesn't seem to know us. His eyes follow us about the room; they look puzzled."

"Eet is," Jiménez put in, "like he was try so hard to remembair. At firs' hees eyes look very frighten', like he was terrify. Then when he see hees padre and the señorita Polly, he give the great sigh and that frighten' look go way."

"That's something, anyway." Nogales nodded. "Now if we can just get the doctor here, we'll have him fixed up in no time, I'll bet. There's no doctor in Ramrod Ridge, I suppose."

"None at all." Vincent looked dubious.

"The nearest is at San Rivedino. I'd like to have old Doc Stebbings, but it's a long drive here and back. I can't ask Stebbings to give up his practice for three or four days. I know he can't afford that. There are too many young doctors in San Rivedino ready to take over his practice. Oh, I know Stebbings would do it in a minute if I sent word for him to come, but —"

"Shucks!" Nogales said. "It's just a matter of money —"

"Yes," Vincent agreed hopelessly, "a matter of money — money I haven't got. And I won't ask Stebbings to come all the way here for nothing. Tomorrow, if Fred is rested, I plan to put him in a wagon and drive him to Rivedino —"

He paused, looking somewhat surprised at Nogales who had apparently lost interest in the conversation and had stepped off to one side where he was engaged with an in-delible pencil and a small worn leather folder. Within a few moments Nogales had returned and handed a slip of gray paper to Vincent.

Vincent glanced at the paper, frowned, then raised his eyes to Nogales. "What — what's this?" he stammered.

"My banker in Chicago told me to write one out whenever I needed money,"

Nogales replied carelessly. "He called it a check or a draft, or some such word. I reckon it works all right, 'cause I've used those papers a lot and I never had any money refused me yet. You just send that in to Doc Stebbings and tell him you expect him to stay here until Fred is on his feet."

"But — but I can't let you do this," Vincent protested.

"All right," Nogales snapped irritatedly. "I'm asking you to use some sense. You're doing it for your son. You know damn' well he can't stand a trip in a wagon. It's all right to be prideful, but there're times when too much pride is a bad thing. I don't need that money; I've got more than I can use. Now think it over, but get that money to Stebbings as soon as possible, is all I ask."

"Nogales —" Vincent commenced, then choked up. His blue eyes were welling. Finally he found his voice. "All right, I'll gladly accept this. You'll get it back someday —"

"The sooner you get word to Doc Stebbings," Nogales cut in, "the sooner he'll get here."

"But this is too much money."

"Not if Stebbings does his job, it isn't,"

Nogales interrupted.

Vincent nodded. "I'll write a note to him at once and dispatch it with this check by Juan. Juan acts as my major-domo. He's a good rider. He'll get to San Rivedino and —"

At that moment a girl stepped through the house doorway. She was tall and slim, with her father's blue eyes; her hair was black as jet and done in a knot at the nape. She wore a loose gown of flowered calico; there was a string of beads at her throat.

"My daughter, Polly," Vincent introduced her. "This is Nogales Scott and Caliper Maxwell. We owe them a great deal —"

"Glad to know you, Miss Polly," Nogales cut in. He liked the firm, cool pressure of the girl's hand. "It wasn't anything, bringing in your brother, so you don't owe us a thing —"

"But the doctor —" Vincent commenced.

"Yeah, the doctor," Caliper interrupted, while he was shaking hands with Polly. "You'd better get him sent for, Mr. Vincent. You were going to write a note."

"So I was, so I was." The elderly man nodded, turned, and hurried into the house, leaving his daughter to carry on the duty of hostess. Polly invited the men into the main room of the long house. It was tastefully furnished, with goatskins scattered about the tiled floor. The furniture was comfortable. At one end of the room mesquite wood lay ready for a match in the fireplace.

After a time Ethan Vincent entered with word that Juan had saddled and was on his way. Polly rose to leave for her brother's room. Until suppertime the four men sat and talked. Vincent told the cowboys something of his past history. Formerly he had owned a cattle ranch in Wyoming. Then, twenty years before, when his wife died and his own health was failing, he had, on the advice of a physician, sought the healing effects of the California desert, bringing with him his two motherless children, Polly and Fred.

"I liked this place from the start," Vincent was saying. "There's something healthful in the very air. I hired Indians and the native Mexicans. We built up this place. I planted my fig orchard on the advice of men who knew this country. I have an alfalfa pasture. My herd is very small: we keep just a few cows for milk and beef; back in the hills a short distance I have sheep and a few hogs. There's a chicken run out back. Someday I plan — at least I used to plan — to plant a citrus orchard —"

"Citrus?" Nogales asked.

"Oranges and lemons. Some limes too."

"Here — in the desert?" Caliper looked amazed. "Do you figure oranges will grow in this country?"

"They're already growing them farther north. I feel sure that this desert will grow anything, given the proper water. And I have water. Someday, mark my word, this whole desert valley will bloom with farms and fruit ranches."

Privately, Nogales and Caliper thought Vincent was a little too enthusiastic, but they listened politely to his conversation; it seemed to keep Vincent's mind from his son. Eventually Polly called them for supper. They entered a comfortable dining room where they were served by an Indian servant. A bottle of wine was produced. "From my own grapes," Vincent said proudly. "You haven't seen my vineyard yet."

After supper they returned to the main room and found seats before the fireplace. "This desert sure chills off at night," Caliper commented. Gradually Nogales worked the conversation around to Fred Vincent and the missing gold.

"Why, hasn't Esteban told you?" Polly asked, surprised.

"We couldn't get much out of Jimmy-Steve," Nogales said. "I guess he reckoned it wasn't his story to tell, not until you had looked us over."

"I'm think it bes' if the señorita tell it." Esteban smiled.

"It can be quickly told," Vincent put in. "Go ahead, Polly. You've got the habit of keeping your facts in a line; I haven't."

"There really isn't much to tell," Polly said. "You see, Fred and I have always lived here. Three years back Father thought Fred should get some city experience, so a job was secured for him with the Commercial National Bank, in San Diego. Fred became one of their trusted employees. Last September the bank decided to open a branch bank up in San Bernardino. Fred was entrusted with the task of transporting thirty thousand dollars in gold to the new bank. He left San Diego with the money in a strongbox, carried by muleback —"

"Alone?" Nogales asked.

Polly shook her head. "He was given a bodyguard of four armed men. The transporting of the gold was supposed to be a secret, but such things leak out. I suppose the very sight of five men riding with a mule packing a strongbox would give the story away. Anyway, when they neared here

Fred decided to drop in for dinner. He hadn't been home for months. We were delighted to see him. He and his men left with the gold, late in the day. Sometime after dark they were ambushed and the bodyguard shot. Three of the bodyguard were killed instantly. The fourth guard, with Fred, got away with the money-laden mule. They made a running fight of it, and headed for here again.

Polly paused a moment. "I guess the darkness favored them, or they'd all been killed instantly. However, before Fred and his guard could reach here they were cut off by another crew of bandits. Then Fred, the guard, and the mule headed for Quithatz Canyon, figuring they could barricade themselves behind rocks and make some sort of fight rather than be killed in open country. Just as they reached the canyon the mule was wounded, but Fred managed to keep it moving. Then the guard was shot down by the pursuing bandits. Fred and the mule kept going." Polly stopped.

Nogales asked, "What happened to them?"

Polly shook her head. "We don't know. One of our Indians had passed through Ramrod Ridge the previous night and had heard shots. When he spoke of it the next morning, we immediately thought of Fred. Father rode out and found 'sign' leading to the canyon. He discovered the guard who accompanied Fred in a dying condition. Before he died he told Father what had happened. Farther up the canyon Father found the mule, also dead. But there was no sign of Fred or the gold. And until today we've never seen Fred since."

Esteban put in, "An' now the señor Fred sleeps again in hees father' house. Maybe when he wake he tell what has happen'."

Nogales said, "It's certainly a riddle. Where do you suppose that gold disappeared to?" He twisted in his chair, reaching for cigarette tobacco and papers. There came a sudden shout of warning from Esteban. Nogales stiffened, then leaped to his feet. The next instant there came the crash of broken glass and the savage roar of a six-shooter!

X

A Rider Goes Down!

Outside a voice yelled, "Slope fast and sudden!" There was the sound of rapid footsteps along the flag-paved gallery, then the creaking of saddle leather.

Within the house Nogales had felt the breeze of a bullet pass his face even as he leaped across the room where his and Caliper's gun belts hung on pegs driven into the wall. By the time Caliper, who had been seated nearest the table, had extinguished the flame in the oil lamp and rushed to fling open the oaken door, Nogales was at his side, pressing the six-shooter into his hand. Polly had given one startled cry and then was quiet. Ethan Vincent had dashed into an inner room for his Winchester, followed by Esteban.

Outside the night was dark. The moon wasn't up yet. Nogales made out two shadowy figures on horseback, just passing through the wide gateway in the white fence that showed up as a dim blur against the surrounding gloom.

Even as Nogales raised his gun, one of the riding figures turned in the saddle. There came a lancelike streak of orange flame and a leaden slug thudded into the doorjamb near Caliper. Nogales fired once, the report blending with the explosion of Caliper's weapon. They fired twice more in quick succession, just as one of the riders reached the wooden bridge over the irrigation ditch. Hoofs thudded hollowly on the wooden planks, then the horse screamed with pain. A man cursed. A heavy body crashed down, and there came the sounds of splintering wood as the bridge railing gave way.

"We got one of 'em!" Nogales exclaimed.

He and Caliper raised their guns and thumbed quick shots at the remaining rider who was still riding hard. The drumming hoofs ran on, indicating that both Nogales and Caliper had missed. Now it was even impossible to make out the shadowy figure as it fled swiftly between the twin lines of cottonwood trees. Nogales raised his six-shooter and fired one chance shot in the direction of the fast-fading sounds of the running horse. From some distance off there floated back a sudden sharp cry, but the horse kept going.

"I might have winged the buzzard," Nogales grunted disappointedly, "though maybe I just scared him."

Vincent and Esteban appeared in the doorway at Nogales' shoulder. Each had a Winchester cocked and ready. Vincent's steel-blue eyes peered into the surrounding gloom. "No use shooting when you can't see your target," he observed disappointedly. He and Esteban lowered their guns. "Polly has sent an Indian to bring up horses —"

"Might as well countermand that order," Caliper suggested. "That hombre's got too much start for us to catch him. He'll probably hole up in Ramrod Ridge, and we'd never uncover him without proof."

Nogales nodded agreement. Polly returned to the room and relighted the lamp. She mentioned that the shooting hadn't awakened her wounded brother. Vincent, Esteban, and the two cowboys stepped out to the gallery and descended to the ground. Two Indians rounded the corner of the house leading saddled horses. One bore a lantern.

"You can take those horses back, boys," Vincent ordered, and added a few words in the Cahuilla tongue to compliment them on their promptness in bringing mounts. "We'll take that lantern, though."

With Ethan Vincent bearing the lighted lantern, the men made their way down to the irrigation ditch. The dead carcass of a horse barricaded the bridge. The right-hand railing of the structure was shattered, where the hurtling weight of horse and rider had crashed against it. The horse's body had remained on the bridge, though its neck and head hung toward the water.

"Damn!" Nogales growled. "I sure do hate to shoot a horse."

"Maybe it was me dropped that animal," Caliper said. "We both shot together."

"That don't help the horse none," Nogales said shortly.

"But where ees theese *caballo's* rider?" Jimmy-Steve wanted to know.

"I could swear one of us plugged him," Caliper insisted.

"Well," Vincent said, "if you got the rider, that'll help a lot." He stood on the bridge, holding the lantern high and shading his eyes against the light, as he scrutinized the slowly moving waters of the irrigation ditch. Abruptly he gave a sharp exclamation. The other three saw the body at the same instant.

It was lying face down, nearly submerged in the black water, resting against the right-hand bank. There wasn't much movement there — only that made by one end of a floating bandanna that stirred with the sluggish current as though seeking release from the knot at the dead man's neck.

The four men left the bridge and made their way along the bank. Hauling out the lifeless body took but a few moments. Then they turned the corpse on its back. Esteban stooped down and pushed back the straggly wet hair that was plastered across the face of the dead man. Then he straightened up. "Ees Ed Curry," he said quietly. "I'm theenk thees no great loss to anyone."

"Who is Ed Curry?" Nogales wanted to know.

Vincent said wearily, "Just another of that gang that hangs around Ramrod Ridge. One of Simon Crawford's crew, of course, though Crawford always claims he hasn't any crew — that he just stays in Ramrod Ridge to run his general store and bar."

"This Curry an enemy of yours?" Caliper asked.

"No more than any of Crawford's men," Vincent replied. "I've never had any trouble with him, if that's what you mean."

"They weren't after Mr. Vincent," Nogales pointed out. "It was me that slug was aimed at."

"Well, let's go back to the house," Vincent suggested. "I'll give orders to have this horse buried and Curry's body taken care of, then post a guard for the rest of the night."

They returned to the house. While Vincent was giving orders to his men, the others rejoined Polly in the main room. Within a short time Vincent re-entered and sank wearily into a chair, saying, "I'm glad that shooting didn't awaken Fred."

Polly nodded. "All the same, I'll feel better when Dr. Stebbings arrives."

Nogales said, "I wonder who came here with Ed Curry."

Vincent shrugged. "One of the Crawford gang, of course, though we can't prove that, any more than we can prove it was Crawford's men that ambushed Fred when he was carrying that gold. If we could only get something on Crawford —" He broke off. "That's why we sent Esteban to Paraiso to see his brother. His brother once said he'd heard Crawford was wanted for a killing up in Utah. We thought maybe we could interest the law in the case if we could get details. But, as you know, while Esteban waited for his brother, you showed up in Paraiso. I've a feeling Esteban thought you might help us."

"We'll do all possible," Nogales said. "Did the San Diego bank ever send detectives here to look into the situation?"

Vincent shook his head. "That wasn't necessary," he said bitterly. "You see, the bank suspected Fred of having a hand in the gold's disappearance when he, too, vanished. Naturally, we couldn't stand that, so I raised a loan on the Rancho de Paz —"

"On what?" Caliper asked.

"Our place here. We call it the Rancho de Paz. Anyway, I made good the bank's loss. Thereupon the bank lost all interest in the robbery. Worst of all, I was forced to borrow the money from Simon Crawford —" He broke off. "However, you're not interested in my financial difficulties."

"Maybe we are," Nogales protested. He made a shrewd guess: "And now, if I'm not mistaken, you're broke and Crawford is pressing you for the money. Well, maybe I can fix that up."

Vincent shook his head, his lips tightly compressed. Then he spoke. "In the first place, Crawford isn't pressing me for the money. In fact, he doesn't want the money. It's the Rancho de Paz he's after. Crawford is just waiting until the time is up in which I'm to repay the loan, then he'll drop down and take the property. The day will come when this place will be worth many times the amount I borrowed on it. No, wait" — to Nogales — "I know what you're driving at. I appreciate it. But it is one thing to accept money from you to save Fred's life; it's quite another to accept help in saving this place. You've done enough. My only hope is to uncover that missing gold."

"All right." Nogales nodded. "I won't say another word. But how come you didn't go to a bank for your loan? Why put yourself in Crawford's clutches?"

"The banks wouldn't lend," Vincent said bitterly. "After the suspicions against Fred, the banks were afraid to have anything to do with us. The very fact I borrowed from Crawford should prove how desperate I was."

"I reckon," Nogales growled. He sat staring at the floor. "I guess, Caliper," he said, after a time, "we'll have to drop in on Crawford and have a talk with him. We'll take Curry's body in in the morning and at the same time deliver that horse we borrowed to bring Fred here."

"You'd better kept free of my affairs," Vincent advised.

Nogales laughed shortly. "I figure it's my affair when Crawford's jackals start shooting at me through your window." He yawned and stretched. "It's been a long day."

"It has that," Vincent agreed. "If you and Caliper are ready to hit the hay, I'll show you your room. And you'd better think twice about riding in to see Crawford tomorrow morning. He's dangerous."

"So's Caliper." Nogales grinned. "And I'll have him with me. I'm a peace-lovin' soul myself, but Caliper can sure look out for my welfare."

Caliper snorted. "Peace-lovin' soul my eye! If you're a man of peace, I'm a Sunday-school hymn singer — and I never did have any voice for carrying a tune."

Jimmy-Steve put in, "Me, I'm love the peace, but I don't sing so well, neither. I'm theenk I'm go along to visit thees Crawford."

"The more the merrier." Nogales chuckled. "Maybe Mister Simon Crawford's got a surprise comin' one of these days."

They said good night to Polly and followed Vincent from the room. In their bedroom a few minutes later they glanced out and saw Jimmy-Steve making his way down to one of the bunkhouses where the help stayed. The Mexican was softly singing a song of Old Spain as he strode along.

"Humph!" Caliper grunted. "Did that Jimmy-Steve hombre say he couldn't sing? Cripes, if he can fight as well as he sings, we've got Crawford licked already."

"Easier said than done, m'boy." Nogales yawned. "I got a hunch we might have a tough day ahead tomorrow."

XI

Leaden Calling Cards

The following morning Simon Crawford was sitting as usual in his big armchair in the center of the floor of his combination general store and bar. There was a table at his right hand. At the table, with a bottle and glasses before them, sat Deacon Trumbull, Hedge Furlow, Limpy Bristol, and Ten-Spot Nance. Several men were scattered along the bar, and paying no attention to the conversation being carried on behind them — if it could be called a conversation — with Crawford doing most of the talking and the other men at the table listening in respectful silence.

Ten-Spot Nance eventually managed to get in a few words. "All right, boss," he said humbly, "I'll admit you're right — but that damned Nogales Scott made me so mad that —. And besides, I was trying to show you I wasn't yellow —"

Heavy, scornful laughter rumbled up from Crawford's interior. "Nothing you could do," he said flatly, "would convince me you wa'n't yellow. If you wanted to show off, why'n't you go it alone? No! You had to take Ed Curry with you! And where's Ed? Dead, probably. And if he ain't dead, maybe he'll get to talkin' too much. And then where'd we be? Even now I ain't so sure but it was Ed fired that shot at Nogales. I only got your word for what happened."

"Oh, you needn't worry on that score," Nance put in eagerly. "Ed's dead, all right, I saw his horse crash down and he let a yelp out of him at the same minute —"

" 'Judge not according to the appearance,' " Deacon Trumbull quoted piously.

Crawford swore at the Deacon. "Shut off that cant, Deacon," he growled. The Deacon fell silent.

Hedge Furlow sneered, "Any way you look at it, it was a dumb play to make, Ten-Spot. If you'd told us first what you intended, I could have warned you, you and Ed could never get away with it. I know Scott and Maxwell. They're tough hombres."

"*You* could have warned them?" Crawford sneered at Furlow. "Who asked you to cut in on this conversation?" Furlow shut up too.

Limpy Bristol said uneasily, "All this talk ain't doing us any good, boss. You've bawled out Ten-Spot, as he deserved, but supposin' Ed Curry wasn't killed? Suppose he's done some talking? Suppose Scott and Maxwell come here? What you going to say to 'em?"

"I'll tell 'em the truth, of course," Crawford said heavily. "I'll tell 'em I didn't have anything to do with Curry and Ten-Spot shootin' at 'em through the window last night. From that point it's up to them."

The Deacon asked cautiously, "You ain't afraid of that pair, are you, Simon?"

Crawford glowered at the questioner. "Afraid of 'em? Hell, no! But we got other plans, Deacon, as you well know."

"You mean," the Deacon asked eagerly, "that you're figuring to bump off Scott and then forge his name to a will so we can get his money —"

"Not so fast, not so fast," Crawford grumbled. "It's all very well to talk of forging his name, but how we going to do it?"

"I can forge any handwriting ever devised," the Deacon boasted.

Crawford's big head nodded heavy assent. "I don't doubt that, but you've got to know what Scott's handwriting is like first. What you going to do — ask him for a sample of his handwriting?"

The Deacon frowned. "I didn't think of that," he admitted lamely.

"That's the trouble with all you hombres," Crawford grunted. "You never think of nothin'."

"But — but getting a specimen of his handwriting should be easy," the Deacon said.

"Yeah, if we were friendly with him," Crawford nodded, "but we ain't friendly. I aimed to sort of shine up to him and Maxwell and now" — he burst into another profane tirade of abuse directed at Ten-Spot Nance — "now this dumb son of a bustard and Ed Curry has ruined things. Damn you, Nance — !"

"The harm's done, Simon," the Deacon said soothingly. "There ain't much we can do now except wait for Scott's next move. And I don't see any reason why we shouldn't have another drink."

Crawford didn't reply, just sat back in his chair and glared at the luckless Nance who shrank back as far as possible. The Deacon, in an endeavor to bring peace to the situation, lifted the heavy brown whisky bottle and filled the glasses. The last glass — Nance's — emptied the bottle, and the Deacon set it back on the table, saying, as he lifted his own glass, "Well, here's how!"

The others reached for their glasses, all except Crawford who was still directing his angry glance at Nance. Then Crawford laughed shortly. The sound was ugly. Reaching for the empty whisky bottle the Deacon had placed on the table, Crawford said, "Nance, you're a fool. Here's what I'd like to do to your neck . . ."

Holding the heavy brown bottle between his two hamlike hands, Crawford exerted pressure. There came a sharp, cracking sound as the bottle splintered in his powerful grasp. Blood trickled down from a small cut on Crawford's hand. With a heavy growl of disgust, he tossed the fragments of glass toward the bar and then reached for his drink. He gulped noisily as the whisky trickled down his throat. The other men put down their drinks and then eyed Crawford in a sort of awed silence as they always did at an exhibition of the man's tremendous strength. Ten-Spot Nance was as white as a ghost. He huddled back in his chair, eyes wide with terror as he tried to meet Crawford's gaze.

Something in the frightened man's attitude struck a humorous vein in Crawford's huge carcass. A loud guffaw rumbled from his lips. "Scared you, eh?" He grinned widely. His gaze shifted to the men at the bar whose attention had been attracted by the sound of breaking glass. The men immediately turned back to their drinks. Crawford resumed to Nance: "Yep, I could break your neck just like I did that bottle, so let it be a lesson to you, Ten-Spot. From now on don't get any ideas. I'll do the thinking for all of us."

"Yes sir," Nance said meekly.

Crawford went on, "That was just so you wouldn't get an idea I was just an overgrown fat man. Remember that, Nance. A few minutes back the Deacon said something about you should judge not according to appearance. It's a wise saying."

"Yes sir," Nance said again.

Crawford gave another guffaw; called to his bartender to bring them a second bottle of whisky. Drinks were again poured. For a time the men sat in silence. Bright morning sunlight made a warm patch on the floor near the doorway. Flies buzzed about the bar and zoomed through the dust motes floating about the room. The Deacon tore off a good-sized chunk of chewing tobacco and masticated loudly for a few moments.

Hoofbeats sounded outside of town, came nearer. A man entered the open doorway and spoke to Crawford: "Three riders coming, boss. They're leading a fourth horse —"

"Who are they?" Crawford demanded heavily.

"Can't tell for certain, but they look like them hombres that stopped here yesterday. Y'know — Scott and Maxwell and that Mex, Jiménez."

Crawford nodded shortly. The man returned to the porch. The Deacon said, "They're leading a fourth horse, eh? I'm betting they got Ed Curry's body."

"It'll be a break for Ten-Spot if true," Crawford growled. "But if Curry is alive, or has talked, I'm disowning you, Ten-Spot. And don't you do any talking out of turn, either."

"Hell! I wouldn't, chief —" Nance commenced.

"I know damn' well you won't," Crawford said cruelly. He turned to Limpy Bristol, "Limpy, I don't know just how the situation will shape up, but I'm depending on you to see that Ten-Spot don't lose his nerve and talk too much."

"Cripes, boss," Bristol said uneasily,

"how can I keep Ten-Spot from losing his nerve?"

"I don't expect that," Crawford said coldly, "but you can keep him from talking too much. That's why I pay you to wear a gun."

Nance gulped. He didn't say anything as he eyed Bristol with a nervous glance. The hoofbeats outside were louder now. Suddenly silence fell.

Crawford craned his thick neck toward the doorway, but he couldn't see anything of the riders who had, apparently, stopped. A frown creased his forehead. By this time there should have been some words from the man he had stationed on the porch. What was going on out there? The others, too, were straining their ears for the slightest sound. Then there came the scraping of a booted foot on the porch.

The next instant the man Crawford had stationed on the porch backed into the room, his hands raised high in the air. Following him into the big room were Nogales, Caliper, and Jimmy-Steve, their forty-fives drawn and covering the man.

The cowboys were grinning widely as they entered the room, but they were, nevertheless, alert for the slightest hostile sign on the part of any of its occupants. Deacon

Trumbull and the other men at the table started to reach toward their holsters, but Crawford quickly stopped that move.

"Leave be," he growled. "They got us covered."

A number of pairs of arms immediately went into the air. Crawford sat as before, one hand in his lap, the other clutching a glass of whisky. He asked coldly, "What's the meaning of this?"

Nogales grinned cheerfully. "Sorry if we've misjudged you and your gang, Crawford, but we didn't know what to expect. We saw your guard on the porch and figured he was there to tip you off, so we pulled our irons when we arrived and signaled him to keep quiet. He got the idea right off. We figured if you were waiting for us with drawn guns that he'd try to save his own hide by warning you, but I reckon, maybe, we were mistaken."

"Why should we be waiting for you with drawn guns?" Crawford demanded.

"Considering you sent a couple hombres to rub us out last night," Nogales said quietly, "it's only natural to expect the worst."

"*I* sent a couple of men?" Crawford frowned.

"Don't deny it," Caliper burst out. "Ed Curry and one other rider fired on us last night. We got Curry —"

"Outside on the saddle of the horse we borrow'," Jimmy-Steve put in, "we bring thees Curry hombre to you —"

"Look here," Crawford interrupted, "you got me wrong."

"Is there any other way to get *you?*" Caliper asked.

Crawford ignored that. He said, "I had nothing to do with ordering Curry and some other hombre out to the Rancho de Paz. If they went out there, they did it on their own hook. It wasn't any of my ordering."

Despite himself Nogales couldn't help believing the man. Crawford asked for details. Nogales gave them. Crawford again shook his head. "I don't know anything about it," he said emphatically, "nor do I know who went with Curry. Curry has been hanging around here for some time, but he doesn't work for me."

"I sort of doubt that," Nogales said flatly.

The Deacon murmured, "He who doubts is damned."

Nogales flashed a quick grin toward the Deacon. "And there's another saying from that same book, you mealy-mouthed old hypocrite, that says, 'Be sure your sin will find you out.' "

The Deacon's eyes widened; his jaw

dropped. Crawford grunted, "If you hombres didn't come here to hold a Sunday-school class, what did you come for?"

The eyes of every man in the room were on Nogales now.

Nogales said, "Like I told you, we were half-expecting trouble when we came in to let you know we'd returned Curry's body and to warn you not to try anything of the kind again."

"I've told you I didn't have anything to do with it," Crawford rumbled.

"The same warning goes for anybody else in this room that did have a hand in last night's game," Nogales said coldly.

Crawford said sarcastically, "This isn't just a social call, then?"

"Call it that if you like," Caliper replied. "We brought our calling cards. They're made of lead and they come out of a forty-five muzzle. Would you like to see 'em?"

Crawford raised one huge impatient hand. "You can put your guns away. Nobody here is going to pull on you. Cripes! I'd like to be friends with you boys, if you'd give me half a chance. I've got liquor and grub to sell here. That's all I'm interested in. I won't get your business if you and me are on the outs. Tony, set up drinks all around. We'll drink to these hombres who come new to our little settlement."

"We'll buy our own drinks," Nogales said shortly. However, he and his companions put their guns away as they strode to the bar. Tony, the barkeep, at once got busy pouring drinks. With an effort Crawford raised his huge bulk from the chair and made his way to Nogales' side. Only now did Nogales realize how massive the big man was. He towered over Nogales, almost dwarfing him. And Nogales wasn't a small man by any means.

For a few minutes little was to be heard except the clinking of glasses and the smacking of lips. Finally, when the cowboys had put down their empty glasses, Crawford spoke, "If this isn't just a social call, what brings you here? Oh yes, I know, you brought me Ed Curry's body — for which I don't thank you; he's nothing to me — and you've given me a certain warning. However, you're mistaken if you think I bear you any ill will. Now, is there anything else on your mind?"

Nogales nodded. "You hold a paper on the Rancho de Paz. Mr. Vincent borrowed thirty thousand dollars from you."

Crawford nodded warily. "That's right. Did Vincent send you here to talk to me about it?"

Nogales shook his head. "He doesn't even know I intended mentioning the matter. I offered to take the paper off your hands, but he couldn't see it thataway."

"*You* offered?" Crawford sneered. "Where would you get the money?"

"I've a hunch you already know that," Nogales replied quietly. "The fact is, Mr. Vincent owes you thirty thousand dollars."

"With interest," Crawford added.

"Six per cent?" Nogales asked.

"Ten." Crawford grunted.

" 'He that is greedy of gain, troubleth his own house,' " Nogales quoted glibly, with a quick side glance toward the Deacon. The Deacon gulped.

Crawford frowned. "One psalm-singer is enough around here," he growled. "I said 10 per cent and that's what I meant. That's one way I make my living. If you don't like the idea of 10 per cent, why — Hell! it's none of your business anyway."

"Ten per cent it is," Nogales said. He had a stub of pencil out, jotting down figures in a notebook. He put the notebook and pencil away and named a sum. Crawford nodded. Nogales went on, "I'd like to take that loan off your hands."

"Why you cutting in on this business?" Crawford frowned. "Particularly if Vincent doesn't know you're doing it?"

Nogales said bluntly, "I figure that paper will be better in my hands than yours. You figure to get the Rancho de Paz, but I don't see it thataway."

Crawford rumbled, "You can't force me to turn that paper over to you —"

"Correct," Nogales snapped. "But I'm betting ten bucks against a plugged peso that I could talk Vincent into accepting a loan before he'd let you take the Rancho de Paz away from him. And I wouldn't charge him any 10 per cent, either. And once he had that money, you couldn't refuse it."

Slowly Crawford shook his great head. "That loan has got a mite over a month to run yet," he said slowly. "I figure to get all my interest —"

"Cripes!" Nogales said impatiently. "I'll give you your per cent up to the time of the note."

"What you so anxious to get that note for?" Crawford inquired.

"That," Nogales said, "is my business. Either you accept my offer or you don't. I got my mind made up you're never going to own the Rancho de Paz."

"Getting right uppity, aren't you?" Deacon Trumbull broke in.

Caliper snapped, "You, Deacon, keep

out of this financial talk. I've still got a few of my calling cards left, if you'd like to see them."

"Maybe I could show you a few cards of my own," the Deacon snarled.

Crawford interrupted, "Let be, Deacon. We don't want any trouble here." And to Nogales, "Just to prove I want to be friendly, I'll let you have that note, Scott. Got the money on you?"

Nogales said, "You know damn' well I wouldn't be carrying that much cash. I haven't even got my check book —"

Crawford guffawed scornfully. "You ain't thinking I'd take a piece of paper, are you? How do I know it'd be good —"

Here the Deacon cut in, "Simon, I want to talk to you a minute."

Crawford looked angrily at his henchman. "Now, look here, Deacon —" he commenced.

"This is important," the Deacon said earnestly.

Somewhat skeptically Crawford allowed himself to be drawn to one side. The Deacon spoke to him low-voiced, "Take that check."

"It might not be any good," Crawford protested.

"I figure it will be good," the Deacon insisted. "You take that check. We've been figuring how we could get a specimen of Scott's handwriting. Here's our chance."

Crawford's eyes narrowed. "Maybe you're right at that, Deacon. I'm commencing to see what you mean."

He returned to Nogales' side, saying, "I reckon Deacon Trumbull must know something about you, Scott. He figures your check would be good. All right, I'll take a chance."

Nogales nodded shortly. "I'll be in tomorrow with the check. . . . Ready, boys?"

Caliper and Jimmy-Steve nodded. The three walked carefully to the doorway, watching Crawford and his men every step of the way. Crawford said angrily, "You three act like you were afraid of getting shot in the back."

"Never did believe in turning my back on a rattlers' nest," Caliper said coolly.

Crawford ripped out a curse. The Deacon said in injured tones, "You judge us all wrong. We wouldn't harm a hair of your heads."

Nogales nodded shortly. "We know, Deacon, we know. Blessed are the pure of heart and all that sort of thing — but you see we don't feel just right about your hearts. They look plenty black to us."

And with that the three cowboys slipped quickly through the doorway. An instant later there came the swift pounding of receding hoofs. Crawford drew a long, angry breath. "That damn' Nogales," he burst out, "is too damn' smart! He thinks fast. He *knew* I was half-inclined to give the word to plug them three."

"What!" The Deacon looked dismayed. "Before we get a sample of his handwriting? There's no profit in that."

Crawford ripped out a curse. "I ain't yet sure I want a profit from that direction. Maybe we'd just be meddling with trouble if we forge a will with his name on it. I got a hunch it might be safer to forget him. Up to now I felt fair certain that I could get the Rancho de Paz — and here I've thrown over that chance for a gamble. It's all too uncertain. I don't know why in hell he has to come into my country —"

"Forget it, Simon," the Deacon said soothingly. "By tomorrow we'll have his signature. Once we have that, you leave things to me. I'll show you plenty!"

"You'd better," Crawford said threateningly. "At the same time I got a hunch it'd be safer to have Scott bumped off right now. Maybe we'll do that yet. There's no use running chances."

XII

"Don't Let Them Escape!"

By the time Nogales, Caliper, and Jimmy-Steve arrived back at the Rancho de Paz they saw a stranger sitting on the house gallery with Polly Vincent and her father. Vincent hailed the cowboys as they started to rein their ponies around the house. They dismounted and ascended the steps to be introduced to Dr. Zach Stebbings. Stebbings was elderly with sparse gray hair and range-weathered features. He looked efficient.

His blue eyes twinkled as he took Nogales' hand. "So you're the cowpoke with more money than good sense, eh?" He smiled, then, at Nogales' uncomprehending frown, explained, "I mean that check you sent, with word I was to remain here until Fred was on his feet."

"Oh, that." Nogales grinned. "Was it enough?"

"More than enough, son. Don't you know I'm tickled pink for a chance to remain at the Rancho de Paz for a spell? My assistant has taken over most of my practice, anyway, in San Rivedino."

"You got here a heap faster than we expected," Nogales said.

"Doc Stebbings surprised me too," Ethan Vincent put in. "He tells me the Southern Pacific has laid rails clear to Moonstone — Moonstone is a small settlement about fifteen miles northwest of here. Don't know as I should even call it a settlement — just a few 'dobe houses and a saloon or two."

"It'll be more than that, Ethan, within another year," Doc Stebbings said. " 'Course, there isn't regular railroad transportation running there yet, but I happen to know the S.P. agent and he was glad to send me along on a work car. I got a horse at Moonstone and here I am. Juan will be along within a day or so —"

"How is Fred Vincent?" Caliper asked.

Doc Stebbings was noncommittal. "His wounds don't amount to much. I've done all possible in that direction. However, his memory seems gone. He acts as though he'd been through a terrifying experience of some sort. All we can do now is let him gain strength and see if he doesn't regain a normal condition. Right now he seems pretty exhausted."

Jimmy-Steve left to take the horses around to the corral. Polly Vincent appeared on the gallery and sat and talked with the men. Nogales said, rather uncertainly, after a time, "Mr. Vincent, I've arranged to take that loan paper off Simon Crawford's hands. Probably I shouldn't have gone ahead without speaking to you first, but —"

Vincent frowned. "Why did you do that, Nogales?"

"I didn't want to take a chance on you losing the Rancho de Paz to that rattler."

Vincent swallowed heavily. "I'm already in your debt, Nogales. You shouldn't have done it. I'll never be able to repay that money unless we can find that missing gold."

"Look, Mr. Vincent," Nogales said earnestly. "You wouldn't accept a loan from me. There was nothing else I could do if I wanted to see you get a square deal. You're under no obligations. I'll make money from the interest. If you never paid me, I'd have a nice property here —"

"Nogales!" Polly's eyes looked moist. "We know just how much you figure to make money on such a deal. I don't think we know how to thank you. But you won't lose anything."

"I swear you won't," Vincent said earnestly. "When Fred regains his health I feel sure he can tell us what became of that missing thirty thousand. Don't you, Doc?"

Doc Stebbings said, "Of course, of course," but his words didn't sound very convincing.

"Well, that's all settled, anyway," Nogales cut in. "At least you won't have to worry about that loan now." He grinned cheerfully. "One thing I always did crave to do and that was give an extension on a loan note. Now all we got to concentrate on is getting Fred on his feet."

"And," Caliper put in, "getting Simon Crawford and his sidewinders off'n theirs. Maybe it's a good thing we got a doctor here. There might be some shooting occur from time to time."

"There's a bad crew hanging out at Ramrod Ridge, Ethan tells me," Doc Stebbings said. "I'm glad I didn't have to come through there on my way here. Why don't they have a law officer there? The idea of a man like Crawford, whom I understand is black clear through, running that town, is pretty bad."

"I've written the county seat about getting a law officer," Vincent said, "but it seems the authorities there don't pay any attention to my requests."

"Maybe," Nogales said thoughtfully, "that will be attended to in time."

The following morning, accompanied by Caliper and Jimmy-Steve, Nogales rode into Ramrod Ridge to take over the note Crawford held. The three weren't pushing the ponies hard. Nogales looked thoughtful. Caliper said, "What's on your mind, pard?"

"My hat." Nogales chuckled.

"Funny, ain't you?" Caliper sneered. "Probably if the truth was known you have to wear that hat to keep your brains from blowing away."

"Probably," Nogales agreed, much to Caliper's surprise.

Jimmy-Steve looked at Nogales in amazement. "What, you do not give the argument? Mus' be you are seeck."

"It's this way," Nogales explained. "I've got a hunch it might not be good sense to give Crawford a check for that money. Don't ask me why. It's just a hunch. First Crawford refused a check, then Deacon Trumbull said something that made him change his mind. I'd like to know what Trumbull said. But there's something in the setup I don't like. Maybe we better keep right on riding, clear to San Rivedino.

We can get the money there and be back in plenty time. Besides, maybe I'll have some other business in that town when we get there."

Caliper and Jimmy-Steve didn't ask questions. The rest of the ride to Ramrod Ridge was made in silence. The horses were pulled to a halt before Crawford's store and bar building. Nogales said, "Wait here, I'll be out in a minute."

Caliper and Jimmy-Steve waited while Nogales entered the building. A couple of rough-looking customers sat sunning themselves on the store porch, but they had nothing to say to Caliper or his companion. Within a few minutes, Nogales emerged, grinning widely, and climbed up to his saddle.

Caliper said, "What's up?"

Nogales' grin widened. "We head for San Rivedino. I don't know why, but it threw a monkey wrench into the works when I told Crawford I'd get him the money instead of giving a check. Deacon Trumbull nearly had an apoplectic fit. The two of 'em tried to talk me out of the money idea. They were more than willing to take a check. They were so willing, in fact, that I decided it would be bad business to fall in with their plans. Let's ride!"

The three gathered their reins, jabbed spurs into the ponies' ribs, and headed out toward the desert floor.

Inside Crawford's store there was considerable cursing going on. "Damn that Nogales!" Crawford raged. "He's too smart!"

"But what do you suppose made him change his mind?" the Deacon asked furiously. "Here, we had the whole thing worked out — all but a specimen of his handwriting, then he announces he's going to give you cash instead. I don't understand it."

"There's a hell of a lot you don't understand," Crawford said wrathfully. "I've listened to your plans long enough, Deacon. Now we'll do things my way."

"What you aiming to do?" the Deacon asked.

Crawford struggled to hold his voice to normal. "Use your head, dammit! Scott said he was going to give me cash instead of a note. The nearest place he can raise that much cash is San Rivedino. All right, he'll have thirty thousand cash, plus the interest owing me. Somebody will have to meet him and his pards on the way back and relieve 'em of their load — and of their lives too."

"But, Simon —" The Deacon started a protest.

"I said I was doing the thinking from now on," Crawford said savagely. "Deacon, you got a job to do. Take enough men —"

"All right," the Deacon said meekly. "I'll take Limpy and Hedge and Ten-Spot. That'll make four against those three."

"You talk more like a fool all the time," Crawford growled. "You'll take those three and seven others. Who you pick is your business, but I want the job done right. You've got to get that money and wipe out Scott and his pals. Understand that? Don't let 'em escape!"

XIII

Nogales Runs a Bluff

Nogales and his two companions didn't push their ponies hard through the desert heat. There was considerable wind blowing, hurling sand and dust in their faces. They rode with their bandannas drawn up across the lower half of their features. Ahead rose two mighty mountain peaks, San Gorgonio and San Jacinto. Here, where they traveled, however, were great expanses of yellow sand dotted with creosote bush and catclaw. Overhead, the sky was a great stretch of turquoise that, at times, seemed almost like blue flame. Miles ahead, above the mountain peaks, were a few clouds of fleecy white, but here on the desert floor the sun beat down with savage intensity.

"Dam'd if I know," Caliper grumbled, "why we're making this hot ride to San Rivedino when you could just as well have given Crawford a check."

"Don't know exactly why, myself," Nogales replied cheerfully, "except that

Crawford and Deacon Trumbull were too damn anxious to get my check. Danged if I understand it. They were sure put out, all right."

"I'm theenk they were up to the crooked business," Jimmy-Steve said sagely, "if you make them so disappoint'."

They rode on. Shortly past noontime they stopped in Moonstone, which proved to be a collection of shacks surrounded by desert willows. Near by a gang of section hands were engaged in laying railroad tracks to the accompaniment of much cursing on the part of a burly foreman. Pausing at one of the saloons for a drink, Nogales recognized the bartender as a man he had known in Texas, named Waco Brown. Brown was a husky, hard-featured individual for whom Nogales had once turned a favor.

"Well, I'll be damned," Brown said, recognizing Nogales as they strode into the saloon. He thrust out one hand.

Nogales and his companions moved up to the rough board bar and Nogales performed introductions. "Long time no see, Waco."

"Too long a time." Brown grinned widely. "What'll you have? This is on me."

They ordered drinks. Brown placed

three bottles of beer on the bar. While the beer was consumed, Nogales and Waco exchanged gossip relative to former days spent in Texas. Brown asked, after a time, "What you doing here?"

"Just rambling around, like usual," Nogales replied. "Last few days we've been visiting at the Rancho de Paz, over near Ramrod Ridge."

Brown frowned. "Every once in a while I hear rumors about Ramrod Ridge. Fellers drift in here, passing through, and after a few drinks their tongues start to wag. I gather there's a rather tough crew of hombres over that way."

"They just think they're tough," Caliper put in. "Maybe they're due to be whittled down a mite."

Brown's face lighted up. "If it wa'n't for this wooden leg of mine I might enjoy throwing in with you fellers for some lead throwing. But them days are past for me. You know" — to Caliper and Jimmy-Steve — "if it wasn't for Nogales I probably wouldn't be here now. He saved my life once, when I got caught in front of a herd of stampeding cows. Damned if he didn't ride right in among 'em and h'ist me off'n the ground. I was sure battered up plenty. Right leg had to come off. Lemme see,

146

that's dang nigh twelve years ago, ain't it, Nogales?"

"Pretty close." Nogales nodded. He settled his hat more firmly on his head. "We've got to go to San Rivedino on business, Waco. We'll probably see you on the way back." He paused a moment, then lowered his voice, "Should any of those sidewinders from Ramrod Ridge get over this way don't mention that you know me."

"Not a word," Waco said.

The men talked a few minutes longer, then took their departure and climbed back into saddles. They rode steadily for an hour, their heads bent against the swirling dust and wind. Now, when they glanced up, San Gorgonio Peak seemed much closer.

It was evening by the time they rode down the main street of San Rivedino. The town was growing fast; even though the banks and stores were closed, there was plenty of activity on all sides. Farmers' wagons passed through the streets; cow ponies were lined at hitchracks. At one edge of the town locomotives puffed and snorted through the railroad yards. In the residential sections were to be seen flower-covered porches. At other points the cowboys stared in wonder at orange trees flourishing while not so many miles away snow still capped San Gorgonio Peak.

"Mighty up-and-coming burg," Nogales mused, as the three walked their ponies down the main street. "Maybe Vincent knew what he was talking about when he said this was the coming country — once the rough element had been stamped out."

"I got a hunch we'll play our share in that direction too." Caliper nodded.

The three found rooms at a hotel for the night, then started out to find something to eat. The evening passed quickly, and by bedtime Nogales had located the various spots he intended to visit the following day.

The next morning, after breakfast, while Jimmy-Steve and Caliper waited under a tree in San Rivedino's plaza, Nogales paid a visit to the bank. Within an hour he was back, carrying with him a small canvas sack which he turned over to Caliper.

Caliper "hefted" the sack. "Thirty thousand in here?" he asked. "Don't feel very heavy."

"There's more than thirty thousand there. Don't forget Crawford's interest. Bills, gold, and silver. It's all there, cowboy. Guard it careful." He started to turn away.

Caliper said, "Where you going?"

Nogales motioned down the street. "There's a drugstore down the line. I want to stop in there a minute, then I'm figuring to pay a call at the county building and see the sheriff of Rivedino County."

"What for?" Caliper asked.

"Cripes! Do I have to tell you everything?" Nogales grinned.

"I don't think you know enough for that," Caliper returned insultingly. "Hey, there's a drugstore just across the way. It looks like a right nice one too."

"That's why I'm not going there." Nogales chuckled. "The drugstore I got in mind hasn't got that kind of reputation."

He strode off, leaving Jimmy-Steve and Caliper staring in bewilderment after him.

Jimmy-Steve shook his head. "Now I'm wonder' to what he is up."

"I am too," Caliper admitted. "Nogales is cooking something in that noodle of his, but he won't tell us what it is until the time comes to spill it."

They sat in the plaza, watching horses, wagons, and men stream past. Some time slipped by. Caliper muttered, "Now what would a drugstore have to offer Nogales? C'mon, Jimmy-Steve, let's you and me go cross to that drugstore over there. Might be we'll see something that'll give us an idea. We ain't getting any place just sitting here thinking about it."

"Already I hav' theenk too much," Jimmy-Steve said. "Maybe I'm need some headache powder', no?"

"I'm inclined to say yes." Caliper nodded. Carrying the sack of money, the two made their way across the plaza to the drugstore.

Meanwhile, Nogales was just completing a transaction in the drugstore he had visited, situated in one of the rougher sections of town. The proprietor, a shifty-eyed man, gave Nogales a small paper-wrapped package. Some money passed between the two, and Nogales strode outside, murmuring, "Sleep sure comes high sometimes."

From the drugstore he made his way back to the main section of town and fifteen minutes later was entering a two-story brick building with a sign over the main doorway which proclaimed it as the Rivedino County Building. A corridor ran straight through the building, with doors opening to offices on either side, and a flight of stairs to the second story at the far end. Before long Nogales found the office he sought: a door stood open and over it swung a sign reading: Hamilton Burger, Sheriff, Rivedino County.

Nogales read the name and chuckled, then stepped through the partly opened doorway into the sheriff's office. There were two men within, both seated at desks. One desk — the smaller one — stood in a far corner, and behind it was a long, raw-boned individual bent over some ledgers — probably monthly expense accounts, Nogales surmised. The man was dressed in a new suit of stiff black and his white collar fitted too tightly about his neck. He looked like an outdoors man, however; his skin was sun-bronzed, and his fingers, clutching a pen, appeared as though they might be more familiar with bridle reins.

"Sheriff Burger?" Nogales asked.

The clerk looked up briefly, nodded toward the other desk against the opposite wall, and resumed his work on the ledgers. The other desk was much larger, though there was nothing on it except a pair of booted feet. The boots were well shined and little worn; the spurs attached were shiny and clean. They didn't look like the boots of a man who worked hard at his job. At the other end of the boots was their owner, slumped back in his desk chair. He seemed to be about half asleep though a fat cigar protruded from one corner of his fleshy lips.

"You Ham Burger?" Nogales asked.

Sheriff Burger cocked open one drowsy eye and surveyed Nogales. He didn't look pleased at having his nap interrupted. He was inclined to flesh and his jowls sagged. His shirt was open at the throat, displaying a hairy chest. Finally his other eye opened. He looked at Nogales with ill-concealed irritation before replying pompously, "I'm Hamilton Burger — Sheriff Hamilton Burger, of Rivedino County. What you want?"

"My name's Scott. I'm here on behalf of Ethan Vincent. Vincent owns the Rancho de Paz down near Ramrod Ridge."

Burger removed the cigar from his mouth. "Am I supposed to get excited about the information?" he sneered.

"From what I've seen," Nogales drawled insolently, "I can't imagine you getting excited about much of anything — unless maybe it would be losing your job." He added darkly, "Maybe that can be attended to too."

Burger's feet came down from the desk; he sat straighter in his chair. "Say, what do you want anyway?"

"Co-operation from your office."

"What sort of co-operation?"

"Mr. Vincent wrote you sometime back,

asking that a deputy be appointed at Ramrod Ridge. He's heard nothing since."

Burger frowned. "Ramrod Ridge . . . Ramrod Ridge . . . Oh yeah, that's that little collection of shacks down south of here a spell. Humph! What does Vincent figure a deputy is needed there for? Lemme see, seems like a feller named Crawford runs a general store there —"

"That's why a deputy is needed. Conditions in Ramrod Ridge are pretty bad."

"Oh, pshaw!" Burger ejaculated impatiently. "We can't appoint a deputy for every jerkwater town in this county. Yeah, I remember Vincent's letter now. Ethan Vincent the name was." He twisted sidewise in his chair to speak to his clerk. "Peters, you ought to remember Vincent's letter. I turned it over to you to answer. What did you tell him?"

The clerk raised his head. Nogales saw now he was a rather well-featured young fellow with a lean, muscular jaw. He spoke with a Texas drawl, direct and to the point, "You told me, Sheriff, to file the letter and forget it — that we couldn't waste time on anybody that far off." Having spoken, the clerk resumed his work.

Burger's face flushed. He couldn't quite meet Nogales' eyes now. After a moment he blustered, "Peters must be wrong. I wouldn't give an order of that kind."

Again the clerk raised his head. "I'm not wrong," he said emphatically, and again went back to work.

Burger looked angry but lacked the nerve to contradict his clerk. He said to Nogales, "Peters is new here — only been with me a month. Really couldn't afford a clerk in my office — trying to save the taxpayers all I can, y'understand — but Peters' uncle happens to be a representative up at the capital and a job had to be found for the man —"

The clerk cut in calmly, "You asked for a clerk. I was sent here. God knows I don't like it any better than you do."

Nogales said, "So you're trying to save the taxpayers' money, eh, Burger? And I come in here and find you dozing at your desk. Oh, this will be a lovely story to tell at Sacramento."

"Dammit!" Burger snapped. "I do my duty —" He broke off suddenly, then, "Where do you say? You mean at the capital?"

"Sacramento's the capital, isn't it?" Nogales said coldly.

"Who do you know up there?" Burger demanded.

Nogales laughed scornfully. "Do you mean to say you never heard the governor speak of Nogales Scott?"

Burger turned pale. "You a friend of the governor's?"

Nogales gave a disgusted sigh and turned toward the doorway. "I might as well be on my way," he said sadly. "I always like to turn in good reports on members of the party holding office, but this is one time I'll just have to tell the facts as I see them. There's going to be a lot of votes lost to the party, I'm afraid, unless we make some radical changes right now. We can't afford to antagonize our constituents. This is going to create an uproar at the capital —"

Sheriff Burger stumbled up out of his chair and frantically seized Nogales' arm. "Don't go away, don't go away," he pleaded. Perspiration beaded his forehead. "My Gawd, I wouldn't want the governor to get an idea I wasn't doing what was best for the party. Let's talk this over."

"Too late for that," Nogales said sternly. "There's a report to be made and I'll have to tell the truth." He allowed himself to be drawn back into the room while he talked. "I'd heard things were bad in this neck of the range, but until now I couldn't believe it. I said to him, 'No, I can't believe Ham

Burger would disregard the welfare of the party —' "

"You said to who?" Burger quavered.

"Who in hell are we talking about?" Nogales snapped irritatedly. "Can't you even wake up enough to listen —"

"The — the governor," Burger said shakily.

Nogales could scarcely keep his face straight. He shook his head as if he couldn't believe the evidence of his ears, then bent a steely glance on the shivering Burger. "I'm sorry for you, Burger, but it's your own fault. Don't say I didn't warn you and give you a decent chance. I could have headed straight for Sacramento, but I decided I'd give you a chance to tell your story first. Well, what I've heard is true, I reckon. I'll be getting on —"

"Wait, wait," Burger said almost tearfully, grabbing at Nogales' arm. "Just tell me what I can do. I wouldn't for anything have the governor think that I let the party down. Just give me a decent chance, Mr. Scott —"

"Did you give Mr. Vincent a chance," Nogales asked, hard-voiced, "when he asked for a deputy at Ramrod Ridge? Hell! You don't even know conditions there —" He paused, as though struck with a new thought. "Or maybe you do. Maybe you're working hand in glove with Simon Crawford. Lord! What a dirty mess this is!"

"Don't say that, don't say that!" Burger begged. "Maybe I've been lax, but I'm honest. I swear it! Just tell me what to do. I want this cleared up before you see the governor —"

"Look!" Nogales' manner changed suddenly. "I'm willing to give you a break. All I ask is that you appoint a deputy for Ramrod Ridge."

"I'll do it, I'll do it," Burger gasped gratefully. "I'll have one there within a week."

"Phaugh!" said Nogales disgustedly. "I want one there now. I want a deputy who can leave right off."

"But, look, Mr. Scott," Burger pleaded, "I can't get a deputy out of thin air. Where could I get one on such short notice?"

"Peters," Nogales said, taking matters into his own hands, "how'd you like to be a deputy?"

Peters smiled suddenly. "I'd sure welcome a chance at it."

"But — but," Burger protested, "Peters is only a clerk. What would he know about enforcing the law? Let me pick you a good man."

"I prefer my own judgment," Nogales

snapped, after what I've seen of you. Now I've wasted enough time. You going to swear Peters in, or aren't you?"

"Certainly, Mr. Scott," Burger said humbly. Peters, raise your right hand while I administer the oath. . . ."

Five minutes later Nogales and Peters were leaving the office. On Peters' chest was pinned a deputy's badge. Sheriff Burger looked fearfully after the two. "I — I hope, Mr. Scott," he said in shaky tones, "that you give the governor a good report of my co-operation."

"I'll think about it," Nogales said shortly. "If you don't hear from him right off you'll know your job is safe for a spell longer."

On the street Peters — whose first name happened to be Roderick — looked curiously at Nogales. "Say, is the governor of California really a friend of yours?"

Nogales chuckled. "I'm sure glad that Ham Burger didn't ask me the governor's name."

Peters heaved a long, appreciative sigh. "I had a hunch you might be running a bluff." He grinned. Suddenly he ripped off the stiff white collar he was wearing. "I'll be so damn' glad to get into some comfortable clothes again. Say, is this Ramrod Ridge as bad as you made out?"

Nogales nodded soberly. "Bad situation there. I don't know how you'll take to it."

"I reckon to make out all right," Peters drawled.

"You're cow-country stuff," Nogales commented.

"Some," Peters admitted.

"How come you took a job pushing a pen?"

Peters explained that. "My uncle John Newbill, he's a member of the California legislature, he got me to come out here, figuring I might like to work in some new country. He got me the job. You know how politics are. I finally ended up as a clerk in Burger's office. Never could make the fat clown understand that I wasn't meant for that sort of work, but he wouldn't even listen to what I had to say. He's so damn' lazy he just wanted a man to do his clerical work."

"What was your last job before you came to California?" Nogales asked.

"I was a member of Company M, Texas Rangers, before I resigned to come out here," Peters said quietly.

Nogales' jaw dropped. "You — a Texas Ranger?" Suddenly he burst into a howl of laughter. "Good lord! I reckon the joke's on me."

XIV

Hardware for Crawford

They found Caliper and Jimmy-Steve waiting impatiently in the plaza. By this time Rod Peters had gone to his hotel and got into his "working togs," as he called them, and which consisted of corduroys, woolen shirt, riding boots, and Stetson — not to mention his holstered Colt's gun and Winchester rifle.

"Meet Rod Peters, boys," Nogales introduced. "Rod is an ex-Texas Ranger so I don't figure he'll have too much trouble administering the law in Ramrod Ridge."

They shook hands. "Cripes!" Caliper said, surprised, "I didn't think they ever would get around to appointing a deputy, as Mr. Vincent requested."

Peters smiled. "Mr. Vincent can thank Nogales for that. Nogales sort of used his persuasive powers on our sheriff." He went on, giving details. When he had concluded, Caliper and Jimmy-Steve howled with laughter.

"Say, Nogales," Caliper asked, "what did you go to that drugstore for?"

"Still curious, eh?" Nogales grinned. "You'll find out in good time — maybe. I'm working on something that may not come to a head."

Jimmy-Steve put in, chuckling, "Caliper and me, we make the visit to the drugstore across the street, but we could not see anyzing you might buy."

"You probably wouldn't in that drugstore," Nogales said. "Did you buy anything?"

"Gosh, I almost forgot to tell you," Caliper burst out. "That drugstore across the way sells a new kind of drink. It's called soda water. It's just bubbly sort of, with flavors in it."

"What kind of liquor do they put in?" Nogales asked.

"Not none," Caliper replied. "Just flavors — I had three vanillas and a strawberry. Jimmy-Steve, he sort of went for lemon and cherry. They're danged good. Maybe I'll never touch whisky again."

"I'm glad you put in that 'maybe,' " Nogales said dryly.

"I mean it," Caliper said earnestly. "Come on across and have one on me."

Nogales shook his head. "Nothing doing.

One more vanilla and you'd be rolling in the gutter, making a disgraceful spectacle of yourself. When Caliper Maxwell swears off whisky, I know he's headed straight to perdition."

"Best way to forestall that," Rod Peters said seriously, "is to saddle up and get out of town pronto. I'd like to get to my new job as soon as possible."

"Right." Nogales nodded. "We'll get our horses. Bring that money, Caliper, if you haven't lost it."

"Money?" Peters looked surprised.

Nogales motioned toward the canvas sack in Caliper's hand. "There's thirty thousand plus in that sack."

Peters said, "My God!" and moved his gun nearer the front. He was commencing to wonder just how crazy these punchers were. Ten minutes later the four men were riding out of San Rivedino.

The sun was directly overhead by this time. It was hot going and the dry wind hadn't abated any. Bandannas were drawn up across mouths and noses.

"Maybe," Caliper commented, "we should have grabbed our dinner before we left San Rivedino. I'm getting hungry." He was riding at Nogales' side. To his right was Jimmy-Steve. On Nogales' left was

Rod Peters, on a clay-colored gelding.

"You're always hungry," Nogales complained. "Being full of vanilla, like you are, I don't see where you got room for food."

"I always got room for food," Caliper stated firmly.

"Room hell! You got a whole house." Nogales laughed. "Try to keep from fainting and I'll buy you a bait when we get to Moonstone."

The men rode on, bending their heads to the sharp sand whirling about them. They were still twenty miles from Moonstone when Nogales spoke to his companions. "I'm going to push on ahead, fellers. You keep right on the way you are. I'll be back before you reach Moonstone."

"Where you going?" Caliper asked suspiciously.

"I'm heading for Moonstone to see that they have plenty vanilla ready when you get there."

"No fooling," Caliper said irritatedly. "What you got on your mind, something pertaining to drugstores?"

"You guessed it." Nogales grinned, knowing Caliper wouldn't believe him. "I tell you what, pard, you tell Rod what's happened around Ramrod Ridge while I'm gone. Give him the whole story. I'll be back before you know it, almost."

Without waiting for further protestations or questions, Nogales pressed spurs to his pony and plunged ahead. Before he had gone a mile his form was lost in the swirling clouds of dust and sand. . . .

Something less than two hours later Caliper, peering anxiously ahead, saw a rider looming up on the horizon. The wind had dropped somewhat by this time and visibility was higher.

"Rider coming," Caliper announced. The others straightened in their saddles.

"Eet does not look like Nogales," Jimmy-Steve said, after a moment. "That ees, eet ees not Nogales' *caballo.*"

"That certain ain't Nogales' horse," Rod Peters added. "Though it looks a heap like Nogales. But where did he get that paint horse?"

"You sure got eyes to make it a paint pony at this distance," Caliper added admiringly. "I was just wondering myself if it wa'n't a paint." And a few minutes later, as the rider rapidly approached, "It's a paint sure enough. And Nogales is forking it. Now what in hell has he been up to?"

It was Nogales sure enough. Five minutes later he rode up in a swirling of dust and gravel on a half-wild pinto horse that

164

was half-inclined to buck the instant Nogales drew rein. The pony was streaked with sweat and dust; its withers were foam-flecked. By this time the others had come to a halt.

"Whoa! You hammerheaded streak of lightning!" Nogales yelled through the settling dust. He surveyed the pinto horse with some admiration. "Cripes! After the pounding I gave you, you still hankerin' to sunfish me out of the saddle?" He grinned at his companions. "Boys, this here pony is one sweet traveler; he fair eats up distance. I wouldn't be surprised none if he had a streak of devil in him too. Started to buck the minute I forked him, but I threw in my hooks and he lit a shuck out of there so fast I sure figured we were flying part of the time —"

"Lit a shuck out of where?" Caliper demanded.

"Where you been?" from Peters.

"Who is belong to theese *caballo?*" Jimmy-Steve wanted to know.

Nogales laughed. "One at a time, boys, one at a time, and I'll give you the whole story. This paint horse belongs to Waco Brown — at least he's holding it as collateral for drinks served to a Cahuilla Injun that hangs around Moonstone, for which said Injun didn't have the money to pay."

"You really been to Moonstone?" Caliper's eyes widened.

"Quiet, Jug-head," Nogales chuckled. "Told you I was going there, didn't I? I can't tell you what happened if you insist on doing all the talking. Did you give Rod the setup around Ramrod Ridge?"

Peters nodded. "Caliper told me the whole story, Nogales. You — we're really up against something, the way I figure it. But now I'm interrupting. What's the idea in changing horses?"

"Just about rode the hoofs off my pony getting to Moonstone in record time," Nogales explained. "Didn't have the nerve to make him carry me back to you fellers again; figured he deserved a rest. So I borrowed this horse from Waco while my horse was getting rested."

"But what did you go to Moonstone for?" Caliper demanded. "Jeez! It's like pulling teeth to get information out of you."

"It's just as hard on the ears to hear you asking questions too," Nogales snapped back. "If you only had the brains you were born with — or maybe you weren't born with any — you'd know just about as much as I do. Listen, Nit-Wit, what happened when I decided not to give Simon

Crawford a check?"

"He got mad," Caliper said promptly. "Leastwise, you told me he did — him and the Deacon both."

"Exactly." Nogales nodded. "I told Crawford I'd give him cash money. Got that much clear?"

"Wait a minute, wait a minute," Caliper put in, his brow clearing. "I'm commencing to get what you're talking about."

"Light always dawns if you wait long enough," Nogales said dryly.

"Look," Caliper said excitedly, "here's how it is — Crawford knows you haven't thirty thousand cash on you, so he makes a shrewd guess that you'll go to San Rivedino to get it. Is that what you mean?"

"That's what I mean. Congratulations on your astute mentality." Nogales grinned.

"And knowing Crawford like we do," Caliper ran on, "you figured he'd send the Deacon and some other riders to hold us up on the way home and relieve us of that thirty thousand."

"Go to the head of the class, Meat-Ball," Nogales said. "Besides the Deacon there's ten other riders, to be exact, waiting for us at Moonstone. I reckon they figure to make sure we pass through and then follow us."

"An' make the wipe out of us," Jimmy-Steve said excitedly.

"Right." Nogales nodded. His face turned grim for a moment, then he smiled. "Maybe we can surprise 'em a mite."

"You mean to say," Caliper exclaimed belligerently, "that Deacon Trumbull and a bunch of skunks are waiting in Moonstone for us to come through?"

Nogales nodded. "They're waiting in Moonstone — and I figure they're waiting for us — and that money you're totin'. Leastwise, they weren't doing missionary work when I saw 'em."

"You saw 'em?" Caliper's eyes widened. "What did they say to you?"

"They didn't see me. There's a back room in the rear of Waco Brown's saloon, where he sleeps. I got one of those Mex kids hanging around Moonstone to tip Waco I'd be waiting for him in his back room. Then I crawled through a window and waited. Waco showed up in a few minutes. He told me the Deacon and his pals had been asking if we passed through on the way to San Rivedino, but Waco told 'em he couldn't remember everybody who passed through. Howsomever, they're right sure we'll be coming back that way with the money, and they're figuring to stay right in Moonstone until we show up."

"The dirty sidewinders," Caliper growled.

"They're all that," Nogales said quietly. "I got a peek at 'em through a crack in the rear wall, and they all looked right determined. I explained to Waco what I wanted. He fixed me up with this paint horse I'm riding. I'll change back to my own horse when we get there."

"Look here," Rod Peters proposed, "supposing when we get to Moonstone I put this Deacon hombre and his pards under arrest?"

"On what charge?" Nogales asked.

"Plotting to rob and maybe kill you fellers," Peters replied.

Nogales shook his head. "Won't do. We haven't any actual proof of that. Besides, they won't start anything right in Moonstone. They were figuring, no doubt, to get us after we left town."

"I'm theenk we should ride hard for Moonstone," Jimmy-Steve proposed, battle light shining from his dark eyes. "The sooner we make the mix weeth them the bettair."

Rod Peters looked thoughtful. "Maybe," he proposed, "it might be better to wait until the Deacon and his pards start something. Then I can make my arrests. In that way we won't need proof — rather, we'll have the proof, through catching them red-handed."

"You got the idea." Nogales nodded. "Let's get going."

After a couple of preliminary bucks Nogales got the paint pony straightened out and it caught up to the other three riders, who were impatiently holding their mounts down to a steady, loping gait. . . .

At the end of three quarters of an hour the riders approached Moonstone. Nogales checked his pony a trifle; the others did the same. Nogales said, "I've got the plan all worked out. Give me a couple of minutes start. I'll go ahead, tie this pony out back of Waco Brown's, and enter his barroom by the rear. You three hit town together and head straight for Waco's place. Rod, you let Jimmy-Steve and Caliper enter by the front door, then you come along about five minutes later. By that time things should be boiling hot enough to give you all the proof needed to make your arrests."

Peters frowned. "I just don't like it, Nogales," he protested. "You going in the back way while Caliper and Jimmy-Steve approach those sidewinders by the front is all right. But there'll be eleven of them against you three. You'll be outnumbered, should they start anything in Waco Brown's place. If I wait five minutes, you might all three be wiped out. I'd better enter with Caliper and Jimmy-Steve —"

"I see what you mean, Rod." Nogales nodded. "But I think we can stall 'em off until you get there. I've worked it out my way and knowing those hombres like I do, I figure the plan will work out all right."

Caliper put in, "If Nogales says it will work, Rod, it will work."

Peters gave in. "All right. You're the boss, Nogales."

"Thanks," Nogales replied. "Just give me a mite of headstart, now, and when you fellers come in the front way, come with your Colts ready. Anyway you look at it, this is going to be tough going. We can't afford to take chances."

Nogales gave a brief wave of the hand and was off. Caliper and the other two riders watched anxiously until he had disappeared beyond the first adobe shacks of Moonstone.

Then Caliper said grimly, "Come on, fellers, we don't want to leave him alone too long."

The three went tearing into the town, leaving clouds of dust in their wake. Three doors distant from Waco Brown's saloon they pulled their ponies to a halt and flipped reins over the nearest hitchrack. By this time all three had whipped out their six-shooters. Their faces were tense. Not far away the railroad section hands stopped their work in amazement and straightened up to watch what was happening. Even the profane-mouthed section boss forgot to curse his laborers as he, too, stood in drop-jawed surprise. Suddenly it occurred to him that the situation looked dangerous: "Bullets due to be flying in a minute," he gasped, and dropped on his face behind a pile of railroad ties.

Unaware of this, Caliper was speaking swift words to his companions. "Better not wait five minutes after we enter," he said tersely to Peters. "Just give us a minute's start, then you come a-running. Come on, Jimmy-Steve!"

With Jimmy-Steve close at his heels, Caliper stepped lightly and swiftly in the direction of Waco Brown's saloon, the open doorway of which was just a few yards away by this time. Their guns were clutched tightly in right fists, thumbs bent across hammer prongs. At any instant they expected to hear the loud crash of exploding guns.

Suddenly, within three steps of the saloon entrance, Caliper stopped. "Wait," he whispered tensely to Jimmy-Steve. "I don't like the look of this. It's too quiet there. I can't even hear a voice. By Gawd! Maybe they've overpowered Nogales. Maybe they took Waco Brown captive and — Cripes! Jimmy-Steve, we've got to move fast. Come on!"

They made a flying leap for the doorway!

Inside Waco Brown's saloon Nogales was quietly drinking a bottle of beer at the bar and conversing with Waco Brown. There weren't any other customers in the bar. Both men were intently watching the entrance to the saloon.

The next instant Caliper and Jimmy-Steve leaped inside the entrance, their faces hard and determined, the guns in their right hands ready to hurl leaden death at anyone who barred their path. Then, seeing Nogales peacefully drinking at the bar, they stopped short, jaws dropping and guns slowly falling at their sides. At the same instant Waco Brown and Nogales burst into howls of laughter.

As the laughter roared out, Rod Peters came charging into the saloon, colliding with Caliper who was standing dumfounded just in front of him. He, too, came to a sudden stop, then a silly grin spread over his features as he realized he'd been fooled.

"Run a whizzer on us, didn't you, Nogales?" he said sheepishly.

Nogales nodded, then went off into fresh peals of merriment. Caliper swore under his breath, then a grin twisted his features. After a moment Jimmy-Steve started to chuckle. "Nogales, he make the rib on us, no?" he said.

"Dang you, Nogales!" Caliper growled good-humoredly, "I suppose you think it's funny to scare us half to death."

"Funny?" Nogales choked, tears coming to his eyes. "If you three could — could have —" A howl of laughter left his lips before he resumed, "Seen the looks on your faces as you came bounding in, all ready to sling lead — Oh — ah — haw-haw-haw!"

"I reckon the drinks are on us." Peters laughed.

"Waco don't — don't keep vanilla, Caliper." Nogales laughed. "You need strong drink, anyway, after having a whizzer like this run on you."

Waco Brown grinned. "I can give you some real nice sarsaparilla pop, Caliper."

"Give me a bottle of beer," Caliper

growled. Jimmy-Steve and Rod Peters lined up at the bar, looking sheepish, and gave their orders. From time to time Nogales went off into fresh peals of laughter. "Goldarn it!" Caliper looked reproachfully at Nogales. "You don't care how far you go, just so you can pull a joke on me, do you? S'help me, I'll get even. See if I don't. But what a sheepherdin', billy-be-damned liar you turned out to be. Telling us the Deacon and his gang was here."

"They are." Nogales wiped tears of laughter from his eyes. "I didn't lie about that. I saw 'em from Waco's back room, just like I told you."

"Aw," Caliper grumbled, "I wouldn't believe a word you say."

"If they were here," Peters asked, "what became of 'em?"

"They had too much to drink and passed out." Nogales chuckled.

Jimmy-Steve laughed and shook his head. "That one I'm not believe, I'm don't get fool' two times in one day."

"Ask Waco, if you don't believe me," Nogales advised.

"It's the truth." Waco Brown nodded. "They got pretty belligerent here for a spell, and scared out all my regular customers. Then, a while later, they passed out one by one."

"Where are they now then?" Caliper demanded.

"Sleeping it off in my back room," Waco said, laughing.

"T'hell you say!" Caliper exploded. He strode to the door leading to the back room and threw it open. Then he stopped short, jaw dropping once more in sudden amazement. "Well, I'll be damned!" he exclaimed.

"That's more than likely." Nogales grinned.

Jimmy-Steve and Rod Peters had crowded close behind Caliper. Now they, too, stopped short in amazement.

Sprawled on the floor of the back room in various attitudes of slumber were eleven hard-boiled individuals, including Deacon Trumbull, Hedge Furlow, Ten-Spot Nance, and Limpy Bristol. But they didn't look hard-boiled now: their mouths were open and their features covered with perspiration. The Deacon's plug hat had rolled off and lay on its side near his head which was pillowed on the legs of one of his companions. A varied assortment of snoring noises filled the stuffy room to mingle with the buzzing of flies.

"Cripes!" Caliper exclaimed in some awe. "Can you imagine such drunken sots. Phew! This room don't smell too sweet."

"It was some job lugging them in here," Waco Brown said. "I'd be much obliged if you fellers would help me cart 'em outside, where we can leave 'em back of my building until they wake up."

"Why not leave 'em there until they come to and walk out of their own accord?" Rod Peters asked.

"I want to get to bed tonight," Waco said. "These hombres won't wake up until tomorrow morning, I'm figuring."

A suspicious light entered Caliper's eyes. He glanced quickly from Waco to Nogales. Suddenly he exclaimed loudly, "Drugstore! Mickey Finn!"

"You guessed it, pard," Nogales chuckled. "That's what I visited that cheap drugstore for. I figured I could get knockout drops there. You see, I sort of figured Crawford might send a gang to wait for us here, so I got the Mickey Finn dope while we were in San Rivedino, then rode here and passed the drops to Waco. Waco did his stuff and here we are — and here the Deacon and his gang are. Pleasant sight, isn't it?"

"Nogales! You devil!" Caliper exclaimed

joyously. "I can forgive you, now, for that joke you played on us."

"Wait a minute." Nogales started to laugh again. "Simon Crawford runs a general store. A general store is supposed to stock hardware. Suppose we furnish him a supply?"

Caliper let out a yell of pure enjoyment. "Pard, your head is really working. Waco, have you got a burlap sack?"

Waco produced a sack and the men collected from the snoring Deacon and his companions their guns and cartridge belts and dropped them into the sack. The armament made quite a hefty load.

Jimmy-Steve grinned as he looked down on the sleeping men. "I'm bet this teach them the lesson not to dreenk, no?"

"Yes." Rod Peters laughed.

"C'mon, pards," Nogales proposed, "let's cart these stiffs out back, then I'll exchange that paint pony for my own horse and we'll head back for Ramrod Ridge."

Ten minutes later the work was done and the men were once more in their saddles. Waco Brown came out to the street to bid them good-by. Nogales said seriously, "I hope when the Deacon and his crowd wake up they don't get sore at you."

"They won't worry me any," Waco

Brown said contemptuously. "In the first place, they'd have a tough time proving I put knockout drops in their drinks. In the second place, I've faced gangs just as tough. If you'll remember, Nogales, I can handle guns myself. Besides, I got friends in this town who like my saloon. Anyway, by the time those hombres open their eyes again, they'll feel too miserable to start any trouble. I've got a hunch they'll hightail it back to Ramrod Ridge as fast as possible."

He and Nogales shook hands. Nogales said, "I'm sure obliged, Waco."

"Hell's bells! I already owe you more than I can repay. I just wish I could be there, though, when you hand that sack of hardware to Simon Crawford."

"I'm figuring the look on Crawford's face should be good for a laugh." Nogales grinned. "Well, *adiós, amigo!*"

Good-bys were said all around and the riders headed their ponies out of Moonstone, across the desert, in the direction of Ramrod Ridge.

XV

Law Comes to Ramrod Ridge

It was four in the afternoon by the time Nogales and his friends rode into Ramrod Ridge. They pulled rein before Simon Crawford's general store and dismounted. Several of Crawford's henchmen lounged on the store porch but none of them had anything to say. They scowled at the riders, but that was all.

Nogales spoke low-voiced to his companions. "Let me go in first, then you fellows bring in that sack of weapons. Caliper, let me have that money."

Caliper lifted the money sack from his saddle and handed it to Nogales. Nogales turned, mounted the steps to the general store entrance, and passed inside.

A few men stood at the bar, drinking. Simon Crawford, himself, stood behind the counter of the store section of the building, engaged in eating crackers and peaches from a tin can. His heavy form moved ponderously behind the counter as he took a couple of steps to reach a can of sardines from a near-by shelf. At that moment he spied Nogales just coming through the doorway. A scowl crossed his heavy features to be replaced by a look of some surprise as his small eyes spotted the sack in Nogales' hand.

Nogales said, "Howdy, Crawford. Got that note of Vincent's handy? I've got your money for you."

Crawford didn't reply for a moment, then he grunted, "I got the note, but I ain't sure if I want to release it."

Nogales' face hardened. "Look, Crawford, we went all through that before. I can't force you to turn that note over to me, but I've talked to Vincent. I know he's more than willing to accept a loan and pay the money himself. So, one way or the other, you've got to give up that paper."

"All right, all right," Crawford rumbled, "you can have the note — providing you got the money. But I ain't counted your money yet."

"Maybe you didn't expect me to get here with it," Nogales said innocently.

Crawford's pig eyes narrowed. "Any particular reason why you shouldn't?" he countered.

"You should know as well as I," Nogales said dryly.

"Scott," Crawford demanded heavily, "what you driving at?"

"I happened to notice," Nogales replied, "that the Deacon isn't around today, nor Furlow, nor Bristol. In fact, several of your steady customers seem to be missing."

"Cripes A'mighty!" Crawford bellowed angrily, "I can't keep tabs on everybody who comes in here to buy from me. Matter of fact" — toning his voice down somewhat — "the Deacon and some of the boys mentioned something about heading down toward the Border, to see if they couldn't pick up a few cows from the Mexes, bring 'em up here, and sell at a profit. I don't know if they left or not, but I ain't seen 'em today."

"That so?" Nogales said softly. "When we passed through Moonstone I heard that the Deacon had been seen there."

Crawford's face turned red with anger, then paled. For a moment he couldn't speak. He wondered what had become of the Deacon and the others. *Why hadn't they stopped Scott and his friends and secured this money that Scott was about to pay over?*

"Goddam it!" Crawford thundered. "I said I didn't know where the Deacon is and I don't care. If you've got the money for that note, hand it over. I ain't got time to stand here talking all day."

"Right," Nogales said and swung the money sack on the counter. "You'll find it all there — every penny that's owing to you. Count it yourself."

"I intend to," Crawford snarled. He seized the sack, jerked open the drawstring, and poured a shower of gold, silver, and bills on his counter. Nogales watched narrowly while the big man's hamlike hands pawed the money in the process of counting it. Finally he finished, replaced the money in its sack, and put it below the counter.

Nogales said, "Right amount?"

"It's correct," Crawford said grudgingly.

"Hand over the note," Nogales snapped.

For just an instant Crawford hesitated. *Why not,* he considered, *call on the men at the bar to shoot Nogales? Then he'd have the money and the note both.*

"Hand over that note." Nogales spoke a second time.

It was then that Crawford noticed that Nogales' right hand rested on the butt of his six-shooter.

"All right," Crawford growled. "You needn't be in such a hurry. Nobody's going to cheat you."

"I know that damn' well." Nogales smiled.

From an inner pocket of his coat Crawford produced a billfold inside which was Vincent's note. Nogales took the note, spread it open and read its contents, then refolded the paper and placed it in his pocket.

"And now," Nogales smiled coolly, "you can give up all hope of ever owning the Rancho de Paz."

"Don't be too sure of that, Scott," Crawford commenced angrily. "I'm not through with you —" Then he stopped short, upon noticing Caliper and Jimmy-Steve, followed by Rod Peters, just entering the doorway. It was the deputy-sheriff's badge of office on Peters' vest that caught Crawford's attention. The three men sauntered across to join Nogales.

Nogales said, "Crawford, let me make you acquainted with Rod Peters, our new deputy. The sheriff's office in San Rivedino has just appointed him to Ramrod Ridge."

Neither Peters nor Crawford offered to shake hands. Crawford stared steadily at Peters for a moment, then grunted, "Never no telling what fool moves these politicians will make. It's just like that windbag, Ham

Burger, to send a deputy down here. Hell! This town doesn't need the law."

"It's here, whether you think it's needed or not," Peters said coldly. "And said law is going to be enforced. I'll be opening an office in one of the buildings here. I understand there are several deserted shacks —"

"Take what you need," Crawford snarled. "I suppose you'll be erecting a jail building next."

"Maybe I won't bother taking prisoners," Peters said quietly. "Maybe I won't have to. It's going to depend a lot on Ramrod Ridge inhabitants. So far, I don't like what I've seen of 'em. From now on, any man that hasn't visible means of support gets out! Do you get what I mean, Crawford? This town has been a sanctuary for crooks long enough. So if you know of anybody that might be on the wrong side of the law, you'd better tell him to get. Because he's sure due to tangle with me if he doesn't."

"Pretty tough, ain't you?" Crawford's voice shook with anger.

Peters said, "Yes, I am. And the longer I stay here, the tougher I'll get. I'll thank you to pass that warning around."

Crawford checked the hot retort that rose to his lips. *After all, Peters represented the law. Crawford had better go easy.* His voice changed suddenly. "Sure, sure, Deputy Peters," he said ingratiatingly, "no use you and me having any misunderstanding. I still don't think a law officer is necessary here, but that's neither here nor there and not for me to say. I want to see things run lawful. I make a small living with my store and bar and I certainly wouldn't want to see things go bad here. Just call on me if you need my assistance in any way. And take any of the buildings in town that you need. You can count on me for full co-operation."

Peters said dryly, "Thanks."

Caliper could hold in no longer. "Say, Crawford, how's your stock of hardware holding out?"

"Hardware?" Crawford looked suspiciously at Caliper. "Well, I ain't had so much call lately for hardware. Depends on what you need. I got some nails and hammers and axes, some pots and pans. Mostly I run to canned goods and beans and flour and such. Just what do you mean by hardware?"

"I had guns in mind," Caliper said seriously.

"I got a right good stock of firearms —" Crawford commenced.

Caliper interrupted, "Well, we had a hunch you'd have some customers right soon for six-shooters, so we brought you in a supply." He lifted the heavy burlap sack of guns and belts and tossed it on the counter.

Crawford eyed the well-filled sack with suspicion and some distaste. "What's that?" he demanded warily.

"Six-shooters, belts, holsters, cartridges," Caliper replied.

By this time the others were grinning widely. Crawford looked from man to man. "Where'd you get 'em?" he demanded.

"Over in Moonstone," Caliper answered.

"Who'd you get 'em from?" Crawford snarled. He felt in some way he was being baited and he didn't like the idea.

Nogales seized the sack and upended it, tumbling out on the counter a miscellaneous assortment of hand-arms, belts, and holsters. Crawford stared at the weapons as though hypnotized. Nogales said, "Don't you recognize 'em?"

"How in hell would I recognize 'em?" Crawford snorted, though a horrible suspicion was entering his mind. *That one gun certainly did look like Deacon Trumbull's. What in the devil had happened to Trumbull and the others?*

"You've seen 'em around here enough," Nogales grinned, "to spot 'em right off, if you were real observant."

"Never saw 'em before," Crawford growled.

"I figure that's open to argument," Nogales returned, "but just in case you really don't know, these guns belong to Deacon Trumbull and that gang that was with him in Moonstone."

Blood rushed to Crawford's face. "So that's it," he shouted furiously at Rod Peters. "Scott got you appointed so you could unarm my men. By God! You're not going to get away —"

"*Your* men?" Nogales asked softly. "Thought you didn't have any men working for you. You slipped that time, Crawford."

Crawford thought fast. "I didn't say 'men,' " he protested. "I said 'friends.' "

Nogales laughed skeptically. "At any rate, Crawford, I figured your *friends* were waiting in Moonstone to hold us up and take that money —"

"You're wrong!" Crawford bellowed. "Wrong as hell! I didn't even know that Deacon and his pards were going to Moonstone. So far as I know they headed down toward the border to buy cows —"

"That Deacon," Caliper put in, "never bought anything he could steal, so that yarn don't go down, Crawford."

"I don't give a damn if you believe me or not," Crawford raged. "I'm telling you what I know."

By this time the attention of the men at the bar had been attracted. They had swung around and were watching intently the scene at the store counter.

By this time Crawford was so angry he could hardly contain himself. He turned furiously to Rod Peters. "You, Peters," he demanded, "what right you got disarming those men?"

Peters said quietly, "My right of office, Crawford. I agree with Nogales that Trumbull and his pards were set to steal that money."

"Did they pull their guns on you?" Crawford ranted. "What excuse did you have — ?"

"Look, Crawford," Nogales cut in, "taking these guns was my idea. I admit frankly that I thought it would be a good joke on the Deacon, Furlow, Bristol, and those others. If we hadn't taken them, somebody else might have while they were asleep."

"Asleep! Asleep?" Crawford bellowed,

his small eyes widening. "What do you mean? Where were they asleep? What are you talking about? How could they be asleep in the middle of the day?"

"I didn't say it was the middle of the day." Nogales grinned. "But as a matter of fact it was. They must have had too much to drink or something, because they passed out in Waco Brown's bar. Waco, being kind-hearted, lugged them back to his bedroom. Besides, he didn't want them sprawled around on the floor of his barroom. It might set a bad example for the customers —"

"You expect me to believe that cock-and-bull yarn?" Crawford blustered. "Now look here —"

"I reckon you'll have to believe it," Caliper interrupted. "They were sure sleeping peaceful. It was a real pleasure to hear all the different kinds of snores. Some of 'em sounded like somebody tearing a rag and some were almost like a locomotive starting. Boy, I'll bet they drunk a skinful. So when we saw 'em layin' there so harmless like, we figured we'd better bring their guns to you before somebody stole 'em —"

Laughter had broken out among the men at the bar. Crawford was the only man in the room who wasn't grinning. He

190

shot a baleful glance across the room and the men at the bar instantly fell silent.

"Peaceful really ain't no name for it," Nogales said tenderly. "Just the sight of all those men resting there so quiet brought out all of Caliper's maternal instincts. He wanted to sing lullabies to 'em."

"That's a fact." Caliper nodded. "Nogales was all for taking the Deacon on his lap and rocking him too. We all got fans and kept brushing the flies off'n the poor helpless critters. Maybe you'd better have some of your men take some nightgowns over to Moonstone — not to mention nursin' bottles. Especially nursin' bottles!" Caliper went off into a howl of laughter.

"And maybe a couple of guardians," Nogales snickered. "Those hombres sure need guardians. Innocent as newborn babes, they lay there, having sweet dreams — I hope —"

Crawford interrupted with a long blast of profanity. His features were purple with anger.

"Just like a big violet flower," Caliper said gravely to Nogales. "I hope he don't swell up any further. He'll bust sure!"

"By the way, Crawford," Nogales straightened his face long enough to ask seriously, "you don't happen to carry cra-

191

dles in stock, do you? I got a hunch the Deacon would just love a nice trundle bed."

Crawford swore some more. Finally he quieted down a trifle and turned to Rod Peters. "You, Peters," he growled. "Maybe you can give me the straight of this. These damn idjits ain't got a sensible idea in their heads."

"I agree with that." Peters chuckled. "You already got the straight of it, as much as we can tell you. Your men were asleep and for a joke we took their guns. In their condition they might have hurt themselves when they woke up."

Crawford glared at Peters. "There's something damn' funny about all this," he rumbled.

"Uh-huh." Nogales grinned. "We thought it was awful funny!"

Crawford bent an evil glance on Nogales. "All right, you've had your laugh," he said threateningly. Maybe when I get the right of this, you'll laugh on the other side of your face. Now if you haven't any more business here, I'll thank you to get out!"

"You can't make him get out," Rod Peters interposed. "This is a public place of business, by your own statement. So long as Nogales isn't disturbing the peace, you can't make him —"

"We're disturbing the peace all right." Nogales chuckled. "Crawford's peace. Come on, fellers, let's ramble."

Nogales and his three companions strolled through the doorway, followed by a venomous stare from Crawford's pig eyes. The instant they were outside Crawford snarled savagely across the room to one of the men at the bar, "You, Catlett, fork your horse and get over to Moonstone. See if you can get the straight of this business — No, you fool, don't leave right away; wait until that deputy and those cow nurses are out of sight."

He moved ponderously across the room and stopped at the bar. "Put out the bottle, Tony," he growled at his bartender. "I'm needin' a drink bad." A long sigh welled up from his huge form and broke into a curse. "Goddamit! Why can't I have men to depend on?"

XVI

"It's Risky Business"

As Nogales and his companions neared the
Rancho de Paz they saw Ethan Vincent,
Polly, and Doc Stebbings seated on the gallery. Polly was just in the act of handing the
other two long, cool glasses. Vincent had already sighted the riders and called to one of
his men to come and take their horses. The
man was there by the time the riders dismounted.

On the gallery Nogales introduced Rod
Peters to the others. He noticed at the time
that Rod held Polly's hand just a trifle
longer than seemed necessary. Polly's face
colored, but she gave Peters a friendly
smile as she said, "If you gentlemen will
find chairs, see what I can do about finding
something to take the desert heat out of
your throats."

They sat down while Polly vanished inside the house. Vincent said, "So the sheriff's office in San Rivedino finally got
around to sending us a deputy. We're

194

mighty glad to see you, Rod Peters."

"I'm mighty glad to be here." Peters laughed. "Though I reckon you can thank Nogales more than the sheriff's office." He told how Nogales had bluffed Ham Burger, and the others were still laughing when Polly emerged holding a tray on which were four frosted glasses which she passed around. "My gosh!" Nogales smacked his lips. "What's this?"

Doc Stebbings' eyes twinkled. "This is Polly's specialty. It's just a little something she fixes up with mint and bourbon and sugar and water. It's guaranteed to brighten a man's outlook on life."

"Mint juleps!" Caliper exclaimed. "Ain't had one of these since I went East to Houston that time."

"I'm think I'm go farther than that for the señorita's dreenk." Jimmy-Steve laughed.

Vincent laughed. "My little mint patch comes right handy these hot days."

"But — but —" Rod Peters sounded amazed. "You've got ice in these drinks, Miss Polly. Ice!"

"I'll have to show you our icehouse," Vincent explained. "Every winter I have my Indians go up in the mountains and bring down enough ice to last through the warm months."

Peters shook his head. "You Californians sure enough know how to live," he drawled. "I'm liking this country better all the time."

Polly laughed. "You wouldn't go back on your native Texas, would you, Deputy Peters?"

"Never thought I would," Peters said warmly, "until just a few minutes ago. Now I'm not so sure."

His eyes were steady on Polly's as he spoke. The girl met his gaze a moment, then looked away. "One thing is certain," she said, "you're welcome here. . . . You know, Ramrod Ridge does need a deputy."

Nogales mentioned Fred Vincent and asked how he was. Doc Stebbings replied that he seemed stronger, that his temperature was down. "His wounds appear to be healing already. They weren't serious, of course. It was mostly lack of blood that weakened him. But he doesn't seem to remember much of anything. He spoke Polly's name once today when she came into his room, but that's about all we could get from him. However, another week of uninterrupted rest might make a vast difference."

They talked of Fred for a few minutes, then Nogales produced the loan note he had secured from Crawford and passed it to Ethan Vincent. Vincent looked at the note and swallowed hard, then passed it to Polly. For a moment neither of the two spoke. Polly's eyes were moist as she handed it back to Nogales. To their surprise Nogales tore the note to bits, saying, "I'll feel better now that that doesn't exist."

Vincent said, "I'm intending to write you another note right off, Nogales. I don't know how we're going to thank you."

"Forget it, please." Nogales smiled uncomfortably.

To cover Vincent's confusion he rushed into talk. "Say, if you knew all that's happened to us — Well, like I told you yesterday, before we left, Ethan, I might change my mind about giving Crawford a check and get the money in San Rivedino —"

"You didn't tell me you thought of going to San Rivedino," Caliper broke in, to help along the conversation. "I thought that was just a sudden idea you got on the way to Ramrod Ridge."

"One of Ethan's men was in Ramrod Ridge when you left the town," Doc Stebbings put in. "He said you looked like you were headed San Rivedino way. We were sort of worried about you bringing cash all the way from there."

"No need to be worried." Nogales grinned. "We did encounter some of Crawford's sidewinders — Deacon Trumbull and some others — but they were all asleep by the time we passed through Moonstone with the money." From that point on Nogales told of relieving the Crawford men of their hardware. By the time he had finished telling that and of Crawford's reactions, the long gallery echoed with laughter and Vincent had found his voice again.

"Knockout drops, eh?" Doc Stebbings chuckled. "I know just the drugstore in San Rivedino you bought those drops, I'll bet. Feller named Mauchwitz runs it doesn't he?"

"That's the name." Nogales nodded. "Kind of a poisonous-looking place. I figured I could get what I wanted there."

"You figured correct, all right," Stebbings said. "Mauchwitz indulges in a lot of shady practices. Sells liquor without a license and so on, liquor that he makes himself, out of raw alcohol, brown sugar, and red pepper. It's terrible stuff. What sort of knockout drops did he sell you — hydrate of chloral, or sulphate of morphine? Or was it something else?"

Nogales shook his head. "You got me. He named a lot of dopes that would turn the trick. I just told him what I wanted and took what he gave me. Anyway, it did the work."

Vincent looked serious. "Right now it's laughable, but I reckon you've made some dangerous enemies, Nogales. It's always risky business to laugh at men like that."

"I'm not worrying," Nogales replied. "They were enemies before, and there's nothing like laughter for cutting down a tough hombre's prestige. Some of those would-be hard fellers in Ramrod Ridge will realize that the Deacon and his men aren't so tough as they make out."

Vincent shook his head. "I'm afraid it won't end there. If something serious doesn't come of this joke I'll be surprised. Men like Deacon Trumbull don't accept such a situation without fighting back."

"The sooner they start fighting back, the better we'll like it," Caliper put in.

"Amen to that." Peters nodded.

A short time later Polly said it was time to go in to supper, and the men put down their glasses and rose from their chairs. Vincent said earnestly to Nogales, just before they passed through the door, "I haven't said all I want to say about saving the Rancho de Paz for me, Nogales, but you'll get that money back. If we could only find that missing gold —"

"We'll find it, Ethan," Nogales said confidently. "I've got a hunch luck's going to start coming your way right soon. Forget that money for now." He grinned suddenly. "Darn it, man! Can't you see I can't talk business when a good supper is waiting?"

The following morning Rod Peters, accompanied by Nogales, Caliper, and Jimmy-Steve, rode into Ramrod Ridge to establish his deputy-sheriff's headquarters. The four men moved about the almost deserted town, examining various empty buildings. Finally Peters found a place of stout construction and two rooms that suited him, the length of a city block from Crawford's store.

"That back room could even be made into a jail," he pointed out, "with a mite of work; meanwhile, I'll have to get this place redded up and a sign hung out."

The men worked until noon, cleaning out the place with the aid of brooms which they had procured from Crawford's store. Jimmy-Steve had gone to make their purchase and came back with the report that Crawford hadn't been anywhere in sight;

that the bartender, Tony, had waited on him. From a couple of other vacant shacks they secured a table to serve as a desk and a couple of straight-backed chairs.

Peters surveyed his office with pride. "Not bad," he announced. "A mite of paint might help a heap, but that can be taken care of later. Still, it wouldn't hurt to get a sign painted right now. Let's drift over to Crawford's store and see what sort of paint he keeps."

Crawford had emerged from his sleeping quarters back of the store by the time the four men entered. He glared at them resentfully, demanding, "Well, what do you want now?"

"Paint, a small brush, a hammer and nails . . ." Peters went on and gave a list of his requirements. Crawford grunted in surprise, then called his bartender to reach the various articles from shelves. The bartender handled the transaction, while Crawford stood moodily at his bar, his back to the customers.

"Nice, pleasant place to deal," Nogales said loudly.

Crawford made no move to turn around.

"Say, Crawford," Caliper asked, "heard anything from your sleeping beauties yet?"

Still Crawford didn't turn, though he

growled over one massive shoulder, "What business is it of yours?"

"I take it you haven't," Caliper said sweetly. Crawford didn't reply.

Peters and his companions were just leaving with the purchases when the sounds of horses were heard stopping before the store. A few moments later Deacon Trumbull, followed by his pals of the previous day, came pushing slowly through the doorway. The men's eyes were hollow and bloodshot; their clothing was badly wrinkled; they looked as though they'd been drunk for a week; they were dirty, unwashed, uncombed.

"Look, Nogales," Caliper snickered. "Here comes the Charge of the Light-Sleeping Brigade."

"You're wrong on two counts, pard." Nogales grinned. " 'Light' and 'charge.' In fact, that crew can't scarcely move. They sure look peaceful, though. Look, they don't even wear guns."

Peters and Jimmy-Steve started to laugh. The Deacon and his companions turned a resentful look their way but lacked the ambition to reply to the taunts. One by one they stumbled up to the bar and called feebly for drinks. Crawford's fat features crimsoned as he glared at the men, then he cursed disgustedly.

Still laughing, Peters and his companions left the store and headed back toward the new deputy's office.

XVII

The Score Is Evened

Two hours later the Deacon and his doped companions, seated near Crawford's big armchair, were still trying to figure out what happened. Crawford had given them a tongue-lashing they would long remember, but even the big man's profanity couldn't make them forget their aching heads.

"A fine bunch you are," Crawford was saying in ugly tones. "Send you out to do a job, and you get drunk and go to sleep — not to mention losing your guns. Why, you'll be the laughingstock of this whole country!"

"Cripes, Simon," the Deacon complained, "there's no call to rub it in. I don't know how it happened. I've told you all I know. Last thing I remember, we were laughing and drinking —"

"I know damn' well you were drinking," Crawford cut in. "And you passed out. Swifty Catlett told me that much."

"What's Catlett know about that?" Ten-

Spot Nance asked. "He wasn't with us."

"Thank Gawd I wasn't." Catlett grinned. He was a rangy individual with pale blue eyes, at the present time wanted for murder in New Mexico. "You hombres sure were sleeping —"

Crawford interrupted, "You don't even know I sent Catlett to Moonstone to see what had happened to you. I've told you that already. Won't your brains ever clear up? Catlett rode there and back, and brought me word you were all sound asleep back of Waco Brown's saloon. He tried to wake you up then. Brown even helped pour water on you, but it didn't do any good. Jeez! What a bunch of drunks. Dumb, that's what you are! I wish now I hadn't let you have your guns again."

The Deacon pressed one hand to his head and groaned. " 'Wine is a mocker,' " he quoted piously, " 'strong drink *is* raging —' "

Catlett's raucous laugh broke in. "You sure had something more than wine," he commenced, "and as for strong drink, it must have been plenty strong —"

"Shut up, Catlett," Crawford said suddenly. "I've got an idea. I just thought of something." Deep frown wrinkles creased his forehead. Abruptly he snapped his fin-

205

gers and jerked out a savage curse. "I've got it!" he gritted angrily. "Deacon, I've watched you stow away a heap of drink in my time, but I never yet knew you to get absolutely blotto. I want the truth now: how much did you fellers drink in Brown's place yesterday?"

"We only had two-three rounds," the Deacon replied promptly. "That's why I don't understand it."

"I do," Crawford ripped out. "Waco Brown Mickey Finn'd you!"

"Mickey Finn?" Ten-Spot Nance exclaimed. "You mean he gave us knockout drops?"

"Exactly," Crawford thundered. "By God! I see it all now. That Scott hombre is too damn' smart. He outguessed us. Maybe I've underestimated him. He figured you hombres might be waiting when he came through Moonstone with that cash money. I'm betting he sneaked into town when you didn't see him and persuaded Brown to put those drops in your drinks."

A low growl of hate rose from the other men. Excepting the Deacon, they rose to their feet and started examining six-shooters. Crawford glanced angrily at them, then, "Sit down, you fools! What do you think you're going to do?"

Ten-Spot Nance said, "I'm figuring to go across the street and wipe out them hombres. They're still over there in that new deputy's office."

"Damn them!" Hedge Furlow snarled. "There's enough of us here to handle —"

"The sooner the better," Limpy Bristol commenced.

"Sit down!" Crawford thundered. The men resumed their seats. Crawford went on, "Cripes! Nogales Scott and his pals aren't fools. Don't you think they've figured as far ahead as we have? You start slinging lead with them and you'll pull Peters into the argument. Either we get jammed up, or we kill him. If we kill him, there'll be an investigation down here. We don't want that. Nope, you fellers just leave things to me. Let me think up a way to handle this. When I give the word, we'll act. Until then, just sit tight."

"By geez!" Furlow rasped. "I got a score to settle with that Waco Brown. I'll —"

"You'll sit tight until I tell you to move," Crawford growled.

The men settled back in their chairs. After a time a few of them rose and drifted to the bar for drinks. No one had a great deal to say, though Furlow was engaged in a low-voiced conversation with Ten-Spot Nance. Nance listened closely. After a time he nodded his head. "We'd catch hell if the boss found out," he reminded Furlow.

"Not if we finished the job clean," Furlow said earnestly. "And you and me could do it. We wouldn't need to say a word to a soul until after it was done. Then I'm betting Crawford would be mighty pleased."

"All right. I'm with you," Nance consented.

Shortly after midnight two riders pushed their ponies across the desert sands in the direction of Moonstone. There weren't many lights in the small settlement when they arrived there. A couple of lamps still burned in Waco Brown's saloon, but by this time the last section hand had rolled drowsily into his bunk, and such Mexicans and Cahuilla Indians as were still awake were in their homes. Overhead the sky was spotted with drifting clouds that continually blotted the moon from view.

The two riders pulled their ponies to a walk as they neared the town, then swung them wide to approach Brown's place from the rear. They dismounted beneath the limbs of a large mesquite tree and dropped reins on the earth. Then, moving with the stealth of Apaches, they slowly commenced to close in on the saloon building.

In the barroom Brown stood yawning behind his bar as he counted the day's receipts. A lamp burned on the back bar behind him. Another swung from the ceiling. Brown finished counting his cash, scooped it into a small canvas sack, and locked it inside a wooden drawer placed beneath the bar. Turning to the oil lamp at his rear, he puffed out the flame and then started around the end of the long counter to extinguish the lamp swinging from the ceiling and lock the front doors of the building. He had taken only two steps when a noise at the doorway caused him to swing back. Ten-Spot Nance was just entering.

Brown gazed steadily at the man a minute, then said, "Oh, it's you, eh? What do you want?"

"A drink, of course," Nance said harshly. He came up to the bar and rested one foot on the bar rail. His right hand dropped to the holstered gun at his side.

Brown said, "Rye, bourbon, or beer?" in a level voice.

"Rye — and hurry up," Nance growled.

Brown nodded coolly and reached below

his bar. His hand again came into view holding a six-shooter instead of the expected bottle. The six-shooter was aimed directly at Nance's body. Nance stiffened and commenced, "What the hell you —"

"Hold it," Brown said coldly. "Don't try to draw on me. I saw in your eyes what you intended when you came in here. Now, what's eating you?"

Nance gulped. "You — you put knockout drops in our drinks," he accused.

A cold smile crossed Brown's face. "Yes, I did," he admitted. "I figured you had something like that coming. Didn't like your introduction to Mister Mickey Finn, eh?"

Nance called Brown a name. Brown said, "Take it easy, Nance. I don't take anything like that from any man —"

At that moment Hedge Furlow softly pushed open the door leading to Brown's back room. Brown's eyes, intent on Nance, didn't see the newcomer.

Furlow's right hand lifted, then exploded abruptly into a mushroom of orange flame. Brown swayed against the bar, caught himself, and lifted his gun, fired once, but missed as he started to fall. Again Furlow triggered two murderous shots. Nance leaped on top of the bar and poured a killing fire into the sagging man.

Brown's hand caught at the back bar, pulling it down on top of him. There came a crashing of glasses and bottles to mingle with the roaring reports of forty-five guns as Nance and Furlow vented their hate on the man below them.

Suddenly their hammers were falling on empty shells. The room was thick with powder smoke. The man on the floor back of the bar was silent. Someplace in town a voice was raised in shrill alarm.

"Come on." Nance spoke quickly. "We've emptied our guns. We've got to get out of here."

"That damned bustard!" Furlow spoke hoarsely. "We've evened the score, Ten-Spot." He stood as though petrified, gazing down on Brown's silent form.

Nance tugged at Furlow's sleeve. "C'mon," he urged nervously. "We've got to slope. I hear people coming. Move fast, damn it!"

Turning, they ran swiftly through the rear of the building, climbed into saddles, and jabbed savage spurs against their ponies' hides. By the time the first of the aroused townspeople arrived at the saloon only a steady, soft drumming across the desert sands told the direction the murderers had taken.

XVIII

Due for a Gunning

The news was brought to Nogales about three-thirty in the morning by a young Indian riding the pinto horse that Nogales had borrowed the previous day. A cluster of men on the Rancho de Paz gallery surrounded the man while he told the story in broken English. Nogales' face grew grim while he listened.

"Can you make it out, pard?" Caliper asked.

Nogales said, steady voiced, "Waco Brown has been shot. I don't know who did it, or how bad he's injured, but he sent this Cahuilla to get me. I'll be riding. Doc" — to Dr. Stebbings who stood shivering in his nightshirt in the chill desert night air — "you'll come with me." It was a statement rather than a question.

"Certainly," Stebbings replied. "I've already asked Ethan to have a man saddle up for us. I'll get dressed and get my bag."

Caliper, Jimmy-Steve, and Rod Peters,

who was staying at the Rancho de Paz until he could get a cot for his office, all offered to go, but Nogales vetoed that. "No use of more than just Doc and me making the ride. This Injun says the fellers that did the shooting left town in this direction. Maybe you could do more by working in Ramrod Ridge come morning. You might learn something."

"We won't wait until morning," Peters said grimly. "I'm figuring to ride in now and rouse Crawford and the rest of his gang. They're due to answer some questions."

Five minutes later Nogales and Doc Stebbings were in saddles, riding hard across the desert wastes. They swung wide of Ramrod Ridge, taking a short cut that led through desert willow, mesquite, and catclaw. By the time they were once more in open desert country the sky was growing pink in the east.

The sun was just lifting above the horizon as they pounded their foam-flecked ponies into Moonstone. Dismounting before the open doorway of Waco's saloon, they stepped inside. The oil lamp swinging from the ceiling had long since burned out, but a faint odor of oily, charred wick still lingered in the air together with the scent of burned gunpowder. A half-dozen men stood at the bar, talking in hushed tones. None of them were drinking. Back of the bar a splintered shelf and a litter of whisky-smelling glasses and bottles hid the dark stain that had seeped into the floor boards.

Nogales looked at the men at the bar. "Where is he?" he demanded.

"You Nogales Scott — the feller Waco asked for?" The usually profane boss of the section hands had stepped forward.

"I'm Scott," Nogales said tersely. "This is Doc Stebbings."

"I sort of took charge here," the section boss explained. "There wasn't much I could do though. We got Waco into bed. He asked for you and then went uncon-scious. It was me sent that Injun to Rancho de Paz. Waco ain't come to since. He's in that back room."

Nogales and the doctor pushed into the back room. Stretched silently on a cot was Waco Brown's unconscious form. All the blood seemed drained from the man's rugged features. He breathed with diffi-culty. An Indian woman sat near the cot, placing wet cloths on the wounded man's forehead. She looked up and started to rise as the two men entered. Stebbings spoke to her in a mixture of Cahuilla and

214

English: "Don't go; I may need you." He drew up a chair and opened his bag after throwing back the blankets that covered Brown's body. After a time he swore softly.

Nogales asked, "What's the matter?"

Stebbings snapped, "I'm damned if I know what's keeping this man alive. He must have the constitution of an ox. He should have been dead long ago. I reckon whoever shot him figured he'd die instanter —"

"You mean there isn't any hope —" Nogales began.

"I tell you," Stebbings said irritatedly, "he should be dead now. His body's riddled with lead. Whoever did this sure aimed to make a complete job of things."

"Look, Doc," Nogales said tensely, "you've got to pull him through. You're here. I'm counting on you."

"Dammit, man!" Stebbings said impatiently, "I can't do the impossible. There isn't a chance to save him. The best I can hope for is to bring him to consciousness before he dies so we can learn who did this. Now get out of here, will you? I can't work when you're always asking questions. This job demands concentration."

Nogales walked grim-faced back to the barroom. He questioned the men there, then passed out to the street. For a time he moved around Moonstone, talking to everyone he could find who had heard the shots the previous night. By the time he returned to the saloon his information covered only two brief facts: after the shots had been heard, two riders were heard leaving town. Already hoofprints had been found heading in the direction of Ramrod Ridge.

He again entered the saloon and passed through to the back room. Stebbings was still working over the unconscious form. He glanced up as Nogales paused in the doorway. "No news," Stebbings said briefly. "I'll let you know if anything happens."

Nogales went back to the barroom. The men there eyed him questioningly. Nogales shook his head, then went around the bar and found an unbroken bottle of liquor and some glasses. "I reckon we all need a drink," he said, his voice quiet.

The section boss and the other men nodded assent. The section boss added, "We've been feeling that way for some time, but we sort of hated to help ourselves to Waco's liquor."

An hour passed, then two hours. The next time Nogales entered the back room

Doc Stebbings was seated quietly in a chair puffing on a brier pipe. He didn't take his gaze from the dying man's face as he said, "I don't know if he'll regain consciousness, Nogales. He's sinking rapidly now. I've done all I can."

Nogales strolled back to the street. He stood in the saloon doorway, rolling a cigarette, his gaze steely hard in the direction of Ramrod Ridge. "It's got to be one of Crawford's men," he muttered. "Two, rather. There were two riders."

The sun was beating down now, making black shadows between buildings. Nogales finished his cigarette, dropped the butt in the street, and stepped on it. A man spoke at his shoulder: "Doc wants you, Scott."

Nogales hurried to the back room. Stebbings sighed and said, "He can't last but a minute or so more. Figured you'd want to be here."

"Not a chance, eh, Doc?" Nogales asked.

"Not a chance," Stebbings replied. "Hell, feel his pulse."

Nogales' fingers sought the dying man's wrist. After a minute he looked up, frowning. "I can't feel any pulse," he said.

Stebbings said shortly, "Now you know what I mean."

At that instant Waco Brown's eyes fluttered open. His gaze rested on Nogales' face. "Hi-yuh, pard." He spoke feebly. "Looks like they got me, eh? Glad . . . you got . . . here . . ."

"Waco," Nogales pleaded, "tell me who did it. Do you know?"

"Cripes, yes. Two of . . . 'em. Ten-Spot Nance . . . came at me . . . from the front. Furlow . . . came in . . . rear way. I never . . . had a chance . . ."

"I'm squaring that, Waco." Nogales spoke swiftly. "But now you rest easy. Doc Stebbings here will —"

"Don't run . . . risks . . . my account . . ." Brown's eyes closed. Now his lips barely moved, and Nogales had to bend close to catch the words: "Seems like . . . you're always . . . doing somethin' . . . for me . . ."

Nogales gripped the man's cold hand and felt a feeble answering pressure. Then, abruptly, Waco Brown died.

Nogales rose to his feet. "Gone," he said briefly.

Stebbings nodded. "Damned if I know what kept him alive this long."

"Maybe I do," Nogales said, level-voiced, "but I reckon it's something neither you nor I understand complete. I guess it just wasn't in the cards for Waco to die without letting us know who did it."

He thrust one hand into his pants pocket and drew out a roll of bills which he thrust on Doc Stebbings. "Do me a favor. Go to San Rivedino and make funeral arrangements. Waco had folks back in Texas and we'll send the body there. I'll give you the address later."

"Sure, sure." Stebbings frowned. "But what are you going to do?"

"I'm heading for Ramrod Ridge pronto," Nogales jerked out. "There's a couple of skunks there due for a gunning."

"Now wait a minute, Nogales." Stebbings caught at Nogales' arm. "Don't you rush off half-cocked. We've got a deputy at Ramrod Ridge now, remember. He can't make arrests if you insist on taking the law into your own hands."

"I'm not forgetting that," Nogales said grimly. "This is one instance where there aren't going to be any arrests. Nance and Furlow don't deserve that much chance. I'm gunning for the murderous sidewinders myself!"

XIX

Powder Smoke

It wasn't quite noon when Nogales rode into Ramrod Ridge. There wasn't a soul in sight along the single street; at this hour everyone was staying within doors, out of reach of the broiling midday sun. A few ponies stood limp and droop-headed before Crawford's general store. Farther along the street, on the opposite side, a brand-new sign proclaimed one of the buildings to be the office of the deputy sheriff. Here, too, stood three saddled ponies, but they were in the shade at that point. Of their riders nothing was to be seen. Nogales judged that they were all in the deputy's office.

Nogales drew his pony to a walk. His eyes narrowed. Should he go first to the deputy's office and tell what he had learned? He gave the thought consideration, then vetoed the idea. "Nope," he muttered, "Peters would want to arrest Nance and Furlow. I'd have to back him in carrying out the law. Reckon I'd better go direct to Crawford's place. If those rattlers aren't there, I'll be surprised."

He touched spurs lightly to the pony and the animal quickened pace until it had carried its rider abreast of Crawford's general store and bar. Here, Nogales pulled it to a halt and dismounted. There was no one on the store porch, but from inside came the clinking of glasses and loud voices.

Nogales stepped lightly up the steps, crossed the porch, and pushed his way inside. Within the store he hesitated but a moment to accustom his eyes to the light after the brilliant glare of outdoors. Men were strung along the bar, drinking and talking. Crawford was ensconced in his big armchair. At the table, beside the chair, sat Deacon Trumbull and Limpy Bristol, talking low-voiced to Crawford.

Nogales' keen gaze flashed quickly along the line of men at the bar and picked out Nance and Hedge Furlow near the far end. Without removing his eyes from the pair, Nogales started directly toward them, his arms swinging easily at his sides.

By this time Crawford had spied Nogales crossing the floor, and sensed that something unusual was in the air. The big man heaved himself out of his chair, took two quick steps, and barred Nogales' passage.

"Where do you think you're heading, Scott?" he growled.

Tall as he was, Nogales had to look up to meet Crawford's baleful glance. "I'm looking for the murderers of Waco Brown," Nogales snapped.

By this time the men at the bar had swung around to see Nogales. One or two of them laughed sneeringly. Nance and Furlow backed away a trifle, hand going to gun butts. Crawford, standing in front of Nogales, obstructed Nogales' view of the action.

"You won't find those murderers here," Crawford rumbled. "Cripes A'mighty! Do you always have to come here when there's been trouble? Like as not somebody in Moonstone shot Brown."

"I know better," Nogales said coldly. "Out of the way, Crawford. I've got a job to do."

"Not so fast, not so fast." Crawford lifted one huge arm to bar Nogales' advance. "Must be you ain't talked to Deputy Peters."

Nogales hesitated. "What's Rod Peters got to do with this?"

Crawford swore. "He had plenty to do with it. Didn't he get me out of my bed early this morning and start asking questions — him and that pal of yours and that Mex? Dammit! They went all through the town asking questions. Every one of my men were in their blankets —"

"That don't go down, Crawford," Nogales cut in. "The murderers had plenty of time to ride back here from Moonstone and get to bed."

"Well, they ain't here," Crawford said emphatically.

"Don't lie, Crawford. They're here. I saw 'em when I came in. Out of my way!" Nogales' eyes burned with small pinpoints of angry flame.

"Hold on, Scott!" Crawford bellowed. He placed one huge paw against Nogales' chest and tried to force him back.

Nogales swore, swiftly sidestepped, whipped his right foot around behind Crawford's right knee, and gave the big man a sudden push. Crawford was already half off balance; the push sent him falling back. He struck the floor with a heavy jar.

Nogales didn't even wait for him to get up. He strode on until he had stopped a few yards from Ten-Spot Nance and Hedge Furlow. The two gazed at him a second, then their eyes dropped. Other men at the bar commenced to scatter out of the way. "You two — Nance — Furlow"

— Nogales' words cracked like shots from a Winchester — "it's a showdown. Go for your guns!"

Furlow backed another step. He was white as death. He didn't say anything. Nance put out one protesting hand. "We didn't have anything to do with Brown's killing," he said nervously. "You got us wrong, Scott —"

"Liar!" Nogales snapped. "Brown didn't die instanter like you figured. He lived long enough to name you two. Now, you dirty skunks, will you draw, or have I got to shoot you down like the dogs you are?"

Nogales waited, tense. Neither man made a move toward his holster. They backed another step and started to spread out, each trying to divert Nogales attention from himself. Behind him, Nogales heard Crawford cursing angrily as the big man heaved himself up from the floor.

Nogales threw caution to the wind. He lifted both hands high in the air. "Now, will you jerk your irons?" he pleaded. "I'm giving you this chance. It's your last one."

It was the chance Nance had been waiting for. His right hand swooped to his holster. Nogales' hand flashed down, came up. A lancelike stream of white fire darted from the muzzle. Nance screamed and went down, clawing at his breast as he fell, his gun, even as he pulled trigger, falling from his hand. Nogales heard the bullet thud into the bar front as he whirled to face Furlow.

Furlow had already fired two shots, both of which had missed. He was still trying to steady his shaking aim when Nogales' next bullet took him in the middle. Furlow groaned, swayed a moment. Then his body jackknifed and he pitched to the floor, still clutching his weapon.

Powder smoke swirled through the big room. There were excited yells. Limpy Bristol had whipped out his six-shooter and was covering Nogales, waiting for the expected order from Crawford who was approaching from behind. Crawford's huge right hand fell on Nogales' shoulder, whirling him around. The big man's face was aflame with rage.

"You claiming those two did it — ?" he commenced. From the doorway came an interruption. "Stick 'em up, you scuts. We've got you covered!"

Caliper, Rod Peters, and Jimmy-Steve were advancing into the room, drawn guns in their hands.

"Up with 'em!" Peters snapped. "You, Bristol, put that gun away and move mighty cautious. Quick, now!"

Crawford had thrown a quick glance over his shoulder at the newcomers, then turned his attention back to Nogales. "What right you got coming in here and —"

"I had a score to even up," Nogales said quietly. He twisted away from Crawford and approached his friends. "Thanks, pards. You arrived about the right time, I reckon."

"We heard the loud voices here and came on the run," Caliper panted. "Then, just as we reached the door, the shooting broke out —"

"There won't be any more shooting for a spell." Crawford spoke heavily. "You hombres can put your guns away. I want to get to the bottom of this. Don't any man make to lift his gun. All right, Peters, call your men off."

Nogales reloaded his forty-five and shoved the gun back in its holster. The room quieted down. The others holstered their guns. Crawford sank ponderously back in his chair. "You, Deacon," he ordered, "go see if there's any life left in Nance and Furlow. I'd like to get at the truth of this business. I got a suspicion maybe Scott was right."

The Deacon rose and crossed the floor, kneeling first at Furlow's side. Instantly he arose, saying, "Furlow's passed to his reward, whatever it is." He stooped by the motionless form of Nance for a moment, then called for whisky. Tony, the barkeep, brought him a glass. A few drops of the liquor were forced between Nance's lips. After a moment the man opened his eyes. The Deacon spoke to him. The others crowded near, but no one except the Deacon could catch the dying man's low-voiced reply.

Finally the Deacon let Nance's head fall back. The men scattered again. "And that's the end of Nance," the Deacon said, adding, "They that take the sword shall perish with the sword."

"Cut out the cant," Crawford roared. "Did those two do it, or didn't they?"

The Deacon came back to his chair. "They did." He nodded. "Nance and Furlow killed Brown last night, then hurried back here and turned in. They —"

Crawford swore, then faced Nogales and his friends. "I don't expect you to believe me," he rumbled, "but those two acted against my orders. They were all for wiping out Brown yesterday. I said no. Oh, we figured out what had happened, Scott. That knockout-drops stunt wasn't funny. You had no business doing that —"

"I wasn't trusting your gang any, Crawford," Nogales said coldly. "I figured that was better than crossing guns with 'em — and a heap funnier."

"You and me will tangle yet, Scott," Crawford growled.

"You'll keep the peace, that's what you'll do," Rod Peters snapped.

"I'll do my share of keeping the peace," Crawford snorted. "Peters, I figure it's your duty to arrest Scott for the murder of Ten-Spot Nance and Hedge Furlow —"

"Murder?" Peters ripped out. "Are you crazy Crawford? The guns of both men are out, both fired their weapons. You call that murder? To me it's a clear case of self-defense, so there's no need of arrest —"

"Dammit!" Crawford roared. "Scott taunted 'em into drawing."

"Take my advice and let matters drop," Peters said coldly. "And while we're on the subject of obeying the law, yesterday I gave orders that every man here without visible means of support had better make track out of Ramrod Ridge. I meant that. I haven't noticed any visible lessening of the population so far. Maybe I will have to make some arrests."

"Not in here, you won't," Crawford replied, and a sly smile creased his fat features. "Every man here is on my pay roll in one capacity or another. Mostly, they make trips buying cattle for me. Some of 'em wait on the store when I'm not here —"

"I get it." Peters nodded coldly. "You probably just put 'em on your pay roll last night so I couldn't run 'em out."

Crawford smiled mockingly. "Cripes, no! These fellers have worked for me for years — and I defy you to prove otherwise, Peters."

"Anyway," Nogales put in, "we've finally made Crawford admit he has a gang. That's something he'd never do before. From now on any skulduggery that breaks out — Well, Crawford, you'll be held responsible. If we can't tie your hands one way, we'll do it another. And don't think we're avoiding a scrap. We're just waiting for one. The sooner you get tough, the better we'll like it."

The men at the bar moved nervously and looked at Crawford for reply. Crawford's face reddened; he opened his mouth to speak, then thought better of it. Finally he said, ingratiatingly, "I've told you fellers a hundred times all I want is to be let alone to run my business peaceful. I don't want trouble. Anybody that knows me well, knows that too. Nope, Peters — Scott — — you can't push me into fight with your talk of getting tough. Any trouble that breaks from now on it'll be of your making. All I ask is peace."

"I wish we could believe that," Nogales said scornfully.

Peters said, "We'll give you plenty of opportunity to prove what you've said, Crawford."

"I mean it," Crawford insisted earnestly. "What say we have a drink all around and be friends?"

Nogales shook his head. "Me, I'm not thirsty right now."

It proved none of his companions was thirsty either. A few minutes later they left Crawford's store and trooped across the street to head for Peters' new office.

XX

Imported Gunmen?

A month passed. Apparently Crawford meant what he said when he had stated all he wanted was peace. Nothing untoward had taken place and the days slipped by in undisturbed tranquillity. Nogales and Caliper were growing restless; both felt the quiet was just the lull that precedes the storm and they waited impatiently to see where Simon Crawford would strike next — as they felt certain he would.

The weeks of rest had worked wonders for Fred Vincent. By this time he was up and around, though Doc Stebbings had not yet judged him strong enough to do any riding. Now that he was in clean clothing, with his hair trimmed and his pale features shaven, he bore little resemblance to the "wild man" who had roamed the hills only a few weeks before. Nogales, Caliper, Jimmy-Steve, Stebbings, and the three Vincents were seated on the long gallery of the ranch house one day, enjoying

Polly's mint juleps. Below on the desert flats the days were hotter than ever, but in the shade of the gallery roof life was pleasant.

"No, Fred," Stebbings was saying, "you'll have to take it easy for a spell. You went through an ordeal that would have killed most men. We can't take chances of a relapse."

Signs of that ordeal were still present. Fred Vincent's face was lined and haggard, though still youngish appearing when set against his premature white hair. At times his blue eyes took on a vacant look; there were huge blank spots in his memory, though bit by bit traces of the fateful night of his running fight returned to him; fresh details welled up almost daily from his consciousness.

"I know, Doc," Fred replied earnestly, "but I've a hunch that if I could just fork a horse into Quithatz Canyon I might remember what happened to that gold. I can recollect herding that pack mule ahead of me into the canyon — then things go hazy. Maybe I fainted from my wounds; I don't know. I remember one slug slicing skin from my neck; another ripped a furrow across my shoulder. But there were days that consisted of just one fainting spell after another. I'd come to in a different place than I had been —"

"There's old scars from those wounds," Stebbings broke in. "There's one scar on your head that looks like it come from a fall."

Fred frowned. "Seems like I remember climbing up above Quithatz Falls, but I'm not sure. And then, someplace along the line, maybe I slipped and fell. It's all like a bad dream. I remember things up to a certain point, then they vanish. I know there were days when I fainted several times. Maybe more than one day passed while I was unconscious. I don't know. Those days I didn't even remember where I was, let alone who I was. I remember once looking in a pool and seeing my hair was white. That struck me funny at the time, but the thought quickly left —"

"Suffering that will turn a man's hair white," Nogales said sympathetically, "must be kind of tough to talk about."

Doc Stebbings said, "Talking will do Fred good now."

Fred went on: "I dug up roots and ate them. Once I came on a cache of piñon nuts hidden by some animal. I stole food from Indian villages; I trapped ground squirrels and rabbits. Somehow, I never thought of shooting them, though I'd kept hold of my six-shooter right along. I've no idea how many miles I've traveled through these mountains. I only knew, those days, I was deathly afraid of humans." He turned to Nogales with a wan smile. "You say I attacked Tim Church, Nance, and Jack Schmidt that day you found me. I wonder why? Were they three of the men who attacked me that night? Did I remember them, or what? Maybe I instinctively recognized enemies. That's an animal's way, and I was living right close to the animals those days. Sometimes in my wanderings I'd approach a settlement, but I always got away as fast as possible. I was afraid of people. Self-preservation was my sole thought. I remember seeing some men tracking me one day. I kept just ahead of them. They never did see anything but my tracks, or brief glimpses far off. Oh, I certainly reverted to the primitive. Small wonder I can't remember what became of that gold."

"We'll find it one of these days," Caliper said. "You'll remember it all of a sudden."

"I sure hope so."

"You will, sure," Ethan Vincent assured his son. "Think of all the things you've remembered and pieced together just this past month."

Here Doc Stebbings broke in on the conversation. "Time for your afternoon nap, Fred. Go in and stretch out. Every wink of sleep you can get is that much energy stored up."

Fred nodded, rose, and stepped into the house. After he had left Ethan said anxiously, "Doc, do you really think he ever will remember everything?"

Stebbings shrugged his shoulders. "I've got to tell you the truth, Ethan. I don't know. I do think there's a mighty good chance of it. Just the past week he's made a marvelous improvement. But the mind is a funny piece of equipment. It might take some great shock to clear Fred's mind. As I say, we doctors don't know yet all there is to know about the human brain."

"Shock, eh?" Caliper speculated aloud. "That night when Fred was held up and shot there was a lot of shooting. Maybe if we could take him up to this Quithatz Canyon and shoot some guns, it might snap his memory back."

"It might, it might," Stebbings conceded, "but I'd be afraid to risk it. It might have the opposite effect of plunging his mind back into darkness again. The mind is a pretty delicate piece of mechanism and it requires only a trifle to throw it out of gear sometimes."

"Don't you think by next week," Polly asked, "that Fred should be strong enough to ride? I've promised to ride with him out on the desert. The cactus plants are in bloom now and the ocotillo. And think how blue that smoke-tree forest must be by this time. All that to look at and the desert sun should do him good, I think."

"I think so myself, Polly." Stebbings nodded. "But let's go slow. As a matter of fact, if he had to, he's strong enough to ride now, but the longer he waits the better his condition will be. We've just got to be careful. That gun fight the night he was jumped by that gang cracked his mind temporarily; I'd like him to take things slow, now, for a spell. I don't mean it was the gun fight alone, but his sufferings later —"

"Ridair comeeng," Jimmy-Steve announced.

Ethan Vincent rose and gazed from his gallery, off across the tops of the trees in his fig orchard to the winding road that led to the Rancho de Paz. "Looks like Rod Peters," he announced.

"Coming fast?" Caliper asked.

Vincent shook his head. "Just riding easy."

Nogales grinned. "Probably no faster than he ever rides to get here, but it always seemed to me he didn't waste much time once he was started. What'll you bet, he's either coming to see Polly or —"

"Why should he come to see me?" Polly asked, her cheeks crimsoning.

"Maybe he likes your mint juleps." Nogales laughed.

"I sort of figured," Doc Stebbings said, "now that Rod has got a cot in his office, we wouldn't see so much of him, but he manages to find some excuse to ride in every evening —"

"Long about suppertime," Caliper finished with a chuckle.

"He often has news of San Rivedino too," Polly defended Peters. "Now that Sheriff Burger sends a man to Ramrod Ridge once a week, to see if Rod needs anything, we hear about happenings in the outside world."

"I'm surprised that Burger showed that much initiative," Stebbings commented. "I wonder what came over him."

Nogales grinned. "He's probably still afraid I'll report him to the governor."

Polly and the others laughed. Caliper

said, "I wonder if he's ever seen the governor. I'd sure like to dress up some night and pretend —"

"You and your disguises!" Nogales said scornfully. "I remember that time you fixed up at Christmas time to fool the school kids. Remember?"

Caliper shook his head. "I don't want to remember," he said ruefully.

Polly asked, "What happened?"

Nogales grinned. "Caliper came into the schoolroom with a red suit and whiskers on and started giving out the presents on the tree when a little tike about five years old asks if Santa Claus got those bow laigs riding reindeer, and another little kid, 'bout the same age, says Mister Maxwell looks real nice since he growed a white beard. Nope, Caliper didn't fool any of those kids."

"That ain't saying I couldn't fool Ham Burger," Caliper said.

"You might be right at that," Nogales conceded.

As Rod Peters arrived and ascended to the gallery, Polly came out of the house with a cold glass in her hand.

"Just what the doctor ordered." Rod laughed, and dropped into a chair. He took a long, cold sip of the drink, blissfully closed his eyes, and rested his head against the back of the chair. "I'd be plumb happy if I could have one of these every day of my life," he murmured.

"That same drink every day?" Nogales asked.

"I wouldn't want any of it changed," Rod said, opening his eyes again. "Not even —" He stopped suddenly, his face growing red.

"Sounds like a proposal, Polly." Nogales chuckled.

Polly was covered with confusion, as was Peters. The rest were laughing at them. Peters tried to explain just what he had meant to say, but it didn't work. Finally he stopped stammering and said boldly, "All right, it was a proposal. What do you say, Polly?"

"No," Polly said promptly. "When I receive a proposal, I don't want an audience on hand."

"Meaning," Nogales said, "that if at first you don't succeed —"

"Suck eggs," Caliper cut in.

The laughter quieted down after a time. Polly entered the house to see how supper was coming along. Ethan Vincent said, "Anything new happening, Rod?"

Peters sobered. "Yes, there is. Something I don't like."

Nogales said, "What's up? Trouble in town?"

Peters shook his head. "Not yet. Everything is peaceful there as far as I can determine. Crawford and the rest of his gang pretend to be friendly. There's nothing I can take offense to, though I know they'd all, every one of 'em, like to put a slug in my back. It's this way. I had my weekly word from Sheriff Burger today, asking if everything was all right and if there was anything I needed to just pass the word to his messenger. But he added a few lines in his note that I didn't like."

"What about?" Caliper asked.

Peters said, "Burger says there's three gun fighters hanging around San Rivedino. They've just come from New Mexico where they played a part in that TIX-Rafter-H range war sometime back. Burger heard one of them say one night in a saloon that they had an appointment to meet Simon Crawford on business —"

"T'hell you say!" Nogales exclaimed.

Peters nodded. "I don't like it either. To top that off, Crawford went to San Rivedino yesterday. Just got back this afternoon. I passed him on the street just as I was about to leave for here and he gave me a smile that reminded me of the cat that

240

just swallowed the canary. He's cooking up something, or I'm a liar."

"You say Crawford went to San Rivedino?" Caliper asked. "I didn't think that big hulk ever moved out of Ramrod Ridge. It must take a mighty powerful horse to carry that load."

"He drives in, in a buckboard," Peters explained. "Yes, I understand he goes to San Rivedino once a month to order a bill of supplies which are brought down later, mule freight —"

"I'd sure like to get a look at the buckboard," Caliper interrupted. "It must be plenty strong."

"Anyway, I don't like the looks of it." Peters frowned.

"I wonder," Nogales said slowly, "if Crawford is importing gunmen."

"That's the way it looked to me," Peters said.

"Did Burger know who they were?" Nogales asked.

"He got their names." Peters nodded. "Wait a minute." He drew an envelope from his pocket and consulted the note that was enclosed. Then he looked at Nogales. "Their names are Nevada Blake, Jim Muttershaw, and Squint Merrick. Know any of 'em?"

"Blake and Merrick are strangers. I had a scrap with Muttershaw, once, back in Oklahoma." Nogales looked thoughtful. "His slug put me in the hospital for six months. He's plenty fast with his irons. I managed to wing one arm, but he got away with the horse we had the argument about. It was my horse. I was just a kid those days, but I've always hoped to meet up with him again. He owes me a horse."

"Maybe this is your time to collect?" Caliper asked.

Nogales laughed mirthlessly. "Maybe I'd be better off without the horse." He repeated, "Muttershaw's plenty fast with his irons."

At that moment Polly came to the doorway to call them for supper. The men rose, somewhat depressed, and filed inside the house.

XXI

Council of War

Crawford and his henchmen were holding a council of war in the back room of the big store building. This back room held a desk, a small safe, a stoutly reinforced bunk where Crawford slept, a table and some straight-backed chairs, as well as the oversize chair at present supporting Crawford's bulk. A pair of windows let light into the room. The floor was of pine boards. A swinging oil lamp was suspended from the center of the ceiling. The voices and clatter of glasses of the men at the bar, beyond the closed door, came but faintly to the ears of Crawford and his companions. With Crawford were Deacon Trumbull, Limpy Bristol, and Swifty Catlett, Catlett having been recently elevated to a position of confidence.

The Deacon had been talking steadily for five minutes. Finally Crawford raised a hamlike hand for silence. "I'll tell you why I haven't done anything," Crawford rumbled. "I wanted time to think things over and lay out plans before we acted. And when we act, I figure all hell's going to break loose. When it does, I want a stronger crew than I've got now."

"There's about twenty men out at that bar and us," Catlett said.

"Do you think that twenty is to be counted on?" Crawford said heavily. "Me, I don't. They're all right for small business, but I'll bet there ain't a man in that twenty who wouldn't fold up and quit if the going got tough — and it's going to get tough right soon. Oh, I know those hombres out there are all right for cattle rustling and changing brands and h'isting stages and so on, but man to man — well, they lack guts. I don't want to act until I got men I can count on."

"What you planning to do?" the Deacon wanted to know.

"Foremost in my mind," Crawford explained, "I want the Rancho de Paz. Someday I'm going to have it, but that can wait for a spell. Then, there's that missing thirty thousand in gold. We want that. And, Deacon, I haven't yet given up the idea of rubbing out Nogales Scott and forging his name to a will — but so far we don't even know what his writing looks like. Howsomever, securing that thirty thousand comes first."

"That's a start," the Deacon agreed. "But where is it? You've had somebody watching the Vincent place every day. If Fred Vincent knows where that money is, nobody at the ranch has gone after it. Fred, himself, hasn't moved away from the house, hardly. Mostly he sits in the sun, or walks around the ranch-house grounds."

"I'll tell you what I think," Crawford said thoughtfully. "I think Fred Vincent hid that money that night, and he hid it so good nobody but him can find it. He's not strong enough yet to lead his pards to the place, but when he does get enough strength back — Well, if we don't act sudden, we're going to lose thirty thousand dollars."

Swifty Catlett frowned and said, "What do you mean — act sudden?"

"Suppose," Crawford said heavily, "we grabbed Fred Vincent and held him captive until he told us where that gold is?"

"You mean kidnap him?" Limpy Bristol said.

Crawford's big head nodded ponderously, his tiny pig eyes darting from man to man to see how the idea affected them.

Deacon Trumbull said shrewdly, "Kidnaping Fred is one thing; making him speak is another. He might refuse to talk."

Crawford said cruelly, "There's more than one way to loosen a man's tongue, once you got him where you want him. Before I got through with him, he'd be glad to talk."

The others were silent, mulling over the idea. Finally Swifty Catlett said, "You mentioned sometime back that you wanted to own the Rancho de Paz. Have you ever thought of taking all our men and raiding the place some night — wiping out everybody? Then you could take what you wanted. We got enough men for that —"

"You talk like a fool, Swifty," Crawford rumbled. "I couldn't get the deed to the place that way, for one thing. For another, there's a deputy stationed here now —"

"I meant to rub Peters out too," Catlett said.

Crawford shook his head. "Nope. If Ham Burger didn't hear from Peters he'd want to know why. The first thing you know there'd be more law officers down here. We couldn't carry on as we have been. I don't want to have to move. I like Ramrod Ridge and the setup here. I don't want that interfered with. We've got to move easy, so nobody can get any proof against us. I still think that grabbing Fred

Vincent is the best thing to start with — and we mustn't leave any clues as to who does it."

"Where you aiming to keep him, once you've grabbed him?" the Deacon asked. "We'd be suspected right off. Scott and Maxwell and Peters would drop down on us like a ton of bricks. They'd search every house in this town —"

"Wouldn't keep him in town," Crawford grunted. "There's plenty hide-outs — caves and so on — in these mountains and canyons hereabouts."

"That's an idea." Catlett nodded. "I know of one dang good cave over in Quithatz Canyon. The opening is hid with tall brush. Nobody'd ever find it once we had Vincent inside — not less'n somebody led 'em to it."

"Keep it in mind." Crawford nodded.

The Deacon said thoughtfully: "I'm getting what you meant, now, when you said we needed a stronger crew, Simon. Our most dangerous opposition is Nogales Scott and Caliper Maxwell. Now if we could only put them out of the way for a spell — but I'm admitting frank that they're too fast for us if it come to a showdown — and none of that gang, out at the bar, would face their guns."

Crawford grunted, swung his huge body to one side, and pawed a heavy gold watch out of a fob pocket. He consulted the watch a moment, then pushed it back in place. "After four-thirty now," he growled. "Those hombres promised to come this afternoon."

"What hombres?" the Deacon asked.

"Three fellers I contacted in San Rivedino yesterday. They come in answer to a letter I wrote a friend of mine in New Mexico about three weeks back. We're going to have three new hands on the pay roll."

The Deacon was curious. "What sort of hands?"

"Well," Crawford said slowly in his deep rumble, "I ain't hiring 'em to wait on counter, nor yet to rustle cattle. They just got through working in a range war in New Mexico. Their guns were for hire and I hired 'em."

"Are they any good?" Swifty Catlett wanted to know.

"They'll be the reinforcements we need," Crawford replied.

"How'll they stack up against fellers like Scott and Maxwell?" Limpy Bristol asked.

A slow smile creased Crawford's fleshy features. "If it comes to shooting, I figure they'll shoot rings around those two. But I'm hoping it won't come to that. I've a feeling that Scott and Maxwell will start minding their own business when they learn what they're up against."

"How about Deputy Peters?" Catlett said.

"He'll have to furnish proof that we're breaking the law before he can do anything," Crawford chuckled fatly. "And I don't figure to give him that proof —"

A knock at the door to the inner room interrupted the words. At Crawford's "What do you want?", Tony, the barkeep, opened the door and stuck his head into the room, saying, "There's three hombres out here to see you, boss. They claim they had an appointment with you."

"Send 'em in," Crawford grunted.

The door closed, reopened a few moments later, and three men entered. "Howdy, boys," Crawford said genially. "Draw up chairs and help yourself to the whisky." He gestured toward the bottle on the table, then introduced the newcomers: "Jim Muttershaw, Squint Merrick, and Nevada Blake."

Muttershaw was a tall, dour-looking individual with a sinewy jaw and thin lips, Merrick was mean-looking with a queer habit of squinting when he talked. Nevada Blake was nearly as tall as Merrick, but heavier. He had quick, restless movements and shifty eyes. All three men were in range togs and all three carried a Colt gun on each hip.

"Two-gun men, eh?" Swifty Catlett commented breezily.

The three turned cold glances toward Catlett. Two of them didn't say anything, just looked. Muttershaw said sourly, "You any objections, feller?"

Catlett wilted. "Now don't get me wrong. I was just trying to be friendly."

Squint Merrick said sarcastically, "Did we come runnin' in here yelpin' for friends? Either you like us or you don't — and we don't care which."

"Take it easy, boys," Crawford rumbled.

Nevada Blake said tonelessly, "Crawford, you said you'd have a job for us. What's it all about?"

"I'm going to put you on my pay roll," Crawford said genially.

"What doing?" Muttershaw demanded.

Crawford smiled. "So far as the rest of the world knows, you'll be special accountants I've hired to audit my books."

The joke didn't go down. Blake swore and said in his flat, toneless voice, "T'hell with the rest of the world. It's us we're asking about."

Deacon Trumbull, hardened sinner that he was, felt a tremor course his spine. These three were coldblooded cases if he'd ever encountered any. Professional killers, all three; no doubt about that.

Crawford got down to business: "I can put you on a regular salary of two hundred a month and keep, or you keep yourself and cut in on a share of the profits —"

"What profits?" Merrick asked coldly.

"There's thirty thousand gold around here waiting to be picked up," Crawford said.

"I don't think we want a regular salary," Blake said flatly.

Jim Muttershaw asked, "Any individual jobs?"

"I reckon," Crawford said. "There's two hombres hereabouts been cutting in on my game. I'll pay five hundred each if you arrange a funeral for 'em. I ain't so anxious though to have one of 'em killed right off; I'd like to get his signature first."

"What's his name?" Muttershaw asked.

"Scott," Crawford replied. "His pal's name is Caliper Maxwell —"

Muttershaw stiffened a trifle. "It wouldn't be Nogales Scott, now, would it?"

"That's the name. Know him?"

Muttershaw nodded reminiscently. "Had a brush with him a number of years back. He was just a kid, then, but like greased lightning with his shootin' iron. I took a horse of his and he tried to give me an argument. Damn' if he didn't put a slug into my right arm that day. Only I had more experience in lead-slingin', he might have got me. I figured I'd finished him, but I heard later he got well. So Nogales Scott is out here. Well, well, I owe him something for that slug in the arm. My arm always has been a mite stiff ever since. Hell! The sooner I can square with him, the better —"

"Wait!" Crawford boomed. "You get that idea right out of your head. Before you bump off Scott I'd like to get his signature —"

"Why?" Merrick demanded.

"He's worth plenty money," Crawford explained. "We've talked some of forging a will. But for the present if you'd like to put him in the hospital for a spell, that's okay with me."

Muttershaw swore carelessly. "I licked him once. Reckon I can put a slug where I want to the next time we meet —"

"If you meet," Crawford said. "It wouldn't surprise me none if Scott and

Maxwell would draw in their horns a heap when they learn you fellers are here."

"Not the Nogales Scott I knew," Muttershaw protested. "Say what you like about him, he wa'n't yellow."

"Take another drink and I'll tell you the plans," Crawford said. Drinks were poured around.

"Here's to crime," the Deacon proposed.

"Drink hearty!" Crawford said. "It looks like luck would be coming our way, now, for a spell."

XXII

Fred Vincent Vanishes

The following morning, after breakfast, Ethan and Fred Vincent, Caliper, and Nogales were standing on the bridge over the irrigation ditch, smoking cigarettes and enjoying the early-morning sunshine. "It's just too dang bad," Nogales commented, "that Crawford and his kind can't be run out. I wonder when those hired gunmen of his are due to arrive."

"I wouldn't care if they never arrived," Caliper said. "It's so dang pleasant here that I'm getting plumb peaceful. I never saw such a place. Here there's water flowing and trees and flowers and green things — and just a few miles away there's the hottest desert I ever laid eyes on."

"This irrigation ditch is responsible for much of the green things you mention." Ethan Vincent smiled. "Without water — well, I guess these hilly slopes would be pretty deserty too."

Nogales glanced down at the water

flowing silently beneath the bridge. "Gosh! Does this water keep running year after year? Doesn't it ever dry up?"

Ethan nodded. "We've been without water twice within the last ten years," he said. "This water comes from up in Quithatz Canyon, you know, from the falls. Well, a couple of times we've had dry winters and the falls just about petered out. But the fall rains always come along in time to save us. After an unusually dry winter, the succeeding winter seems to bring more rain than ever. Last summer this ditch was a mud ditch, and then a terrific rain came —" He stopped.

Fred looked up. "The night my men and I were held up it rained. How it rained! I just happened to think of that. The water came down in torrents." He frowned. "I just happened to remember something that happened that night." A smile suddenly crossed his face. "It started to rain just about the time I was heading that pack mule for the canyon. Those raindrops struck like bullets. I remember when the first slug hit me, for a second I thought it was just a raindrop."

"I recollect it rained three days straight." Ethan nodded. "But we were so wrapped up in Fred's disappearance that we weren't thinking much about rain then. I do remember, though, that tracks were right hard to find. It's queer how things like that will slip a feller's mind."

Nogales said, "We never have got up the canyon to see those falls you speak about. I'd like to see them sometime. Being so close to the desert, it seems mighty odd."

"I'll take you up the canyon just as soon as I'm allowed to ride a horse," Fred said. He looked at his father.

Ethan shook his head. "Not today, Fred." The father smiled. "You know Doc would never hear of it."

Fred sighed. "I sure get bored just sticking around the house. Reckon I'll take a walk down through the fig orchard this afternoon. The trees should be well budded out by this time."

"They are." Ethan nodded. "The walk would be good for you, Fred."

"How far is it to Quithatz Canyon?" Nogales asked.

"Only a few miles from here," Ethan replied. He pointed off toward the southeast. "This range of mountains behind us swings in a great curve to the southeast. Just follow the range with your eye. Now, you see, off there a spell, there's a sort of curved talon of rock that slopes down to the desert floor. See it? Well, that's the entrance to the canyon. It winds back into the mountains for three or four miles before you reach the falls. These mountains are full of canyons. East of Quithatz you can see Morando Canyon, and beyond that, the canyon where the palm trees grow. On the other side of those hills is a big smoke-tree forest —"

"We spotted those smoke trees from a distance the day we first came here," Caliper said, "but we didn't pass through 'em. Jimmy-Steve brought us in by way of that palm-tree canyon."

"Look here," Ethan proposed, "if time is hanging heavy on your hands, Nogales, why don't you and Caliper ride up to Quithatz Falls today? It's a nice ride. Take Jimmy-Steve along. He's been up there many a time and knows the best ways for a horse to take. Those canyon walls are right treacherous at times and the footing is bad if you don't know what you're doing."

"What do you say, pard?" Nogales asked.

"Suits me right down to the ground." Caliper nodded. "I'd like to ride some fat off'n that bronc of mine. I'll go tell Jimmy-Steve."

Three quarters of an hour later Caliper and Nogales were mounted, with Jimmy-

Steve mounted on his pony leading the way. Leaving the Rancho de Paz, the riders followed the irrigation ditch along a gently rising slope. "Many time," Jimmy-Steve said proudly, "I'm work on theese deetch — and on the othair deetch to which we come later. Eet hav' bring life to thees earth."

A half-hour later they passed a second irrigation ditch where it branched from a rapidly running stream. Following the grass-bordered stream, in time they reached the talon-shaped ridge that marked the entrance to Quithatz Canyon. At this point the canyon was probably two hundred yards wide, and the hills on either side were gently sloped, but as they followed the winding stream back through the San Jacinto Mountains, the walls on either side grew steeper and seemed to pull closer together. The horses progressed steadily up the canyon. By this time the mountain stream leaped and tumbled over boulders in its path. Grass grew thickly on either side; an occasional willow and some cottonwoods were seen.

At spots where the stream hugged one wall the riders crossed their horses through the swiftly running water as Jimmy-Steve led the way to the safest footing. As the canyon narrowed, two red rock buttes opened the way to the last stage of the journey. By this time the men were on much higher land, guiding their ponies cautiously along a narrow rock shelf that wound along one canyon wall. The horses were breathing heavily by the time they'd passed between the twin buttes and the men pulled them to a halt for a brief rest.

They sat easily in the saddles, smoking cigarettes. Far below, in the bottom of the canyon, the stream foamed white around great gray-and-white streaked boulders. There were willows and cottonwoods in plenty down there now. Jimmy-Steve said, "Look back and you see the view."

Caliper and Nogales swung around in their saddles and glanced out between the two red buttes.

"My gosh!" Caliper gasped. "I didn't realize we'd climbed this high."

Far out, between the two great red rock sentinels, they were looking down on the floor of the Cahuilla Valley, a vast yellow expanse of desert sand formed in the matrices of continual winds into drifts and rippled dunes as far as the eye could reach. The riders finished their cigarettes and urged their mounts on. The trail wound around one shoulder of a sloping mountainside, climbed and crossed a small rock-cluttered knoll, then commenced to drop. The sun's torrid rays beat down into the canyon, streaking man and beast with grimy sweat. Great boulders barred the way from time to time. Now the stream was lost to view, though occasionally the riders caught the sounds of rushing water moving turbulently in its boulder-littered bed.

The descent became steeper. The ponies braced their muscles and moved stiff-legged down into the shadows between huge rocks, slipping and sliding on the treacherous footing. A few small cotton-woods appeared. Scrub oak grew from cracks in the rock walls at frequent inter-vals. Nogales suddenly became conscious of a steady roaring in his ears and the sounds of leaping waters. Quite suddenly, as the riders rounded a shoulder of yellow-streaked granite, they saw the stream once more, beating itself into a raging white froth along its stony course, heading from a wide pool of tumbling waters. And at the far side of the pool, cascading down a sheer rock wall nearly a hundred feet above the riders' heads, Quithatz Falls formed a broad ribbon of lacy foam that plummeted straight to the surging waters of the pool below. Veils of shimmering spray formed and disappeared and formed again.

Nogales broke an awe-inspired silence: "That's mighty pretty!"

Caliper just stared, mouth agape. Sun filtered down between rocks and tree branches. Jimmy-Steve reined his pony into the pool at a point where it narrowed to form the stream. The other two followed him, stirrup-deep, into the water, through a rainbow of flying spray, and emerged on a grassy bank, shaded by slim aspens, on the opposite side. Here they dismounted and, while the horses ranged along the grassy bank and thrust their noses into the icy waters of the pool, rolled fresh cigarettes.

Far above, through the lacy branches of the trees, they could see the turquoise sky, flecked with a few fleecy clouds.

Caliper commented, "This is really a box canyon, isn't it?"

Jimmy-Steve nodded. There was no need for speech. The canyon ended in that abrupt cliff of sheer granite over which, at one point, the waters of Quithatz Falls had worn a deep groove. It was peaceful here, even with the roar of the cascading waters in their ears.

"And this is where Fred came that night

he was raided?" Nogales said.

Jimmy-Steve nodded. "How far he come — maybe not thees far — we do not know. The pack mule what carry the gold — eets body was found not many yard' from where we now stand."

"Then Fred must have driven it this far," Caliper pointed out. "The gold wasn't on the mule's carcass when it was found. It couldn't have unlashed that strong box itself. Fred must have done it. But what went with the gold? And what was Fred doing?"

Jimmy-Steve shrugged. He eyed the steep rock wall over which the falls dropped. At one side the face of the cliff was dotted with grass and stunted trees growing from the rock. "A man can climb up there," he observed. "I, myself, have made the climb."

"What's up above?" Caliper asked.

"The stream that go' to form Quithatz Falls, rocks, more mountain', and beyon', othair waterfall'. The footing for the climb is ver' bad — but eet can be done."

Nogales surveyed the steep rock wall with narrowed eyes. Yes, he thought, a man could climb up there, but it would be a task almost for a mountain goat. In his mind he saw himself making the climb; he visualized each foothold and saw each stunted tree he would grasp to pull himself farther. There were wide cracks here and there in the rock. At one point there was a narrow shelf. A man could stretch out there and rest, probably. From below, it looked wide enough, though you never knew about those things until you got up there.

"Yes," Nogales nodded, "a man could make to get up there all right. Maybe that's how Fred got out. But it would take a mighty husky hombre to tote thirty thousand gold up that cliff, not to mention the weight of the strong box. And Fred was wounded, besides. He might have started up and fallen back. Maybe he was knocked unconscious. For all we know he might have lain for some time in deep brush, hidden from view of anybody who came into this canyon."

After a time they tossed their cigarette butts into the pool and caught up their mounts. "It's been a nice ride," Caliper said appreciatively. "That waterfall is worth seeing. What gets me is it's so close to desert country."

"It's sure give me an appetite." Nogales grinned.

"There you go," Caliper accused. "And

you're always talking about me getting hungry. For once I was going to keep my mouth shut."

"That would have been a blessing," Nogales said.

They kidded each other all the way back to the Rancho, much to Jimmy-Steve's amusement. An hour and a half later they were once more riding along beside the irrigation ditch, and within a short time after that the three riders came within view of the ranch house.

In front of the house Nogales spotted Polly, Ethan, Doc Stebbings, and several of Ethan's hired men. "Looks like something is wrong," Nogales jerked out. "C'mon, let's hurry." They plunged in spurs and loped ahead.

Something was wrong, as they gathered from the white-faced Polly and the others.

"Fred's disappeared!" Polly announced.

"How long has he been gone?" Nogales asked.

Polly shook her head. "We don't know. We just noticed he was missing a short time back. Then we started to look for him —"

"I was talking with him shortly after dinnertime," Ethan said. "He told me he was going to take a walk down through the fig orchard. You know, he mentioned it this morning. None of us thought much about it —"

"I noticed he wasn't here," Doc Stebbings put in, "but I took it for granted he was taking his afternoon nap."

"Look, Doc," Nogales asked. "Any chance of Fred having a relapse, losing his mind again, and wandering off?"

Stebbings shook his head. "I don't think so. In fact, I feel sure not. But we've looked every place —"

"That settles it," Nogales said grimly. "Caliper — Jimmy-Steve! We're riding to Ramrod Ridge. Crawford is back of this, or I'm a bald-faced liar."

"I'll go with you," Ethan proposed worriedly.

"You stay here — all of you," Nogales said. "For all we know this might be a scheme to draw us all away and leave the Rancho undefended. C'mon, Caliper and Jimmy-Steve! I hope you got plenty ca'tridges. We may need 'em bad!"

XXIII

Bronc Fighters

Arriving at Ramrod Ridge, Nogales, Caliper, and Jimmy-Steve went directly to Rod Peters' office. Hearing the drumming of horses' hoofs, Peters came out and greeted them as they came plunging up. "Something wrong?" Peters exclaimed.

"Plenty," Nogales snapped. "Fred Vincent has disappeared. I've got a hunch Crawford is back of it."

Peters frowned. "That's bad! Wouldn't be surprised if you were right, Nogales. What you aiming to do about it?"

"We're heading to see Crawford. Wanted to let you know first. If anything breaks, you'll know we tried everything legal first. You'll come with us, of course."

"Certainly," Peters replied. "Here's something you didn't know. I was intending to ride to the Rancho and tell you about it. Crawford's hired gunmen arrived. They got in yesterday, but I just got wind of it a spell back. Reckon they have been keeping inside. I dropped in Crawford's store just as a matter of course, and Crawford introduced me to the trio. I recognized the names. Crawford was smiling sly all over that fat face of his when he introduced us. Told me they were special auditors he'd hired to go over his books. He knew I didn't believe it, of course; he was just rubbing it in."

Nogales said quietly, "It looks like trouble all right."

Peters nodded. "All three of those gun fighters carry two guns — well-notched guns. They look plenty mean!"

Caliper shrugged his shoulders. "What if they are two-gun men? That don't mean they can use both at the same time — not and be accurate. Damn' few men can. If they want trouble —"

"We're wasting time here," Nogales pointed out. "Let's get down to Crawford's place."

The riders reined their ponies into motion. Peters followed at a run. Arriving before the store, the men ran up the steps, crossed the porch, and pushed inside, ignoring the few loungers who were standing near the building.

Several men were lined at the bar, among whom Nogales quickly picked out the three gunmen. Though it had been years since he'd seen Muttershaw, he recognized him immediately. Simon Crawford filled his big chair in the space midway between bar and store counter. Seated near him were Catlett, Bristol, and the Deacon.

"Well," Crawford rumbled mockingly, "customers? What can I do for you, Scott? Howdy, Maxwell, Jiménez, Peters. Can I sell you some canned tomatoes, or did you just drop in for a drink? Or maybe you'd like to meet my new auditors —"

"Don't run off at the head, Crawford," Nogales said steadily. "You know what we're here for."

"Am I supposed to be a mind reader?" Crawford grunted sarcastically. "How should I know — ?"

"Liar!" Nogales snapped. "You know. Fred Vincent has disappeared. We want to know where he is."

"Well, well, that's news to me," Crawford said in pretended concern. "Let me see, Fred Vincent. Oh yes, he's the sick feller that's been layin' around the Rancho de Paz —"

"Cut it, Crawford!" Nogales whipped out his gun. "Either you tell me where Vincent is, or —"

"Hold it, Scott!" Muttershaw growled,

leaving the bar and crossing the room in quick strides, followed by Merrick and Nevada Blake. Muttershaw's right gun was already out. "You ain't drawing on no friend of mine. I've got you covered!"

Nogales kept his gun steady on Crawford. Behind him he'd heard the rasp of metal against leather as Caliper drew his gun. "You, Muttershaw" — Nogales spoke steady-voiced — "this isn't your business. Better keep out —"

"Maybe I'll make it my business —" Muttershaw commenced.

"You'll all put your guns away." Rod Peters' voice carried clearly through the big room, his own gun out now. "I'm keeping the peace here, and I'll shoot any man that pulls trigger. You hear me! That goes for you, too, Nogales!"

"Look, Rod —" Nogales commenced.

"The law is the law, Nogales," Peters said determinedly. "There'll be no gun fight here if I can prevent it. Muttershaw, you and your friends get those guns out of sight pronto!"

Reluctantly the men reholstered their guns. Crawford's huge body shook with laughter. "The deputy is an honest man. He's going to really enforce the law in Ramrod Ridge. Congratulations, Peters —"

"Never mind that," Peters interrupted coldly. "We want to know where Fred Vincent is, Crawford!"

The Deacon said, "Why not search the store if you think he's here?"

"I'm going to search this whole damn town!" Peters snapped.

Muttershaw laughed scornfully. "I outshot Scott once and now when we meet again he brings his deputy friend to protect him from another fight."

Nogales' face reddened. "You know that's a lie, Muttershaw. I'd be glad to face you any time, anywhere —"

"I want a hand in this!" Caliper yelled.

"You can have it, hombre," Blake snarled.

Jimmy-Steve said hotly, "I'm crave' to cross some gons myself eef thees third two-gun braggart ees got the nerve —"

"You damn' greaser!" Merrick snarled. "I'll —"

"Keep your hands from those guns!" Peters yelled. "There'll be no fighting here while I'm a deputy in this county." His face was grim, determined; his gun swung in a wide arc that covered every man in the room.

"Nothing like having the law to protect you," Muttershaw sneered.

"We certainly do have a peaceful county." Crawford laughed. "Well, there'll be no fights here. Howsomever, it isn't so very far to the county line where Deputy Peters' authority ends. That's just an idea, of course."

"And a damn' good one!" Muttershaw exclaimed. "Seems like there's a smoke-tree forest hereabouts that's just over the county line. It ain't too far to ride, Scott, providing you and your pals have the nerve to face us. I sort of doubt you have —"

"Damn' right we'll face you!" Nogales cried angrily. "That suits us right down to the ground!"

"I forbid it!" Peters cried. "Can't you see, Nogales, they expected the cards to fall this way? They've worked it out in advance. Don't let them trap you."

"Maybe it won't be us that gets caught in the trap," Nogales said, cooling down somewhat. "Caliper — Jimmy-Steve — are you with me?"

"Right with you, pard," Caliper said quietly.

"The soonair the bettair!" from Jimmy-Steve.

"Nogales" — Peters commenced, his face working with anguish — "don't be a fool. You can't do this. I won't let you. I'll stop this fight —"

"You can't, Rod," Nogales said, level-voiced. "These hombres have hurled a challenge. You can't stop the fight. It's not your county over that way. And you can't leave your district —"

"Cut out the *habla*," Muttershaw growled. "Either you'll meet us in the smoke-tree forest or you won't."

"We'll be there," Nogales snapped. "We'll meet you there. You want to leave first, or shall we?"

Muttershaw produced a four-bit piece from his pocket and spun it in the air. "Call it!" he snarled.

"Heads!" from Nogales.

Muttershaw looked at the coin in his hand. "Heads it is. Take your choice."

Nogales considered a moment. "We'll leave first and meet you there. How do you want it — dismounted or from saddles?"

"Reckon we can fight from our horses' backs," Muttershaw snapped. "I always did hate to get down from my bronc to kill a man."

A thin smile of triumph crossed Nogales' face. "We'll be leaving now. Start any time after us you like. The sooner the better. C'mon, pards!"

He strode from the store, followed by his friends.

Muttershaw called after him, "We start shooting the instant we see each other."

"Suits me," Nogales flung back over his shoulder.

In front of the store Peters said to Nogales, "Damn it, pard, I was trying to keep you from fighting for your own sake. Those fellers are fast. This killing game is old stuff to them. Just stall along a spell and give me a chance to see if I can't stop this fight —"

"Don't want it stopped," Nogales said coolly. "The sooner we have a showdown, the better. They may be faster than us, but I figure we can lick 'em on strategy. We already got one advantage."

"What's that, pard?" Caliper asked.

"I give Muttershaw his choice and he said he'd fight from the saddle. They'll need one hand on the reins most of the time. That means they'll use only one gun."

"Damned if you ain't smart," Caliper said admiringly. "Well, they used to call me a bronc fighter back in the days when I was peeling broncs for the Triple-T horse outfit, but this will be a new kind of bronc fighting."

"The sooner we get to it the better I'll like it." Nogales nodded. "Let's go, gun-throwers."

They shook hands with Peters, climbed into saddles, and headed out of town.

XXIV

Roaring Forty-Fives!

Three quarters of an hour, by hard riding, brought them to the first smoke trees. Here was a wide expanse of sandy soil from which grew the practically leafless thorny shrubs known as smoke trees. A few bluish flowers were already appearing in the branches, giving the trees from the distance the appearance of puffy clouds of smoke. They weren't tall as trees go and they were spaced widely apart in most instances. Some golden spined cholla and desert verbena grew here and there, but mostly the footing was clear for riding.

Nogales and his friends pulled rein in an open space and faced the heavily breathing ponies in the direction of Ramrod Ridge to await the arrival of Muttershaw and his two pals.

"They'll be coming pretty close behind us, I figure," Nogales said quietly. "So we won't have to wait long."

"We're kind of in the open here, aren't

we?" Caliper frowned. "They'll be coming through the trees, partly sheltered. We'll make clear marks —"

"These trees aren't so thick but what we'll spot them almost as soon as they spot us. Then we can wheel our ponies back where the trees are a mite thicker; as they come on it will bring them into this clear space —"

"Damn! That ees smart," Jimmy-Steve said admiringly.

"Mebbe they'll try sneaking up on us," Caliper said.

Nogales frowned and shook his head. "I don't reckon so. One thing about gun fighters like those three, they don't go much for tricks. They figure their guns are too good to bother with tricks. The thing for us to do is to each pick a man. No use all three of us throwing down on one man while his pals knock us out of our saddles. Ten to one we'll sort of pair off. I figure Muttershaw will be coming for me; there's that old score to settle. I remember that Merrick called Jimmy-Steve a 'damned greaser,' so it might be he'll go after Jimmy-Steve first shot. That leaves Nevada Blake to you, Caliper."

"I wish we could be sure it would work out that way," Caliper said. "If we only knew who each one was going to fire on, it might make a difference."

"Maybe we can find out," Nogales said thoughtfully.

"How ees that?" Jimmy-Steve asked.

Nogales explained. "Likely they'll have their minds made up as to which one of us each picks to shoot at. All right. We'll see them coming through the trees, I reckon, before they're in firing range. Like as not they'll be spread out. We'll spread out too. The instant they heave in sight, I'll throw a shot at Muttershaw. Caliper, you fire at Blake. Jimmy-Steve takes Merrick. The range will be too far to do any damage, but if each of them fires back in the order I've named, we'll know who they've picked. If they don't keep that order, we'll change according —"

"Do you figure they'll answer our first fire if the range is that far?" Caliper said.

Nogales nodded. "It's natural to fire back on a hombre that's firing on you, even when you know the distance is too great. Anyway, my scheme is worth trying. And reload the instant you've fired that first shot — load all six chambers. No resting the hammer on an empty shell. We'll need all our loads. C'mon, now, let's spread out."

They widened the spaces between their horses and waited, facing tensely in the direction of Ramrod Ridge, each one of the three alert for the first sign of the enemy.

"Rider coming!" Nogales announced suddenly.

"I see Blake!" Caliper called to his companions.

"There ees Merrick," Jimmy-Steve announced, "comeeng my way."

The trio had spoken almost at the same instant.

The three horses came loping swiftly through the trees.

"Give 'em a volley!" Nogales called.

Three six-shooters fired simultaneously. Their owners at once reloaded. From the approaching enemy there was an instant's hesitation, as though the firing at that distance surprised them. Then came three shots, raggedly spaced.

"Damn!" Nogales laughed coolly. "It worked! We drew their fire before they were ready. Muttershaw's bullet kicked up sand twenty feet in front of me —"

"Blake fired on me," Caliper replied.

"Merrick ees my meat," from Jimmy-Steve.

"Spread out more," Nogales called, low-voiced. "From now on it's every man for himself!"

The approaching riders came plunging on. Nogales and his pards held their fire until the Muttershaw riders had almost reached the clearing. Then their guns blazed again, an instant before they turned their ponies and raced them back to thicker growth.

Now the forty-fives commenced to roar in earnest. Spurring from behind a tree, Nogales saw Muttershaw closing in on him fast. Nogales fired one swift shot. He saw dust puff from the top of Muttershaw's right shoulder. Saw the tall man wince and sway back. Then Muttershaw stiffened. He came bearing in on Nogales, his teeth bared in a savage snarl, his right hand blazing white fire. The breeze of a leaden slug whined past Nogales' body. Then the impetus of Muttershaw's plunging horse had carried him past Nogales.

Nogales wheeled in his saddle and sent a shot winging after the man. At the same instant Muttershaw had turned, raising his gun to beat Nogales to the shot. Nogales' forty-five exploded an instant quicker. Muttershaw emitted a wild yell that blended with the report of his six-shooter and reeled from the saddle. Even as Muttershaw fell, Nogales felt his own horse stumble and go down.

Releasing his feet from the stirrups, Nogales leaped wide to the sandy earth, thumbing one swift shot while he was still in the air. Muttershaw was just scrambling to his feet when the leaden slug struck. The impact whirled him half around, then without a sound he pitched back to the ground.

Nogales closed in fast, upraised gun ready for further action, but it wasn't needed. Muttershaw was done for. Nogales gave the dying man a brief glance, then ran to catch up Muttershaw's pony which stood a few feet away. Nogales' pony was already dead.

"You've owed me a horse for a long time, Muttershaw," Nogales thought grimly as he vaulted into the saddle.

There was firing among the trees on both sides. The firing on the left came nearer. Suddenly Jimmy-Steve came backing his pony into view. Nogales swore. Jimmy-Steve's right side was bathed in blood; his right arm hung useless at his side. But the Mexican's left arm was still functioning. A bullet clipped twigs from a tree near Jimmy-Steve's head even as his left hand lifted the six-shooter for another shot. From beyond the branches came a shrill cry of anguish. Jimmy-Steve gave a short, triumphant laugh then pitched from his saddle to the sandy earth.

In an instant Nogales had dismounted and was standing over him. He started to lift the Mexican, but Jimmy-Steve opened his eyes and said gamely, "I'm all right, Nogales. Go help Caliper. When I see heem he was down —"

Nogales leaped back to the saddle and started through the trees, passing on his way the lifeless body of Squint Merrick whom Jimmy-Steve had just finished. By this time the shooting had ceased. Nogales' pony plunged on its zigzagging course between trees. Abruptly it emerged into a small open space. Here, two men were sprawled on the sandy earth, not far from one another. One horse was down, thrashing about; the other stood quietly near by.

One of the men was Caliper, the other Nevada Blake. Nogales dismounted and went first to Caliper. Blood trickled from a wound in Caliper's left leg to seep into the yellow sand; there was a crimson furrow across the top of his head that wasn't deep enough to be dangerous. The cowboy was only momentarily stunned. Nogales heaved a sigh of relief and hurried to Blake's side.

The gunman was dead, his wide-open glassy eyes staring blankly at the sky. Nogales moved across to Caliper's horse and saw it had a broken foreleg. "I hate to do this, horse" — grimly Nogales drew his gun — "but you'll be better off." As the echoes of the shot died away, the pony ceased struggling.

By the time Nogales returned to Caliper the wounded cowboy was sitting up. He forced a wan smile. "Glad to see you up and doing, pard. How'd Jimmy-Steve come out?"

Nogales told him, then, "What happened to you?"

"My horse stepped in a hole and we spilled. Blake came charging in like a demon from hell. I managed to get in a couple of lucky shots, but his last shot put my lights out for a minute or so."

"Don't try to get up." Nogales nodded. "Let me look at your leg."

Caliper lay back. "My conk sure aches. Leg's all right."

"Lucky that head wound isn't lower. Anyway, we got all three of those sidewinders. I lost another horse to Muttershaw, but I got his in return. I reckon I got the best of the bargain too. . . ."

Nogales talked while he did what he

could for Caliper's wounds. None of the men had brought canteens with them, so the injuries couldn't be bathed. Finally he had Caliper fixed up as well as possible and on the back of Nevada Blake's horse. Caliper swayed unsteadily and Nogales decided to lash him into the saddle. Then, remounting, Nogales went back to Jimmy-Steve, followed by Caliper. Jimmy-Steve was in a sitting position on the ground. He greeted the pair cheerfully, though his face was white and his teeth clenched against the pain. His right arm was broken and a bullet was lodged against his right ribs.

Nogales fixed up the wounds with the aid of torn strips of bandanna handkerchiefs and lashed the Mexican into his saddle. The sun was low by the time he had finished and both Caliper and Jimmy-Steve were in no condition for swift traveling. By this time Merrick's horse had wandered off and Nogales didn't want to waste time looking for it.

He mounted to his saddle, eying worriedly his two wounded charges. "I reckon you'll just have to tough it out for a spell, pards. We'll head straight for the Rancho. Doc Stebbings is there and the sooner I can put you in his care, the better. But we've got to travel easy and not too fast.

Too much jogging might bring on the loss of more blood than you can stand. So grit your teeth and make up your mind that it can't last forever. We'll take a rest, now and then, if the going gets too tough. And when you get back on your feet, we'll go after Crawford and the rest of those skunks. And that's not going to be far off."

It was nearly midnight when they reached the Rancho de Paz. By that time both Caliper and Jimmy-Steve, weakened by loss of blood, were sagging, limp, unconscious, against the ropes that held them in their saddles.

XXV

Challenge

By the time Doc Stebbings finished working on Caliper and Jimmy-Steve and had them resting comfortably in beds, false dawn was appearing in the east. Caliper had at once gone to sleep, but Jimmy-Steve was wakeful and wanted to talk. Though nothing had been said, the Mexican felt in his heart that Nogales would return to Ramrod Ridge as soon as possible.

"You ron too many of the risk', Nogales," he said worriedly. "True, we hav' wipe out the gonmen, but you do not realize the danger of thees Crawford hombre. He ees so much of the powerful, an' sly, also, like the fox —"

"Hush up, now, Jimmy-Steve," Nogales said soothingly. "Try to get to sleep. You need rest. You and Caliper both lost a heap more blood than you can afford. The sooner you get better, the sooner we can get after Crawford —"

"Ah, that ees eet." Jimmy-Steve sighed.

"Weel you wait ontil Caliper and I are able to help?"

Nogales evaded answering. At that moment Ethan Vincent came into the room. "It's a mite early, Nogales, but Polly figured you could stand some breakfast. You didn't have any supper last night and the coffee will give you a lift."

"I'm willing to go without supper any time," Nogales said grimly, "for the sake of wiping out snakes. No news yet of Fred, I suppose?"

Ethan sadly shook his head. He had had his men out all night, searching, but without success. "We found 'sign' down in the fig orchard," Ethan went on, "that showed evidence of a struggle. That's where they seized Fred. There were three horses, but the footprints show only two riders. I suppose the third horse was to carry Fred away."

Nogales accompanied Ethan out to the breakfast table. Stebbings was there, looking weary after his night's work. Polly's eyes were red; she looked as though she'd been crying. But the girl forced a wan smile as she poured Nogales' coffee.

"I don't see why we haven't heard anything from Rod — Deputy Peters," she said once.

"I imagine Rod is plenty busy," Nogales returned. "He's as anxious to get track of Fred as we are. Just as soon as I finish this chow, I'm aiming to ride in and learn what's doing."

Doc Stebbings shook his head. "Before you do any more riding, Nogales, you'd better catch a mite of shuteye. You didn't sleep last night and it looks as though you'd have a tough day ahead of you. Leave Ramrod Ridge to Rod Peters. He knows his business. You get some rest."

Nogales laughed shortly. "I'll get my rest — later. I don't think I can rest while Fred is gone and Simon Crawford and his coyotes are on the loose."

Nevertheless, ten minutes later, when Nogales stretched out on a couch to smoke a cigarette while he was waiting for his pony to be saddled, he dropped almost instantly into sound sleep. Polly took the cigarette from his fingers and threw a blanket over him. After a time the pale light entering the windows changed to gold as the morning sun lifted above the desert flats to the east.

At seven that morning Rod Peters came pounding in to the Rancho. The sounds of his arrival awakened Nogales, who swore at himself disgustedly for falling asleep. They talked to Peters on the long gallery fronting the house. Peters looked drawn; his eyes were bloodshot after a sleepless night. He greeted Nogales on the gallery with a congratulatory nod and, "Nice piece of work you fellows did yesterday, Nogales. I'd like the details."

"You knew we licked 'em then?" Nogales said.

Peters nodded. "When none of you returned to Ramrod Ridge I commenced to get worried. I reckon Crawford was bothered too. Anyway, he sent a couple of men out to the smoke-tree forest to learn what had happened. I saw 'em when they got back last night. They had Squint Merrick's horse with 'em. They didn't want to talk to me, but I put on the pressure and they admitted that Muttershaw and his pards had been wiped out. They found the bodies out there, and a couple of dead horses besides."

"We were lucky," Nogales said quietly, and went on to give the story of the fight. When he had finished Peters said,

"It's not luck that wins against gun fighters like those three. It's guts and headwork. I'm dang glad that Caliper and Jimmy-Steve are going to be all right."

Nogales said, "You didn't pick up anything about Fred Vincent in Ramrod Ridge, I suppose?"

Peters wearily shook his head. "It's not for lack of work, though. I've talked to every blasted man in that town — grilled him plenty, by gosh — but I can't learn a thing. Every one of 'em denies all knowledge of the affair. If they know anything — and I feel sure some of them do — they're backing on Simon Crawford to get them out of any trouble that may arise. Yep, I've been plenty busy all night, until just before I came here. There isn't a shack in town I haven't searched, but I couldn't uncover any clues. I've threatened plenty trouble for anybody that held out on me. I reckon I threw a scare into a few —"

"How come?" Doc Stebbings asked.

"I noticed a few hombres packed up their things and left town. I guess they must have felt trouble was due to break. But the majority of Crawford's skunks are still on the job. Someday I'm going to clean out that rat's nest —"

Polly sighed. "It can't come too soon to suit me, Rod. When I think of Fred, weakened as he is, being held prisoner some place —"

"Now, Polly girl," Ethan soothed. "Don't you fret. We'll find Fred all right."

"Sure we will, Polly," Peters said awkwardly. "You just leave things to us." Seeking an excuse to change the subject he turned back to Nogales. "One of Crawford's gang that left town was Swifty Catlett. He rode out about three this morning, with a sack of grub and a canteen. I reckon he's had enough of Simon Crawford."

"Swifty Catlett, eh?" Nogales' eyes narrowed. "I wonder. Whatever you say about Catlett, I'd never figure him as being yellow and easy to run out —" Nogales stopped suddenly, then swore under his breath.

Peters asked curiously, "What's the matter?"

"I've been dumb," Nogales groaned. "We let ourselves be worked into that fight yesterday. That got us out of the way. Fred was seized in the fig orchard. I'm betting he was held out in the desert some place until nightfall, or later, then he was taken some place else. I've got a hunch that Catlett did said taking. No wonder you didn't find Fred in Ramrod Ridge, Rod. He was probably never brought into the town. Crawford outfoxed me. He got us away from Ramrod Ridge at the very time we should have been searching for Fred.

Now, with the start they've had, no telling how far away they've taken Fred."

"God! I should have thought of that," Peters said disgustedly. "What's to do now?"

"Simon Crawford will know where he is," Nogales said grimly. "I'm aiming to talk to Crawford and, one way or another, force the truth out of his big carcass."

"I'll go with you, Nogales," Ethan proposed.

Nogales shook his head. "You stay here and hold the fort."

Ten minutes later Nogales and Peters were riding furiously toward Ramrod Ridge. Nogales checked rein only once to speak to Peters, "I don't want any interference this time, Rod. You're the deputy in Ramrod Ridge, and you're sworn to enforce the law, but I don't aim to be crossed this time. Do I get a free hand, or don't I?"

"What you aiming to do?" Peters demanded.

"I'm going to throw a gun on Simon Crawford and he's going to tell me or else —"

"Maybe," Peters said slowly, "I'm going to have to resign my office — because I sure don't aim to do any interfering in anything that comes up between you and Crawford."

"Good," Nogales snapped. "All I ask of you is to see that nobody else takes sides. C'mon, let's ride!"

Simon Crawford was, as usual, seated in his big chair in the center of his store when Rod and Nogales entered. There were the customary drinkers at the bar. Limpy Bristol and the Deacon were seated at a table near Crawford.

Nogales went straight up to Crawford, ignoring the other two. Nogales said, steady-voiced, "Crawford, where's Fred Vincent?"

Crawford lifted one questioning eyebrow. "Well, well," he rumbled sarcastically, "if it isn't Scott back. Had a mite of luck against Muttershaw and his pals yesterday, didn't you?"

"Where's Fred Vincent?" Nogales demanded.

"Where's your two pals, Scott? You know, Maxwell and that Mex —"

"They're taking it easy," Nogales said, and his tones were like chilled steel. "One of us is enough to do what I'm aiming. For the third time, where's Fred Vincent?"

"How in hell should I know where he is?" Crawford thundered angrily. "We've told this deputy all we know. Better talk to him. I don't intend to be bothered —"

Nogales whipped out his gun. "Crawford, this town isn't big enough for both of us. You're going to come across with what I want, or I'm going to plug you! So you'd better get on your feet and make to pull that iron."

Crawford didn't stir. "Don't talk like a fool, Scott."

"I'm telling you," Nogales snapped grimly. "You tell me what I want to know, or yank your gun. Or suit yourself. Either way I'm aiming to plug you."

Crawford snorted scornfully. "You trying to arrange a gun duel with me, Scott?"

"Call it that if you like. It's what I want. I'm hoping you've got nerve enough to pull —"

Crawford's raucous laughter broke in on the words. "And I suppose you and your deputy friend would call that fair play? Hell! What you trying to frame me to do? Sign my own death warrant? I'm no gun fighter. I admit I wouldn't have a chance against you with a gun. Why should I exchange lead with you?"

"You refuse to draw against me, then?" Nogales was momentarily baffled.

"I certainly do." Crawford's lips stretched in an evil smile.

"By God!" Nogales threatened, angered by the man's cool pose, "I'll choke the truth out of you then."

"With your bare hands, I suppose?" Crawford said mockingly.

"With my bare hands!" Nogales snapped. The Deacon bent swiftly toward Crawford and whispered something. If Crawford heard him he paid no attention. He laughed sarcastically. "You must consider yourself a fighter, Scott."

"I can take care of you," Nogales said, "you big —"

"You're offering to fight me?" Crawford sneered. "Why, Scott —"

"Sure I'm offering to fight you," Nogales said eagerly. "With guns, or fists. I prefer guns, but if you want —"

"Nogales!" Peters interposed, "you can't —"

"Let be, Rod," Nogales whipped out without turning his head. "You promised no interference. This should suit you. There'll be no gun play —"

"But, Nogales —" Peters pleaded.

"Now, Deputy" — Crawford hoisted his muscular bulk up from the chair — "you don't need to take your pard's part. Of course if he's too yellow to stand up to me —"

Nogales' eyes blazed angrily. "I'll show you who's yellow!" he half shouted. "If I can't lick an overgrown —"

"Look, Nogales!" Peters started again.

"Keep out of it, Rod," Nogales jerked impatiently. "You promised not to interfere."

"He won't interfere," Crawford said in ugly tones. On his feet now, he towered over Nogales. "How do you want it, Scott? Do we fight here?"

"Suits me," Nogales said grimly.

"No holds barred?"

"Suits me," Nogales snapped.

Crawford nodded. "Supposing we clear this room — everybody goes outside, including you. I'll wait here. Then you come in when you're ready. And I" — he smiled evilly, slyly — "will be ready when you come in."

Nogales nodded swift assent, whirled, and headed for the outdoors, followed by Rod Peters. Back of him he heard Crawford ordering everybody else out of the building. Men came pouring out into the street. Nogales headed across the road, where he paused in the shadow of a building. He laughed shortly at Rod Peters' look of concern. "I'll choke the truth out of him —" Nogales commenced.

Peters groaned, "Pard, why didn't you listen to me when I tried to stop you?"

"I didn't want the fight stopped," Nogales said. "I don't like killing a man. If I can get the truth out of him without putting a slug in his fat carcass, so much the better." He smiled at Peters' worried face. "I know you think Crawford is cooking up some scheme, making everybody get out that way. You figure maybe he'll be waiting for me with a gun when I come in unarmed. Is that it?" Nogales commenced to unbuckle his gun belt.

Peters shook his head. "I'll see that there's nothing like that takes place. With me here, Crawford wouldn't dare. He won't need to —"

"Quit worrying," Nogales said shortly, eyes still on the building across the street before which were clustered knots of men. Then he nodded. "Yeah, Crawford and the Deacon are cooking up something, I'll bet. Limpy Bristol is outside, but the Deacon hasn't showed up yet. There's the Deacon now!"

Deacon Trumbull emerged from the store and closed the door behind him. Descending the steps, he came straight across the street where Nogales waited. The Deacon looked very concerned.

Nogales grinned. "What's up, Deacon, Crawford lost his nerve?"

The Deacon shook his head. "I don't think this fight should go on, though," he said seriously.

"Why not?" Nogales snapped.

"Supposing you were hurt," the Deacon said, "and the injury caused your death. You might get knocked down, strike your head on something sharp. You never know —"

"Cripes!" Nogales said irritatedly. "That's my lookout. You'd better be thinking about Crawford —"

"But if you did die," the Deacon insisted, "then Deputy Peters would arrest Simon for murder."

"I'll give you my promise he won't," Nogales said quickly. "You hear me, Rod?"

The Deacon shook his head. "Spoken promises are words written on water," he said unctuously. "But I've prepared two papers for you and Simon to sign. Simon has already signed his. Are you willing to do the same?"

"What kind of a paper?" Nogales asked, eying the Deacon.

The Deacon handed Nogales a slip of paper signed by Simon Crawford. It was simply a form of release, freeing Nogales from all obligations in case of Crawford's death or serious injury in the forthcoming fight. Nogales glanced at it, then passed the paper to Peters. Peters said suspiciously, "I don't like this."

"Looks all right to me," Nogales said shortly. "I'll sign your paper, Deacon, so Crawford won't be responsible for my welfare."

A momentary glint of triumph entered the Deacon's eyes. He handed Nogales a second paper and an indelible pencil. Nogales quickly signed the paper and returned it to the Deacon. "I'll take this to Simon," he said, and hastened back to the store.

Within a moment the Deacon again emerged from the store and closed the door behind him. "Simon's waiting for you, Scott," he called across the street, and quoted mockingly, with a wave toward the watching crowd of men before the store, " 'These wait all upon thee, that thou mayest give them their meat in due season.' " A laugh went up from the assembled men.

Nogales smiled thinly. "It is my intention," he paraphrased, "to kill this whole assembly with hunger." He turned to Peters. "Well, I'd better be starting —"

"Wait!" Peters' face worked with emotion. "I tried to stop this, but you wouldn't listen. Now you've got to know. I've learned things since I've been here. Crawford's looks are deceptive. He's strong as a bull. I've heard that he's killed men with his bare fists. I can't pin those rumors down, but there's something in them. Not so long ago, it's been hinted, he broke a man's neck with one blow. He's lightning fast on his feet. Now do you understand why I tried to stop this fight? Look, Nogales, listen to me now. You can't go through with this —"

"One minute, Rod." Nogales put out one protesting hand. For a full minute he didn't speak. Finally a rueful smile crossed his bronzed features. He sighed disgustedly. "Looks like I've been outfoxed by Simon Crawford again. Dammit! I should have known he wouldn't offer to fight me unless he was mighty sure of himself. But I was so damn' mad at the big gorilla that I wasn't thinking clear. Now it looks like I'm in for something I didn't bargain for."

"But you're not going through with it?"

"I've got to —"

"He — he'll kill you, Nogales, sure as sin. You can't fight a man like Crawford. His strength is abnormal!"

"I've got to," Nogales said doggedly. "I've passed my word. There's something funny about wanting me to sign that paper too. It wasn't just for what the Deacon said it was. Rod, I've got to get that paper back. I'm thinking clearer now. There's something here to be straightened out —"

"But not by fighting," Peters protested, his face pale. "Let me dope out a way to fix this up."

"Nothing doing." Nogales' face was white, but there was a look of determination in his eyes. He commenced to peel off his clothing, down to the waist. "In case — in case anything happens," he said, and his voice shook a little, "tell Caliper and Jimmy-Steve —"

"For God's sake!" Peters broke in. "You can't —"

Nogales shook his head again, gripped Peters' hand, and started slowly across the street, in the direction of Simon Crawford's store. As he approached the building, the men standing before it moved back to let him pass. One or two mouthed epithets as he moved by, but the hard, determined look in his steely eyes stilled their voices as he ascended the steps to the porch, crossed, and flung open the door. A moment he stood there, gazing inside, then he moved on, pulling the door closed behind him. A yell went up from the waiting crowd.

XXVI

The Killer Strikes

For just a moment, after the door closed at his back, Nogales stood peering through the big room, trying to accustom his eyes to the change of light after the sun glare of the outside street. And then it happened:

With the impact of a speeding express train Simon Crawford bore in from Nogales' right, where he had been waiting just inside the doorway. Nogales felt himself caught up in the rush and carried off his feet as Crawford's huge hands fastened on him. The impetus of Crawford's speed and weight carried both men across the room. Then Crawford released his grip, and Nogales went hurtling through space to strike with a spine-thudding jar against the long wooden bar. Glasses and bottles standing there clashed together and toppled, spilling their contents.

To save himself, Nogales caught at the edge of the bar, struggled upright. Then, seeing Crawford closing in again, Nogales swung to one side, scrambled to the top of the bar, and dropped to the floor beyond. At the same instant Crawford plowed into the long counter, causing it to rock on its foundation.

For a moment the two men stood glaring at each other, only the mahogany bar between them. Crawford was stripped to the waist and in his stocking feet. His huge torso was ridged with muscle. Nogales thought with surprise, *There's not so much fat as I expected.* Crawford's little piglike eyes glinted evilly as he surveyed Nogales. "I'm going to kill you, Scott," he thundered.

"Come ahead, killer," Nogales taunted. He was breathing heavily, stalling for time to recover from that first savage rush. His breath was returning now, but his body still ached from that impact against the bar.

"Come out from behind there!" Crawford bellowed.

"Come and get me." Nogales laughed.

Crawford cursed. Quick, light-footed steps carried him around the end of the bar. Nogales waited, tense, ready to move. Crawford started a quick rush. At the same instant Nogales flung out his right arm to reach the back bar, and swept a pyramided stack of glasses and several bottles to the floor in Crawford's path. Crawford tried to stop himself, but he was too late. One foot landed on a bottle, he slipped and lost his balance, going down with a crash. Glass crunched beneath the weight of his huge bulk.

"Cripes!" Nogales spoke in some surprise, "you're top-heavy, Crawford!"

Crawford rose swiftly, far more swiftly than Nogales had expected, voicing angry, animallike cries. Blood trickled from small cuts on his barrellike torso as he came charging after Nogales, bellowing like a maddened steer.

Nogales retreated as Crawford closed in. They moved back to the center of the room, Nogales always giving way before the short, angry rushes with which Crawford tried to come within striking distance.

Suddenly, with the speed of a rattlesnake, Crawford picked a chair from the floor, sent it flying at Nogales' legs. The flying missile caught Nogales at the knees, bowling him over, sending him sprawling on the floor. With a hoarse, triumphant grunt Crawford rushed in, his powerful hands clutching at Nogales.

Nogales rolled out of harm's way and catlike came to his feet again. It was too late to retreat now. Instead, he stepped up close. His fists went *thud, thud, thud!* on Crawford's jaw. He heard Crawford's contemptuous laughter. Just in time he saw Crawford's huge fist coming at him. He ducked in time to take the force of the blow on the side of his head.

For a brief instant everything went black. Nogales felt as though his head had been torn from his shoulders. Then his brain cleared as he found himself again on the floor. He was down with Crawford's hands pawing at his throat. There was a smell of dust and blood and sweat in his nostrils as he squirmed from side to side. And always those hoarse animallike growls kept welling up from Crawford's thick throat.

Frantically Nogales' fingers searched for and found Crawford's eyes. He pressed his thumbs deep into the sockets. Crawford suddenly screamed with pain and drew back. Nogales tried to retain his advantage, but the huge brute was too strong for him. An instant later they were both on their feet again, sparring for time, fighting to catch their wind.

Once more Nogales started his retreat, with Crawford coming closer and ever closer. Suddenly Nogales stepped in, threw two savage punches into Crawford's middle, felt his fists sink deep into fat and muscle, then jumped quickly back in time to escape the sledgehammer blow that flailed past his head.

Round and round the room the two went, Nogales always retreating, until the time was right for a quick attack and a get-away. Time after time he pounded Crawford's middle, then leaped back from the killing ferocity of Crawford's fists. Sweat and blood were streaming from both men now. Nogales' body was scratched and torn from contact with the rough board floor.

Again Crawford started one of his express-trainlike rushes. Nogales feinted a retreat, then stood his ground, swinging his right fist to Crawford's jaw as the big man closed in. What happened next was pretty much blurred in Nogales' mind. He felt his fist bounce from Crawford's jaw. An instant later something like the kick of a mule crashed against Nogales' left ribs.

All of the breath was forced from his body as it went hurtling beneath a table. Again those wild animal growls as Crawford came nearer and nearer. Desperately Nogales threw himself to one side, at the same instant seizing and jerking the nearest leg of the table. The table toppled over, directly in Crawford's path. Crawford cursed as he went crashing down.

In an instant Nogales was up and around the table before Crawford could rise. His fists swung viciously at the big man's face and head. Crawford's face was cut and bleeding now, but he flung out one ironlike arm; his hand clutched at, seized, Nogales' right wrist. Nogales felt his arm bend back. He thought the bone was breaking. He gave way suddenly and, miraculously, managed to slip out of Crawford's sweaty grip.

He retreated to the center of the room, breathing heavily. After a moment Crawford heaved up from the floor and started after Nogales. Nogales backed away, unconscious of the yelling that was taking place outside now. Men's faces were pressed against the windows. Though Nogales didn't know it, Rod Peters stood with his back to the door, drawn gun in hand to prevent any of Crawford's men entering.

Crawford, too, was breathing heavily now. His mouth was open, inhaling great gusts of air. Nogales' cleaner living was commencing to tell. Crawford's left eye was closed; his face looked like a chunk of bruised beefsteak. But he was still dangerous.

A thought flashed through Nogales'

mind: *If I can only close the other eye. I've hit him with everything I had on the jaw — the same with his middle. It doesn't work. But if I can close his other eye . . .*

Suiting the action to the thought, Nogales leaped quickly in on Crawford's left side. His left fist crashed against Crawford's right eye. Then, as Crawford swung, Nogales leaped out of harm's way. Again he backed away, again he leaped suddenly in, and once more his fist punished that right eye.

That was the game: concentrate on Crawford's eyes. It was the beginning of the end for the huge man, though Nogales didn't dare let those powerful hands close on him again. He'd leap in, swing sharp, punishing blows to the eyes, then jump away. The right eye commenced to swell, then it, too, closed. Once, when Nogales missed the eye, his fist contacted Crawford's nose. He felt bone crack beneath his bruised knuckles.

By this time Crawford's bellowing cries were filling the room. He was more than ever like some huge wounded antediluvian monster as he rushed blindly, madly, about, banging into chairs and tables in the furious search for his opponent. Even his sweat-streaked body seemed to exude a strange animal stench. His face was a bloody smear, the features almost lost in the swollen puffy mass, the result of Nogales' savage slashing blows.

Again and again and again Nogales leaped in, his fists striking like thunderbolts. Still Crawford refused to go down. His speed was gone now, but he kept coming after Nogales. He could no longer see, but his ears told him the directions in which Nogales moved.

Nogales spoke, his voice sounding like a hoarse croak, "You're licked, Crawford. Where's Fred Vincent?"

What he said Nogales never knew. The big man's voice was a mingled cursing and bellowing as he started in Nogales' direction. Nogales waited, tense. His arm lifted. Then Crawford took him by surprise. Instead of striking out in his usual killer fashion, Crawford suddenly dived, hurling his weight at Nogales' legs. The two went to the floor together.

Over and over they rolled, scratching, clawing, each seeking a finishing hold. One moment Nogales would be on top; the next he'd be nearly smothered beneath the weight of Crawford's great bulk. Crawford's arms were around Nogales' body now. Their hold tightened, like two constricting steel bands. Fight as he would, Nogales couldn't break loose. He felt the breath leaving his body. His ribs must surely crack. He squirmed desperately around, locked his hands in Crawford's throat. He could feel his fingers sink in and in and in.

Now it was Crawford who was fighting to break loose, but Nogales hung on with bulldog determination. That terrible vise that had enclosed his ribs was gone now, but Crawford was striking again, his fists thudding against Nogales' head and body.

Still Nogales kept his steely grip fastened in Crawford's throat. He didn't know how much longer he could withstand the fearful punishment from those flailing fists, but this was his last chance. He was on the point of losing consciousness when he felt Crawford's blows commence to weaken. Even so, it seemed ages before Crawford relaxed and lay still.

Nogales struggled to his knees. For the moment he couldn't rise higher. The room swirled and momentarily everything went black. Then Nogales managed to get a grip on himself. His vision cleared. Crawford lay stretched out before him, gasping painfully for breath, the sounds echoing through the big room and sounding like two pieces of dry leather rasping against each other. All the fight was gone from him now.

Nogales bent over him. "Where's Fred Vincent, Crawford?"

"Don't — know —" Crawford gasped.

Again Nogales applied pressure to Crawford's throat. After a moment he released his grip. "Where's Fred Vincent?" he asked again, staring down on that red pulpy mass that had once been a face. "You're finished, Crawford — or do you want me to shut off your wind for good?"

"Don't — don't —" The words came painfully. "Vincent — in cave — Quithatz — Canyon —"

"What cave? Where is it?"

But Crawford had lost consciousness. Nogales took a deep breath for added strength, then went through Crawford's pants pockets. He found the paper he had signed for the Deacon, tore it to bits, then rose and walked wearily toward the door.

As he staggered outside he heard Rod Peters say, "My God!"

Nogales tried to be humorous. "I reckon I was struck by an express train . . ." Then Nogales fainted dead away.

XXVII

Quithatz Canyon

Twenty minutes later Nogales opened his eyes to find himself stretched on the cot in Rod Peters' office. He was dripping wet. Peters wasn't there. Nogales glanced around the room and painfully sat up. A pail of water stood near and some court plaster. There were some patches of the plaster on various sections of Nogales' anatomy. Nogales swung his feet to the floor. Every bone and muscle in his body ached, and for a moment his head swirled dizzily. Then it cleared.

The door of the office opened. Peters stepped inside. A look of relief passed over his face as he saw Nogales. "Cowboy!" he exclaimed, "you sure took a beating. You look like you'd been run through a threshing machine."

Nogales forced a wan smile. "Maybe that's what it was. I thought it was a cyclone. . . . How'd I get here?"

"I carried you here. You were just plumb

exhausted. It must have been a fight —"

"It was a killing brawl," Nogales mumbled from between swollen lips. "I don't want any more of Crawford's game. My God, Rod! I hit him with everything I had and most of the time he just laughed. I reckon I'm lucky —"

"I reckon you are." Peters nodded. "But it'll be some time before Crawford laughs again. He's a sight. I don't think he'll ever completely recover. He looks like you'd pounded him with two-by-fours. His neck is all slashed and torn —"

"I didn't use two-by-fours on his neck," Nogales said grimly. He looked at his bruised knuckles. His fingers ached as though they'd been extended beyond their normal strength; the nails were broken. Nogales sighed wearily. "Does Crawford admit he's licked?"

"Hell's bells, cowboy! He can't admit anything. He's still unconscious, or partly so. The Deacon and Limpy Bristol are working over him, but they can't get anything out of him but a moan now and then, then he slips off again. There aren't any teeth left in the front of his mouth. His eyes are swollen shut. There's just a flat spot where his nose used to be. What did you do, go complete crazy, or something?"

"I reckon." Nogales nodded. "He had me on the run most of the time. I guess I was getting pretty desperate." Glancing across the room, Nogales saw his shirt and gun belt. He staggered up, swayed uncertainly a moment, then started to dress.

"What you intending?" Peters asked.

"I'm riding to Quithatz Canyon. Fred Vincent's being held there, in a cave, some place —"

"You're crazy. You better take it easy. I'll go —"

Nogales shook his head, donned his sombrero, and strapped on his gun. "You've got to stay here, Rod. It's your job. I'm all right now. I'll feel better after a ride into the canyon. I was just plumb tuckered for a few moments, but I'm all right now."

"But, Nogales —"

"Don't try to stop me, Rod. Just bring up my horse for me. Eventually Crawford is going to tell the Deacon that he revealed Fred Vincent's whereabouts. Then they'll all be starting for the canyon to cut me off, I'm afraid. It's up to you to stay here and see that nobody leaves town. That's a big job. That gang of Crawford's is likely to turn ugly with the Deacon to urge 'em on. You may have a job holding 'em down."

"I'll hold 'em down," Peters said grimly.

He crossed the room, picked up his double-barreled shotgun, and started shoving buckshot shells into the weapon. "With this and my six-shooter I figure I can stand off quite a crowd."

"Maybe it won't be necessary. I figure they won't do anything until Crawford gets to speaking again. That's why I've got to hurry. Maybe I can find Fred before Crawford commences to give orders. If you'll get my horse I'll be much obliged. If you see anything of Crawford's gang you can tell 'em I'm hurt bad, that I'm heading for the Rancho to see Doc Stebbings."

Peters nodded and stepped outside. Nogales sank down wearily on the cot again. Lord, how he ached! He felt bruised all over. The creaking of saddle leather sounded outside the office. Nogales rose and staggered outside. Peters helped him up to the saddle. Conscious of the sullen eyes watching him from Crawford's porch, Nogales slumped down on the horse's neck.

"Good acting, cowboy," Peters whispered. "They'll never guess you're heading any place but home. Good luck. Got any idea where to look?"

Nogales whispered back, "Not the slightest. I'll follow one side going in, the other going out, if I don't find that cave right off. There should be something, some bit of 'sign' to tip me off, though. I'll be seeing you, Rod."

Peters slapped the pony on the rump and it walked slowly down the street, with Nogales' sagging form slumped above the saddle horn. Once out of sight of the town, he straightened in his saddle and touched spurs to the pony.

The horse made good time into Quithatz Canyon, following the trail Jimmy-Steve had taken the previous day. Nogales made it in even faster time, driving the cow pony along treacherous shelves over which Jimmy-Steve had led a cautious way. As he rode, Nogales was alert for any sign that might lead him to a hidden cave, but he couldn't even see any fresh hoofprints beyond those made by the horses he and his companions had ridden the day before.

The hot sun beat down into the canyon. Sweat streaked man and beast. Nogales wished that he had a canteen on his saddle. His mouth was parched and dry; his head ached terrifically — in fact, his whole being was one solid ache from the beating he had taken at Crawford's hands. His left ribs were so sore to the touch he hated to make the slightest movement.

"Feels like I've got some cracked ribs," Nogales muttered. "Lord, I wish I had a drink." That animal odor of Crawford's still lingered in the cowboy's nostrils. "God! What a beast he is!"

The horse hurried on. Before long they swung down around the big rock that marked the approach to Quithatz Falls. A few more yards and Nogales pulled his pony to a halt at the edge of the tumbling pool of water. Beyond, the falls cascaded straight in a wide white ribbon of lacy froth. The horse moved out into the pool and thrust his nose into the cooling depths.

Nogales relaxed in his saddle and looked around. "So far, no cave that I can see," he mused. "Going out we'll follow the other side of the canyon, horse. Vincent's got to be in here some place. . . . That water taste good, pony? I'm going to have me a drink in a minute. I'd like to get in and wash all over. . . . Well, why not?"

The very thought of the fresh, cooling water on his aching body was gratifying. Guiding the pony across the pool to the opposite bank, he dismounted and stripped off his clothing. Starting back toward the water, he paused suddenly. "Reckon I'm not thinking clear," he muttered. "Vincent is held some place in this canyon. There's a guard over him probably. I'd sure feel like a fool if that guard was to catch me out in that pool, mother naked, without a gun to defend myself."

He picked up his gun and placed it on the bank, close to the edge of the pool. Then he stepped into the water, which proved to be icy cold. Nogales shivered appreciatively and moved on into deeper water, feeling his way carefully over the smoothly worn rocks on the bottom. He moved nearer the falls, thinking, *I'd sure like to stand right under those falls.*

The water was up to his chest now and he stretched out, swimming with slow, easy strokes. The icy mountain water made him tingle all over, washing away much of the ache and forcing the blood to race swiftly through his bruised body. The invigorating depths of the pool were like a caress to his scratched and cut flesh. He ducked his head beneath the surface and came up blowing and puffing in keen enjoyment. "By cripes!" he laughed, "I'm commencing to feel whole again. This was a real idea." And then another thought struck him, "But it wouldn't be such a good idea if some of Crawford's men were to sling some lead my way. I reckon I'd better get back to my gun."

He swam a few strokes back to the bank, then stood up and commenced to wade the rest of the way. At his back, the roar of Quithatz Falls drowned out all other sounds. Suddenly he swore with pain and halted abruptly, having stubbed his toe on some hard, unresisting object. "Damn it!" he swore. "I figured all these rocks on the bottom were worn smooth and round. . . . That didn't feel like rock, though. I wonder . . ."

He dropped down, opening his eyes under water, then abruptly stood up. "Well, I'll be damned!" he half shouted.

Beneath the waters of the pool was what appeared to be a strongbox!

He stooped down again, while the icy waters swirled about his bare thighs. Managing to get one hand under the box, he gave a tentative lift. The box was plenty heavy. Five minutes later, his heart beating madly with excitement, he heaved the dripping strongbox out on the bank and stood over it, panting hard from his exertions, near the spot where he had left his six-shooter.

"If that isn't Fred Vincent's strongbox and if the missing thirty thousand in gold isn't inside, I'm a pie-eyed liar!" he told himself emphatically.

Due to the roaring of Quithatz Falls he didn't hear the first shot as it whined past him, clipping leaves from the aspens growing thickly on the bank of the pool. However, when the second bullet struck a rock, throwing bits of granite in his face, Nogales dropped as suddenly as if he'd been hit and lay still, face down, one bare foot still stretched out in the pool, the other leg drawn up beneath his body.

XXVIII

Catlett's Confession

For five minutes Nogales lay without movement, his body dripping wet. His foot, extended in the pool, commenced to ache from the chill of the water. Now that he had ceased his exertions, the air seemed to grow cold. It was with difficulty that he kept from violently shivering as he endeavored to lay as still as though he had been mortally wounded. His fingers had closed upon the butt of his six-shooter as he went down. He lay now with his eyes opened only enough to survey the scene that spread before him. Near by was the stretch of grassy bank, with beyond the sloping wall of the canyon, almost wholly concealed by heaped rocks and thick brush. Overhead the leafy branches of slim aspens cut off the direct sunlight, throwing a crisscrossed pattern of shadow across Nogales' naked form.

His eyes moved from side to side behind narrowed lids, alert for the first sign of movement from the man who had fired the shots at him. There wasn't anything to be seen at first — just trees and rocks and brush, with the continual roaring splash of Quithatz Falls at the rear.

And then, fifty feet away, Nogales caught a slight movement behind a tree trunk. The next instant the movement was gone. Five minutes more passed. Nogales waited. A man suddenly took form around a shoulder of rock. It was Swifty Catlett, six-shooter in hand, approaching cautiously the spot where Nogales was lying.

Catlett took two more careful steps, stopped again, his gaze seeking movement from the sprawled form on the bank. Still Nogales held his fire. Then Catlett raised his gun to take careful aim.

Like a flash Nogales rolled to one side and came, catlike, to his feet, his right hand throwing a mushrooming cloud of smoke and fire. Shocked, surprised, Catlett held his fire an instant too long. When he did pull the trigger the bullet flew wide as the impact of Nogales' slug ripped through bone and muscle.

Catlett half dove, half spun, to the earth, braced himself on one hand, and again raised his gun. Nogales thumbed a second swift shot. He saw Catlett's body jerk as the bullet plowed in, then Catlett sank to his face and lay quiet.

Nogales lowered his weapon and crossed the intervening space in quick strides. Stooping at Catlett's side, he turned the man on his back. Bloody foam was issuing from Catlett's pale lips. His eyes were already glazing. With an effort he met Nogales' searching glance.

"Where's Vincent, Catlett?" Nogales demanded.

The reply came low; Nogales could just catch the words, "Up in . . . cave . . . not fifty yards . . . from here. . . . I reckon . . . you're . . . too fast for . . . me, Scott, I'm a goner . . . ain't I?"

Nogales said, "You're a goner, Swifty. I'm sorry, but it had to be you or me."

"I . . . know, Scott. No . . . hard feelin's, I was just . . . on the wrong side . . ."

"Just where is this cave?" Nogales cut in.

"Look for . . . two rocks . . . 'bout same size . . . with tall brush growing . . . between them . . . up near canyon . . . wall. . . . Push through brush . . . find cave. . . . You want . . . know . . . anything else?"

"Thanks, no. . . . But wait a minute. Swifty, Crawford was awful anxious to get my signature. Why?"

A thin smile crossed the dying man's ashen features. "Crawford . . . and Deacon

. . . planned to rub you out . . . then forge your signature . . . to a will. . . . They planned to get . . . everything you own . . ."

Nogales waited. A shudder ran through Catlett's frame; he drew a quick choking breath, and died.

Nogales rose to his feet, made his way back to his clothing, and quickly dressed. Reloading his gun, he started in search of the hidden cave, wondering if there were any more guards with Fred Vincent.

He had no trouble finding the twin rocks Catlett had mentioned. Moving cautiously near, he pushed through the brush and came out in a narrow cleared spot. Beyond, in the canyon wall, was a large opening higher than a horse's head. Nogales waited, tense, listening for voices or movements. Only silence met his straining ears. Then, quite suddenly, a horse nickered from within the cave.

Nogales pressed on, gun in hand. Entering the cave, he saw first the rumpled blankets on which was the bound form of Fred Vincent. Beyond stood two horses tethered to pegs driven into cracks in the cave wall. At one side were a stock of canned goods and a couple of saddles.

"Nogales!" Fred exclaimed, a note of glad relief in his voice.

"You all right, Fred?"

"Sure, I'm all right. Just get these ropes off me and — Where's Swifty Catlett?"

Nogales said quietly, "I encountered Swifty down by the falls. He won't bother us any more."

He had his knife out by this time, sawing at the ropes that held Fred's wrists and ankles. After a moment Fred rose to his feet and stretched stiffly. "By gosh, I'm glad to see you! Is everybody all right? What's happened since I was seized and brought here? Say! What's happened to your face? It looks like you'd been scrapping. What happened?"

"Whoa!" Nogales laughed. He gave brief details of the happenings during Fred's absence, then said, "You're sure you're all right? You're not hurt any?"

"Right as rain." Fred laughed. "In fact, I think the activity did me good. No, Catlett didn't knock me around any. He treated me all right. Just questioned me a heap regarding that missing gold, but I couldn't remember a thing. You know, a couple of riders grabbed me when I was walking down in the fig orchard. They held me out in the desert, outside town, all night. This morning, early, Catlett brought me up here, tied in my saddle. After we got here he tied me up and left me on these blankets, then lay down himself and took a snooze. I fell asleep myself. When I woke up, he was gone. I don't know how long he'd been gone. Next thing I knew, you came in —"

"I don't guess he'd left you for very long. He must have come outside to look around and spotted me. I'd been taking a swim down near the falls." Nogales paused and looked narrowly at Vincent. "You're sure you're all right, Fred?"

"Positive." Fred looked curiously at Nogales. "If you ask me I think the ride did me a lot of good. Why, what's on your mind?"

"Figure you can stand a shock?" Nogales asked. "No, wait — don't get me wrong. There's nothing happened to Polly or your dad. This is good news."

"Good news never shocks me." Fred laughed. He sobered suddenly. "Don't tell me you've located that missing gold?"

Nogales nodded. "I'm right sure, leastwise. Anyway, I've found a strongbox that wa'n't packed with feathers. It's too heavy for that. While I was in swimming I stubbed my toe —"

"Wait! Fred exclaimed, holding up one hand. "It's coming back. Now I remember.

Nogales! I can remember everything! You found that strongbox in the pool!"

"I'm telling you." Nogales grinned, laughing at the dawning look of remembrance in Fred's features. "But do you recollect how it got there?"

Fred nodded emphatically, unable for the moment to find his voice. Then the words poured out in a sudden torrent: "It all comes back now, clear as day. I'd herded that pack mule up here. The mule was wounded and dropped not far from the pool. It was raining like the devil. We'd had a long drought. There was scarcely any water in the pool. The falls were just a thin trickle, but I knew before long they'd be pouring over in the usual manner. I unleashed that box and tumbled it into the pool, knowing that the way the rain was coming down the falls would soon cover it up and we could get it later."

"You sure had the right hunch, Fred."

"I'll bet that box was completely submerged in a couple of hours. There was a regular cloudburst on! Once the box was taken care of, I had to think of myself. I was wounded and getting pretty weak. I knew those raiders would be coming into the canyon after me. I started to climb the cliff where the falls came down. I remember getting part way up, then my strength left and I fell back. After that I don't know what happened, except I woke up buried in a clump of brush. If anybody did look for me, they didn't look in the right place. But at that time I couldn't remember what had happened, who I was or where I was. There was a long time of wandering around, being afraid of everybody and everything. It's a wonder I even realized what my six-shooter was and hung on to it — Say, did you make sure the gold was in the box?" His face was eager, questioning, half skeptical.

"Didn't have time for that," Nogales returned.

"Let's go see!" Vincent ran past Nogales and headed in the direction of the pool. Fast as Nogales followed, Vincent arrived there first. There was a broad grin on his face as he looked across the strongbox at Nogales, "This is it, all right. Nogales, how will I ever thank you?"

"Forget that part," Nogales said. "We've got to get inside this box. Now if you only had the key to this padlock — but you haven't. This box is sure water-soaked, but the staple seems to hold fast. I reckon I'll have to shoot off that lock."

"There should be six canvas sacks inside," Fred said excitedly, "each containing two hundred and fifty twenty-dollar gold pieces. Quick, Nogales, shoot that lock —"

Nogales' gun roared. A moment later he threw back the cover of the box which was still partially filled with water. He reached in and swung out a hefty, watersoaked canvas sack and let it to the ground. Fred's fingers fumbled at the wet drawstrings. Finally he had the sack open. Peering inside, he gave a wild yell of joy. "It's here! It's here!"

"Five more sacks like this in the box," Nogales counted.

Fred dropped weakly down on a rock, a silly grin on his face. Nogales sat beside him. They rolled and lighted cigarettes. Within a short time Fred recovered his composure.

Nogales said, "I'll tell you what. No use totin' this strongbox back with us. We'll get one of those blankets from the cave, bundle up these sacks of gold, and lash it on the back of Catlett's horse. You'd better take Catlett's gun too. Then you mount the other horse and head straight for the Rancho with the gold. I'll accompany you most of the way, but I want to get back to Ramrod Ridge as soon as possible. There's a settlement to make and I figure Rod Peters may need my help."

"How about me going with you?" Vincent asked.

Nogales shook his head. "It's your job to get that gold to the Rancho. I'm just worrying whether you'll be up to it or not. All this excitement and —"

"Stop fretting about me." Fred grinned. "My mind's all right, if that's what you mean, and as for my body — Well, if you hadn't already licked Crawford, I'd take him on myself. Finding this gold is just the tonic I needed. I never felt better in my life!"

Two hours later they emerged from the canyon and were following the irrigation ditch that led to the Rancho. By this time it was past noon and a strong desert wind had come up. Here, where they were riding, leading the horse packed with the blanketed gold, the wind wasn't so bad, but down on the desert flats Nogales could see that the atmosphere had turned hazy with flying dust and sand.

"Looks like a sandstorm rising," Fred commented.

"Do they get 'em often in these parts?"

"They're not unusual this time of year."

They rode on, until Nogales sighted the roof of the ranch house. "I'll be leaving you here," he announced. "I want to get to Ramrod Ridge. You push on to the welcomin' arms of your folks and turn that gold over to your dad."

"It'll take a big load off of his mind," Vincent said. "Now he'll be able to pay you. I don't know what we'd have done without your help, Nogales."

Nogales flushed and reined his pony away as though he hadn't heard. "Keep going," he urged through the sound of the rising wind. "I'll be seeing you before long."

He turned the pony toward Ramrod Ridge and plunged in his spurs.

XXIX

The End of Ramrod Ridge

By now the wind was blowing harder than ever. It swooped down in great gusts, hurling biting particles of sand against horse and rider, sand that stung and cut. Nogales' face commenced to feel as though it had been rubbed with sandpaper. He drew his bandanna up across his mouth and nose and bent his head against the fierce blasts. There seemed to be no definite direction from which the wind came. Now and then there'd be a lull, and when the gusts resumed they seemed always to choose fresh points of the compass.

The air was so filled with dust and sand that by the time Nogales neared Ramrod Ridge the town was almost obscured from view. It was impossible to see the sky; the sun was a great brassy disc that glowed feebly through a hurtling sandy fog. Suddenly the vague outlines of a building appeared before Nogales' vision and he realized he was entering the town. Other buildings loomed up as he progressed farther. A section of tin roof went bumping and clanging along the roadway; papers were swept wildly about in the ever-rising gale.

As he drew near Rod Peters' office a man loomed up through the sandy air. It was Limpy Bristol. Bristol peered through the swirling atmosphere, recognized Nogales, and hurled a savage curse.

"What's bothering you?" Nogales yelled through the gale.

But Bristol didn't reply. Instead he took to his heels and headed in the direction of Crawford's store. Within a moment his form assumed shadowy outlines, then vanished altogether.

Nogales dismounted and led his pony into the open space between Peters' office and its neighboring building. Peters' horse was already there, sheltered to some extent from the stinging storm. Peters' door was closed. It required main force to open it against the strength of the wind. Nogales stepped inside and the door banged at his back. Here he stopped and took a deep breath.

Peters was seated at his table, smoking a pipe. He jumped to his feet as Nogales entered.

"You're back, pard! Did you find Vincent?"

Nogales nodded, adding, "And the gold."

"T'hell you say!"

"I'm not fooling." Nogales continued and gave details. When he had concluded:

"Gosh, that's good news. How do you feel now, after your fight?"

"Mite stiff and achy, but not bad. Heard anything from Crawford?"

"I was over there about an hour ago. He's back on his feet again and nearly insane with rage. One of his men had some fight experience at some time or other and knew how to treat black eyes. He took a razor and made cuts in the swollen flesh around Crawford's eyes. That let out the bad blood, or something. Anyway, Crawford can see again —"

"Nothing much happened while I was away then?"

Peters shook his head. "I guess they were all waiting for orders from Crawford, and, like I say, they just recent got him up on his feet. Cripes! There isn't much that could be done in this windstorm. Nice little breeze, ain't it?"

"I don't know as I ever seen worse."

"I'm damned if I know how you could

see to find Vincent or the gold."

"It wasn't blowing up in the canyon — and a few miles back it isn't blowing nearly so hard as it is here. What did Limpy Bristol want?"

"When?" Peters asked.

"Just before I got here."

"He wasn't here."

"I saw him leaving just as I rode up. Didn't you see him?"

"He wasn't in here," Peters repeated and frowned. "I wonder if that bustard was spying on me to see what I was doing."

"Why should he be?"

Peters said, "Crawford's able to give orders again. By this time they all know that Crawford revealed Vincent's whereabouts. Maybe they were ready to ride for the canyon —"

"They know I'm back now," Nogales cut in. "If they're looking for trouble they'll be heading here right soon, Rod. Maybe we'd better get ready."

"Wait," Peters said suddenly. "After your fight with Crawford those coyotes saw you head out of town. I gave it out that you were heading for the Rancho to see Doc Stebbings. Now Bristol will tell 'em you've returned. They'll never dream that you've been to the canyon and found Vincent —"

"I'll tell you what I bet they will do, though," Nogales interrupted. "To prevent me from going to Quithatz for Vincent, I figure Crawford will send some men here to stop me — and stop you as well. Once you and I are out of the way, the gang can go to the canyon and overpower anybody else I may have told. Leastwise, I got a hunch that's the way Crawford's mind will work."

"I think you're right. Well, I've got enough on Crawford to act now. I reckon I'll just sashay over to his place and put him under arrest. We know he planned Vincent's kidnaping and that he plotted to kill you and forge your signature to a will. I'll also arrest Bristol and the Deacon as accessories — and anybody else that shows signs of backing up Crawford. Right now I'm deputizing you to help me make arrests. Ready to go?"

"Ready and waiting," Nogales said promptly. "Come on!"

Peters turned the doorknob, then threw his weight against the door to open it against the force of the howling gale. Sand cut and tore at their faces as they stepped outside. The outlines of houses could be seen but dimly through the dusty fog. By this time the sun was sending down only a pale light on the street.

"Phew! What a wind —" Peters shouted to make himself heard above the howling elements.

"Wait, Rod!" Nogales said suddenly. "There's a gang coming!"

The two men waited. Forms took on shape and came nearer, headed by Limpy Bristol and the Deacon. Behind them Nogales could make out some twenty men at least. Some were armed with rifles. The Deacon was carrying a length of coiled rope.

Suddenly Bristol looked up and spotted Nogales. "There's Scott!" the man shouted. "C'mon, we'll string 'em up!"

Wild yells arose from the followers. Nogales and Peters commenced to back away. Nogales said calmly, "We'd better get back to your office, Rod. We'll have to make a stand there. That gang's sure set to wipe us out, and the fact that you're a law officer won't stop 'em! C'mon."

They turned and started back toward the building. One of the men behind Bristol jerked a rifle to his shoulder and fired. The report sounded flat and thin against the roar of the wind, but Peters saw the bullet kick up dust at his feet. Instantly his six-shooter was out, blazing swift defiance.

A man went down. For a moment the mob halted. Then the Deacon yelled, "Don't stop, men! We've got to get 'em or they'll get us."

Limpy Bristol's forty-five roared. Nogales thumbed two quick shots. He saw Bristol spin half around and then drop. Now firing broke out with savage intensity. Bullets were flying all around Peters and Nogales, but, miraculously, the two managed to get back to the deputy's office without being wounded. Jerking open the door, they leaped inside and quickly shot the bolt.

"We're in for it, Nogales," Peters said.

"I won't go out without taking a few of those scuts with me," Nogales said grimly.

A bullet shattered the windowpane. More bullets thudded into the door. Peters and Nogales dropped to the door until the early volleys had subsided. Then they both leaped for the window and threw shots at shadowy forms dashing past. But this time there were no answering reports.

The two waited, crouching close to the walls. Nogales said, "They've stopped shooting. I can't hear a sound."

"Couldn't hear much in this wind anyway," Peters growled. "Maybe they're trying to make us think they've left, so we'll come out."

"Maybe." Nogales nodded. "But I got a hunch they're up to some deviltry. I don't like it. . . ." He sniffed the air suddenly. "I smell smoke —"

"No wonder! Look!" Peters pointed to the closed door that led to the room back of his office. Smoke was curling through the crack between the door and the jamb. "My God! They've set the back of this building on fire. They're going to burn us out!"

He opened the door and a gust of flame shot into the room. Quickly he shut the door again and turned, pale-faced, to face Nogales. "What are we going to do now, pard?"

"Stay here and roast," Nogales replied grimly, "or leave here and go down fighting. They'll be waiting for us the instant we appear, of course."

They could hear the crackling of the flames in the back room now. The atmosphere grew hotter and hotter. The boards of the back wall grew hot to the touch. Peering cautiously through the broken windowpane, Nogales reported, "I can't see anybody, but I know they're waiting — Cripes! Rod, the building across the street is afire! I reckon sparks from this made it catch."

"With this wind, we'll be lucky if the whole town don't catch. Those damned fools!"

The room was filled with smoke by this time. Both men commenced to choke and cough. "I don't know how much longer I can stand this," Peters gasped.

A sudden orange light appeared in the room. Glancing up, they saw that fire was burning through the ceiling. Embers drifted down on the men's clothing to be slapped out with their hands. Now they crowded near the window, trying to catch as much fresh air as possible.

"Look," Peters said, "I can see a whole row of buildings on fire! This blaze is" — he stopped to cough — "spreading rapidly. How much longer we staying here, pard?"

"Not much longer." Nogales spoke, trying to hold his voice steady. Sweat was streaming down his features now. "I'm hoping the smoke will get thick outside and we can make a dash for it!"

"Smoke or no smoke, I've got to have air!"

"Right! We'll get moving. Let's go through this door with our guns blazing. We'll get as many as we can —"

"I hear shooting!" Peters interrupted. "There's a lot of it." They listened, and heard through the mingled roar of wind and crackling flames the sharp reports of guns and pounding hoofs. Peters stole a glance around the edge of the window.

"Cripes, Nogales!" he yelled joyously. "There's a street fight going on. There's been so much noise we didn't get it!"

"Street fight?" Nogales asked dumbly.

"Sheriff Ham Burger is out there! He's got a crew of riders with him! Things have been happening while we hung back here breathing smoke. Come on!"

Throwing open the street door, the two leaped out. By this time all one side of the street was ablaze, the shifting wind sending flame and sparks in all directions. The sun-warped wood in the buildings caught and burned fiercely.

The street was filled with horsemen as Nogales and Peters stepped outside. Ham Burger spotted them almost instantly. "Wondered where you were, Peters," his voice came bellowing above the sound of crackling timbers. "Hi-yuh, Mister Scott! Glad to see you're alive."

The street was strewn with the bodies of dead men. Two horses were down. Farther along three horsemen were herding a bunch of prisoners before them.

"Seen Crawford?" Nogales yelled.

Burger shook his head and reined his

horse to one side. "Somebody said he was still in his store. I'm not waiting to see. Come on, let's get out of this town. The whole place is going in a few minutes. Hey, Scott, where you going?"

But Nogales was out of earshot now, running swiftly in the direction of Crawford's store. The roof of the building was ablaze, but the rest of the structure was intact. Nogales leaped to the door. It was locked. He threw his weight against it, but the door resisted. Standing back, Nogales took a short run and again hurled his fighting poundage against the barrier.

There came a sharp splintering sound as the door jerked and fell inward. As Nogales stumbled on through, he caught the picture in a brief glance. Waiting there, in the middle of the room, were the Deacon and Simon Crawford. The Deacon's long six-shooter was out. Crawford held a double-barreled shotgun in his hands.

Nogales drew his six-shooter and threw himself to the floor all in one swift movement. He heard the roar of the Deacon's six-gun, followed by the heavy boom-boom of Crawford's weapon, as a charge of buckshot thundered above him. Both men, having missed, were preparing to try again. Crawford was fumbling for fresh shells and the Deacon was raising his six-shooter when Nogales thumbed two swift shots from his prone position on the floor.

He saw the Deacon's long form jerk, then fall side-wise, the six-shooter clattering from his hand. Crawford was still trying to shove fresh shells into the shotgun when Nogales fired once more.

For an instant Crawford swayed unsteadily. Then, like some huge stricken beast, his knees bent and let him to the floor where he lay without movement.

Nogales scrambled up and darted outside, reloading as he ran. By this time not a building remained untouched by fire. Ramrod Ridge had turned into a blazing inferno and the crackling of burning wood was deafening, the heat intense. Smoke billowed up to be swept away by the raging wind.

Sprinting as fast as he could, Nogales ran the flaming gantlet of buildings. By the time he reached the end of town his clothing was burning in a dozen places, his eyebrows were singed.

Suddenly he heard Rod Peters' voice, "God! You did escape! We were worried."

And then, to Nogales' surprise, he saw the relieved faces of Caliper and Jimmy-Steve looking down on him from their saddles.

XXX

Conclusion

"And the more I thought of it," Ham Burger's pompous voice went on, "the more it was borne in upon my conscience that I owed it to my constituents to look into affairs at Ramrod Ridge. My deputy, Rod Peters — and I think you'll all admit I certainly know how to pick good deputies — had kept me well informed how matters stood. With me to think is to act. I rounded up a bunch of fighting riders, deputized them, and came here to put under arrest every manjack of Simon Crawford's crooked outfit. The very thought of his nefarious practices has for a long time made my blood boil. I decided to put a stop to it once and for all. We arrived at — ahem — a very propitious time, I believe. Wouldn't you say so, Mister Scott?"

"No doubt of it," Nogales replied.

"And — er — and," Burger asked cautiously, "do you think the governor might be interested in this affair — that is to say, the small part I played — er — ?"

"I intend to write the governor to-morrow," Nogales said dryly, "for the sole purpose of telling him the way in which you fulfill the duties of your office."

They had all been seated on the ground, back from the heat of the fire, watching the town go up in flames. By now there was little left of Ramrod Ridge save a smoldering heap of desert-dried timbers. The wind was dying, too, as though, having accomplished its purpose, it had departed for other regions.

If Nogales was surprised at seeing Jimmy-Steve and Caliper when he emerged from the flaming town, he was more surprised to be greeted by Polly, Fred, and Ethan Vincent. Their presence was quickly explained by Ethan: "We could see smoke rising and flames from the gallery of the house. Polly got all upset about Rod and wondered if he was in danger."

"Father!" Polly had protested, coloring.

"It's so," the elder Vincent said, his eyes twinkling, "though I wouldn't go so far as to say you were as bad as Caliper and Jimmy-Steve. We couldn't hold those two down, wounded as they were. Doc fixed 'em up and we all mounted and came down to see the doings. We were just in time to see Nogales emerge from the blazing street. I just hope Caliper and Jimmy-Steve won't get a setback from their activity."

Doc Stebbings growled, "You couldn't kill those two. They're too tough."

"I sure wish I'd been in on the excitement, though," Caliper said wistfully.

"Ees so." Jimmy-Steve nodded. "Always, Nogales, he have all of the fun."

"You've all had a hand in the doings," Ethan nodded, "though Nogales gave me the biggest thrill by finding that gold."

"If you got a thrill, what do you think I got?" Fred laughed.

The talk ran on and on. Back some distance from the group Ham Burger was instructing his riders regarding the prisoners who had been taken. The voices of Rod Peters and Polly dropped lower and lower and finally they got into a very confidential conversation of their own.

"Well," Nogales said finally, "Crawford and his gang are wiped out, as well as Ramrod Ridge."

"Good riddance all around, I'd say," Ethan nodded. "We'll have peace in this country now."

Rod Peters got back into the conversation, "Peace is fine when you've got a job. But now I've got to get me another town, and I've got a hunch this county is filled with deputies just waiting for offices."

Nogales glanced over one shoulder where Sheriff Burger was talking to his riders, and said with a wink, "Rod, I'll bet I can get you another office. One word about the governor watching out for your welfare and —"

Rod shook his head. "I don't want to get a job thataway."

"I've been thinking about your job, too, Rod," Ethan Vincent put in. "Before long I'm going to start raising blooded stock to sell to cattlemen who want to improve the strain of their herds. And next winter I aim to put in some citrus trees. There'll be too much work for my foreman. How'd you like to handle the cattle end of the business for me?"

"Why — why," Peters stammered, "that's downright nice, but I don't know if I should take the job or not —" He broke off, his face crimsoning, his eyes searching Polly's face.

"Please take it, Rod," Polly said quickly. Her cheeks, too, were red. Rod looked at the girl steadily, seeking the answer to a certain question. Apparently he found the reply he sought, for he turned back and said, "I'll be glad to work with you, Ethan."

"Fine," the elder Vincent said heartily and patted Polly on one shoulder.

"Gosh," Caliper said, "everything is turning out right. First Rod gets burned out of his job, then he gets another — and plenty happiness besides, I'm betting. You know, I sort of miss the Deacon; he'd probably have something appropriate to say on such an occasion. Nogales, can't you think of anything?"

Nogales pondered a moment, then, grinning, "Behold," he said, "how great a matter a little fire kindleth!"